NATHAN FOX

Dangerous Times

L. BRITTNEY

FEIWEL AND FRIENDS
NEW YORK

A FEIWEL AND FRIENDS BOOK
An Imprint of Macmillan

Library of Congress Cataloging-in-Publication Data Available

ISBN-13: 978-0-312-36962-0
ISBN-10: 0-312-36962-X

First published in the United Kingdom by Macmillan Children's Books,
a division of Pan Macmillan.

Feiwel and Friends logo designed by Filomena Tuosto

First U.S. Edition: October 2008

10 9 8 7 6 5 4 3 2 1

www.feiwelandfriends.com

INTRODUCTION
England, March 1587

ENGLAND is on the brink of war.

Queen Elizabeth I has refused to marry and produce an heir, and her country is beset on all sides by enemies. Since she became queen, she has turned England into a largely Protestant country, and the pope has made it known that anyone who assassinates her would gain "merit in the eyes of God." Philip of Spain, head of the mighty Spanish Empire, has taken it upon himself to restore the Catholic faith to every country he conquers and he constantly has his sights set on England.

In February 1587, Mary, Queen of Scots, had been beheaded on Elizabeth's order. Mary, a staunch Catholic and a claimant to the English throne, had been kept prisoner by Elizabeth for years and had been found guilty of plotting to assassinate the English queen and take her throne. Worse still, Mary had conspired with Philip of Spain to pass the English throne to the Spanish Empire when she died.

Sir Francis Walsingham, England's spymaster general, had

tricked Mary into the conspiracy to prove to Elizabeth that the Scottish queen would always be a major threat if she was not executed. So, reluctantly, Elizabeth signed Mary's death warrant, knowing that the Spanish Empire would now redouble its efforts to conquer England. And she was right.

Walsingham's large network of spies, scattered all over Europe, has now told him that Philip of Spain is amassing his troops and ships to invade England. It is only a matter of time.... Can Walsingham's spies save England from disaster?

PART 1

PROLOGUE

THE BOY IS MARKED OUT

THE boy was suspended above the stage by a rope, and the tall, dark man watched him with some amusement as he twisted and turned with great agility. The boy grasped the rope with one hand and with his other hand he scattered red rose petals over the actors beneath him.

He's strong, thought the man, and he nodded with approval. His next thought was echoed by a whisper from a younger man standing next to him in the shadows.

"He is the finest boy actor I've ever witnessed, my lord. I have heard him do many foreign accents—he's played his age and older—female and male. I've seen him do spirits and hunchbacks, fairies and monsters. He is a marvel."

The tall, dark man turned slightly and permitted himself a wry smile. "I think you spend too much time at the playhouses, Master Pearce, when you should be working for me," he murmured. John Pearce looked at his employer and returned his smile. "Can

I help it, Sir Francis, if, occasionally, I hanker to return to my old profession?"

"What is his age?" asked Sir Francis.

"Just thirteen, my lord."

Sir Francis Walsingham turned back to his observation of the boy actor, who was now shinning up the rope toward the opening in the roof space above the stage. With the ease and agility of a practiced acrobat, he swung his legs over his head to the wooden platform and then disappeared into the darkness. The play was over and the audience burst into a roar of approval, accompanied by much feet stamping and catcalls. As the noise swelled until it threatened to lift the thatching off the roof of the theater, Sir Francis turned and raised his voice to a near shout. "Come, John, we will talk with this boy—but not here, at his lodgings."

The two men made their way toward the back of the theater, dodging the feverish jostling of the actors as they rushed for the stage to take their due praise from the audience. Sir Francis and his companion pressed themselves against the wall to wait for the tide of men to pass. Suddenly, as nimbly as a squirrel, the boy actor dropped down a rope ladder that swung from a hole in the roof and joined the back of the throng. He was flushed and happy, his dark curls stuck to his face with sweat. He barely glanced at the two men as he pushed past them—but long enough for Walsingham to register the boy's arresting ice blue eyes.

"He is much taller than he looked up a rope," murmured Walsingham. "I do not think he will be playing young maids for much longer, my friend." John Pearce smiled and nodded his agreement but Sir Francis had already moved out of the darkness of the playhouse into the bright sun of the alleyway behind the theater.

In the daylight, Walsingham looked old and careworn, but he still carried himself with a quiet authority and strength. His eyes, which were almost black and seemed to see everything, made tremble all who came before him with a secret in their hearts. He was, after all, England's spymaster general. There was no plot, no conspiracy, no deviousness that escaped Sir Francis. No one could enter or leave England without the permission of his office. His formidable intelligence-gathering networks had been built up over a number of years. Many people served England by working for him—actors, poets, pirates, mystics, and noblemen—no one was too low or too high. He spent his own money in maintaining these networks and much of what he did was without the knowledge of the queen—but he did it all for her. To Walsingham, Elizabeth I was the greatest and wisest monarch who had ever ruled England—and he believed that without her, all would fall into chaos.

The two men walked on in silence. They made a strange pair—the tall, somber, older man and the handsome, energetic, younger man by his side. Walsingham was aware that his companion kept his hand firmly on his sword and was ever alert to any threat that might arise. Sir Francis reflected that of all his agents, Pearce was the most loyal and intelligent.

It was John Pearce's intelligence that had first brought him to Walsingham's notice. Pearce had arrived at court, the son of a poor but aristocratic family, and made a good impression. He had once been a boy actor in a company, The Children of the Chapel

Royal, so he knew how to play to an audience. By the time his widowed mother sent him to Elizabeth's court to revive the family fortunes, he was eighteen years old.

He came to Walsingham's attention one evening after dinner. The queen was bored and circulating around the room looking for distractions. She was attempting to flirt with the young men as usual. Such attentions were a trial and most newcomers to court were terrified that her eye would alight on them. When Her Majesty chose to speak to John Pearce, he acquitted himself well. She asked him questions in Latin and smiled when he was able to reply smoothly. Then she asked him, in English, if he could speak Greek.

"Your Majesty," he replied in English, "I did study Greek, but although Homer taught me much about heroism, it taught me little about how to converse with a beautiful woman."

The queen was delighted and raised her voice. "It is an intelligent man who knows his limitations. He will go far." Everyone applauded. What she *really* meant, thought Walsingham, recalling the incident, was that she was pleased to be called beautiful. Vanity was her vice.

Later that year, John Pearce had sought out Walsingham in private, to tell him of a conversation he had overheard in a tavern, which he thought might present a danger to the queen. Walsingham was impressed. The plot was investigated and the guilty men disposed of. From that moment, Pearce became one of Walsingham's agents. The young man had many talents—he could speak several languages, he had an actor's talent for disguising his face and voice, and he was an excellent swordsman. After he had been trained, John Pearce became skilled in many other arts not known by ordinary men. By the age of twenty-two he was the most accomplished operative in the espionage network and Walsingham had him marked for great tasks in the year ahead.

The two men stopped by a door in an alleyway not far from the theater.

"This is the lodging place?" inquired Walsingham.

"Yes, my lord."

"And you say he lodges with his sister?" Pearce's smile told Walsingham that the sister was, most likely, a beauty.

"Four other actors lodge here, and the house is owned by a Mistress Fast."

"Then let us go in and wait for the boy," said Walsingham. The two men entered into the gloom of the doorway to await the arrival of young Nathan Fox, who would shortly learn that the spymaster general wished to recruit him to work for queen and country.

CHAPTER 1

THE RECRUITMENT

THE actors tumbled out of the theater into the spring sunshine, laughing and joking.

"Was I not superb today?" shouted Richard Burbage.

"As usual, you were the great hero," answered Will Shakespeare. "It's a shame you were not a little *less* of a hero." This sly reference to Burbage's growing waistline sent the others into hoots of laughter and Will merited a cuff around the ear from the object of his wit.

"Enough, Will Shakestongue! You have been an actor in this company but five minutes, whereas I . . ."

"HAVE ACTING IN MY BLOOD!" chorused the other three actors, well used to this speech.

"It's my father who pays your wages," roared Burbage in mock anger but a smile played around his lips. The audience had cheered long and hard for him today and nothing was going to destroy his good humor.

At that moment, Nathan Fox came hurtling round the corner and into the group, with the force of a crossbow bolt. Burbage was taken off balance and fell onto the path, sending up a cloud of dust around him. "God's blood!" he roared. "What in the name of all that is holy did you do that for, boy?"

Nathan blushed and struggled to help the heavy actor to his feet.

"Sorry, sir. I was rushing to catch up with you all," he said, brushing the street dust from Burbage's rather fine clothes.

"And why were you in such a hurry, Nathan?" asked Will Kempe, who always looked depressed and worried despite being the comic actor of the company.

"I . . . I found Will's book on the floor. I wanted to return it to him." Nathan held up a battered, leather-bound notebook.

"Thank God, Nathan," cried Shakespeare as he took the book and feverishly fanned through it, as if to check that everything was still there.

"Oh, the famous book," Burbage said contemptuously. "Just when are we going to get some benefit from all these scribblings?"

"When I am ready, Richard," said Shakespeare in a tone that defied any argument.

The group carried on walking in the direction of the nearest tavern. As they turned to go inside, Shakespeare stopped.

"I shall leave you now, gentlemen."

The others turned in amazement.

"What, no food and drink tonight, Will?" inquired Samuel Crosse, the last member of their little group.

"No, I shall eat in my rooms. I have work to do." Shakespeare turned on his heel and set off toward his lodgings.

"I'll come with you," called out Nathan, wisely deciding to forgo the company of Richard Burbage, who had been glaring at him since being knocked into the dust. With a hasty nod to the others, Nathan ran swiftly after his friend.

The actors stood at the tavern door and watched the pair turn the corner. "I wish Will would just concentrate on being an actor," muttered Burbage.

"Ah, but there is a depth there, you know," Will Kempe reflected. "Perhaps we shall be grateful for his words one day. Good plays are hard to find."

Burbage snorted contemptuously at the thought that a great actor should be thankful to a mere playwright and stepped into the tavern to find food for his growling stomach.

Nathan trotted beside his friend in an effort to keep up with him. "When are you going to write your first play, Will?" he asked.

Shakespeare stopped in his tracks and looked intently at the boy. "When I have enough good stories. A good story is the most important thing. Now, tell me ...," he continued, "this play we have done today ... what did you think of it?"

They began to walk again and Nathan thought seriously before answering. "The audience liked it well enough," he began, "but ..."

"Ah yes ... *but*," Will interrupted. "What story was there? None at all. There were some star-crossed lovers—but why did they have problems? This was not explained. There was a comic scene, so that our friend Kempe could clown about and make the audience laugh—but why? There were some effects—your famous acrobatics, Nathan...." He tousled the boy's curls affectionately. "But none of it meshed together. There was no progression from A to B to C. It was just a collection of set scenes, guaranteed to make an audience react. That is not a play, Nathan. Not my kind of play."

Nathan frowned. He felt too inexperienced to criticize older and more experienced actors—let alone the work of a playwright— yet he recognized that Will was making a valid statement. Even during rehearsals, Nathan had sometimes been bored by the aimlessness of the piece they were working on.

"Then what *is* your kind of play, Will?" he asked earnestly, knowing that he could rely upon the articulate Shakespeare to provide an interesting answer.

Shakespeare looked frustrated for a moment, as if struggling with something that he could not quite understand. He took a deep breath. "I want . . . I want to tell a story that will so enrapture an audience that they will forget that they are in a theater. I want them to be totally silent. . . ."

Nathan snorted, remembering today's audience and their constant chatter, as well as the comments and abuse they sometimes hurled at the actors. Then he thought wistfully of the Bible stories he had seen as a small child reverently acted out in front of the church. The crowds had watched them in awe—and silence— hanging upon every word. It was those experiences that had instilled in him a love of theater.

"Yes, silent," said Will softly, as if reading Nathan's mind. "As if the audience were spying at the unfolding of someone's life through a window and they dared not breathe in case they are discovered. I want the audience to care about each character—to care if they live or die. I don't want them to just care about the actors.

To applaud their favorites and to talk all the way through the performances of those they do not care for."

Nathan grinned. "Richard Burbage would be outraged if he did not receive his usual plaudits from the audience."

Shakespeare smiled wryly. "Richard does not understand. He is a great actor but he is too concerned with being a *famous* actor to realize that he is capable of more. But I will cure him of that in time."

Nathan looked at his friend with amusement. "You seem very sure of yourself, Will."

Shakespeare shook his head sorrowfully. "No, what writer is ever sure of himself? Except . . ." He turned and a light appeared in his eyes as he spoke. "When he knows that the story he is writing is so good that he cannot fail. Believe me, Nathan, the story is the thing."

The pair had reached their lodging house and were surprised to see their landlady, Mistress Fast, waiting on the step for them. She looked worried.

"Thank goodness you've come home!" she exclaimed. "I was about to send someone to find you."

Shakespeare looked alarmed. "Why, mistress? Is it trouble with the law?" Nathan shot a sideways glance at his friend. He had heard rumors that Will had come to London to escape some trouble with local magistrates.

"No, no, Master Shakespeare. Young Nathan has two important visitors. Marie is talking to them now. I shouldn't have left her alone with them. I don't like the look of the older man. He gives me chills. . . ."

Nathan felt a surge of concern and he looked at Will anxiously. They did not wait to hear more and pushed past Mistress Fast, taking the steps two at a time. As they pounded up the stairs, Nathan's thoughts were jumbled. *Why are these men here to see me? Am I in trouble?* He racked his brains to try and recall any mischief that he may have got up to with the other apprentice actors but he could think of nothing.

Will and Nathan burst into the room, only to be met with a rather tranquil scene. Nathan's sister, Marie, was pouring ale for an older man, who was seated at the table. A handsome young man sat by the window, watching her. Marie looked up at her brother and his friend with consternation.

"Nathan! Why so rowdy?"

Nathan mumbled an apology and, as he turned to close the door, saw a strange look appear on Will Shakespeare's face.

The older man spoke. "Master Nathan Fox. And someone I believe I know quite well—Master Shakespeare."

Shakespeare bowed. "Good day to you, Sir Francis."

Nathan's eyes opened wide. "*Sir* Francis?"

"Nathan, this is Sir Francis Walsingham," said Marie with a smile. "Her Majesty's *secretary of state*."

Nathan bowed hurriedly as his sister continued, "And, Nathan, Sir Francis has come here expressly to see you."

"Me!" he spluttered. "Why?"

"I fear we are to find out," muttered Shakespeare gloomily.

Nathan looked at Sir Francis Walsingham. His skin was sallow and what hair showed around his black skullcap was graying. He was dressed all in black, apart from the startling white ruff around his neck. His face was stern and his almost-black eyes were piercing. But for all that, Nathan did not fear him. There was something about the man that fascinated him.

Walsingham stood up, leaning heavily on a stick. *He looks tired*, thought Nathan, *perhaps he is ill.* Sir Francis motioned him to sit down.

"Master Fox, allow me to introduce John Pearce. He works for me." The good-looking younger man bowed and immediately put Nathan at ease by giving him a broad grin and a wink. Nathan felt his breathing slow down and gave Pearce a small smile of relief, as Walsingham continued, "Of course, you know Master Shakespeare, but what you do not know is that he also works for me." Nathan's mouth dropped open as he looked at his friend, who seemed more than a little uncomfortable.

"Will? Works for *you*?" Marie was shocked by the news. "Then, sir," she added defiantly, "so do I!" And she produced an embroidered handkerchief from her apron pocket. Walsingham smiled and turned to Shakespeare. "So this is the lady who produces the fine handiwork that enables us to send our secret messages?" Shakespeare nodded and the four adults exchanged knowing looks.

For Nathan, the revelation that Marie had been working for the secretary of state and had never told him produced a surge of sudden annoyance. This, in turn, made him rashly inject a note of sarcasm into his voice when he said to Walsingham, "Begging your pardon, sire, but what exactly is your business with *me*?"

This display of temper caused a small smile to relax Walsingham's usually stern features. "No, *you* must pardon *me*," he replied graciously. "But before I tell you all, our friend John will play guard at the door, for what I am about to say cannot be overheard by anyone." And with that, Pearce left the room.

Sir Francis began pacing slowly.

"Master Fox, I am many things to Her Majesty, the queen. I am the secretary of state; I am a member of the Privy Council; I flatter myself I am her confidante; but above all I am Her Majesty's spymaster general. I operate a network of many agents who are my eyes and ears, and sometimes my sword, both in England and abroad. We protect Queen Elizabeth, in the best way that we can. These are dangerous times, Nathan. You know that the pope, many years ago, excommunicated our queen and called upon the world to depose her by any means?"

Nathan nodded, trying to be patient but all the time wondering when Walsingham was going to get to the point. He glanced around the room. Marie and Shakespeare looked grave.

"And you know that last month, the queen of Scots was beheaded for her part in a plot to kill our queen?" Walsingham's voice rose a little with passion and he did not wait for a response to his question.

"It is certain," he continued, "that the king of Spain will now use force to make England part of the mighty Spanish Empire. My spies tell me that he is building and equipping a massive fleet of ships, an armada the Spanish call it, to come and crush us all. England has many brave men, and doubtless we can call on more, but we will never be able to defeat the Spanish in battle. We must do it by sabotaging their plans in secret. This is what my agents are trained to do."

Walsingham stopped pacing and faced Nathan.

"I know something of your life—that you and your sister are orphans. And that your parents were gypsies from some European state. Is that so?"

Brother and sister looked at each other. Nathan had never thought of himself as a gypsy. He did not really remember his parents and he had no experience of gypsy ways. But Marie's chin rose defiantly. She knew only too well the drawbacks to having gypsy blood. Gypsies were not welcome in any country. Even the famously tolerant Queen Elizabeth had passed a law, in her youth, which gave the death penalty to any gypsies caught thieving or practicing witchcraft.

Walsingham smiled and patted Nathan's shoulder reassuringly. "Your gypsy blood has given you your acrobatic skills, I'm sure. I have watched you in the theater. You are strong and agile. But," Walsingham continued, sounding more sinister, "mark my words, if we are conquered by Spain, your skills and courage will not save you from the tortures of the Inquisition. At this very moment, there are Jews, Moors, gypsies, and Protestants burning in Spanish cities."

Nathan's lips curled in distaste. People in London still spoke of the Protestant burnings that Queen Mary had ordered some thirty years ago. Such religious intolerance was not really to the English people's taste and the present queen knew that. Nathan pushed the image of burning bodies from his mind. He knew that his overactive imagination would take over his senses if he dwelt on such things.

"Such intolerance is not confined to Spain," murmured Shakespeare pointedly, causing Nathan to snap out of his reverie and look at his friend in surprise. Walsingham rounded on him with fire in his eyes.

"You live in a world of make-believe, Master Shakespeare, where good and evil are clearly separate and all stories end well. *I* am forced to live in the real world. Yes, I have executed Catholic priests and queens but not because they were *Catholics* but because they were *assassins*."

He turned back to Nathan.

"I do this work, Nathan, because I have traveled the world and there is nowhere like England. It is a precious stone set in a silver sea—a fortress built by Nature herself against infection and the hand of war—it is a scepter'd isle. This we must protect."

Out of the corner of his eye, Nathan could see Shakespeare scribbling furiously in his book.

Walsingham turned to Will with an amused look.

"Have my words impressed you, Master Scribe?"

"Deeply, Sir Francis," muttered Shakespeare.

"Then let us hope they have impressed Master Fox." Walsingham drew a deep breath. "Will you work for me, Nathan? Will you be Queen Elizabeth's youngest, and perhaps most useful, spy?"

Nathan was astounded, filled at once with a confusing mixture of fear, pride, and excitement. *Is this a serious request? Surely he has the wrong boy? What does a spy do? Isn't it dangerous?* So many questions flashed through his brain but all he could do was blurt out stupidly, "Me, sir? I am only an actor!"

Walsingham laughed. "Then you have some of the very best training—for spying is all about deception and disguise. And where better to learn that than in the theater? But I will not deceive you. It is dangerous work. Many of my agents have been killed or imprisoned. But if you come to work for me, you would have John Pearce as your partner and you could have no better protection. It was he who found you and it is he who thinks you would be of use to him. Together, you would make a formidable team. What do you say?"

The deep honor that Nathan felt at being chosen for John Pearce's partner made him lose sight of the words Walsingham had uttered about danger, death, and imprisonment. But those were the only words that Marie had heard and her lack of enthusiasm was obvious.

"I like it not, sir," Marie said flatly. "Nathan is safe in the theater. I swore to my father that I would take care of him. He is a mere boy. He should not be exposed to such dangers."

Walsingham nodded. "I understand your concern. But he would be trained to take care of himself. I would see to that. And he would be partnered by my best agent. John has survived far longer than many other men, in the most dangerous conditions. Perhaps he can reassure you himself." Walsingham strode to the door and opened it, beckoning Pearce inside. Then he turned to Shakespeare. "Will, stand guard for a moment. I will call you back when we have finished." With a bow, Will changed places with Pearce.

Walsingham put his arm around Pearce's shoulders. "John,

Nathan's sister feels that the work would be too dangerous for him and I said that you could reassure her."

Pearce told Marie that he would pledge his life to take care of Nathan and he spoke of how Nathan would be coached in all the arts of survival. Marie's face softened just a little.

But before she could respond, Nathan cleared his throat and glared at his sister. "*I* will decide whether I choose this service or not," he said forcefully. He was not about to let his sister seal his fate.

"But you are not of an age to—"

"I have earnt money for the both of us since I was eight years old," Nathan retaliated.

"In the theater, where you are safe," Marie countered.

"If we do not save England from war, no one will be safe," stated Pearce plainly. "Nathan can be of more use with me. Especially on my next mission."

"Which is what?" demanded Marie.

Pearce looked at Walsingham for permission to speak and his employer inclined his head in agreement. "I am to go to Venice to set up an alliance."

Nathan suddenly felt dizzy with excitement. Venice! The exotic setting for so many of the plays he had performed in the theater.

"I have always wanted to go to foreign places!" he exclaimed.

Marie remained stubborn. "And how would a young *boy* be of help?"

"He would pretend to be my servant. He would be able to find out things in the servants' quarters that I could not. He could

19

overhear gossip, eavesdrop on conversations. A young servant boy is invisible to the adults around him." Pearce turned to Nathan. "You speak several languages, do you not?"

Nathan nodded eagerly. "Yes, sir. Marie taught me French and I learnt Italian from some traveling actors. Greek and Latin were given to me at school. I learn languages very quickly."

Walsingham murmured his approval.

Marie looked defeated. "Do you want to do this, Nathan?"

Nathan's chest felt tight and his face hot. Who could refuse the promise of such adventure? "Yes, I do. More than anything."

"Then I will allow it," said Marie in a small, almost sad, voice. She turned to Walsingham, her eyes suddenly steely. "But if any harm comes to him, you will find that I am your greatest enemy, sir. I will lay a gypsy's curse on you forever."

"God forbid that any harm would come to the boy, but if it did, you may find yourself at the back of a very long queue. Come, John, we shall go now. Mistress Fox, please pack Nathan's bags tonight, for John will come and take him away for training tomorrow. He must be ready to sail with Sir Francis Drake before the month is out."

Nathan's eyes widened. "Sir Francis Drake!"

Walsingham looked amused. "You like pirates, do you, boy? I like pirates too. They have a poor reputation but they do good work for me."

With that, England's spymaster and his chief spy made their good-byes and left. Will Shakespeare returned to the room. "So the puppet master has signed himself up another puppet," he said cynically.

"A puppet just like you, Will," Nathan reminded the playwright, cheekily. "So, what is it exactly that you do for Sir Francis?"

Shakespeare smiled. "Show him, Marie."

Marie delved into her apron pocket and produced the embroidered handkerchief, along with a piece of parchment. "Read it," she said, handing Nathan the parchment.

He scanned the verses on the page and recognized them as Will's.

My heart is longing, ordinary mortal I,
No warmth to greet, no sweet murmurings
From your cruel lips, sweet Elizabeth.
Of't fond of telling, fair nymph of the land,
Our two souls must ne'er share those happy states
Where parlous love lies in gravest beauty tamed
And sighs are merely like mere wisps of clouds.

Perchance your ill thoughts of me
Arise from whispers that assail the ear.
Would I might remove the slurs of other's spite
And in this action we then should be
Entwined in all embraces, all lies forfend.
And now I beg that you might cast away all doubts,
To talk of hopes and not besmirch my name.

I know that I am kept at length with cold visage.
My dream is broken, spare your sour notes.
We needs must part and we must break our troth,
All joining in sweet remembrance, though
We are together, tied in past sorrows.
God will judge my heart, e'en though I be not well with you.

"So?" asked Nathan.

"Is that all you can say—'so'? Does not the beauty of the verse strike you?" asked Shakespeare, exasperated.

Ignoring Will's frustration, Marie instructed Nathan to place the parchment on the table and lay the handkerchief over it. Tiny strawberries, flowers, and leaves were sewn all over the fine linen in a random pattern. Each flower had a small hole in its center. Nathan laid the handkerchief over the square of parchment. It fit exactly on top and certain letters were visible through the holes in each tiny flower. Slowly he read out the message.

My heart is longing, ordinary mortal I,
No warmth to greet, no sweet murmurings
From your cruel lips, sweet Elizabeth.
Of't fond of telling, fair nymph of the land,
Our two souls must ne'er share those happy states
Where parlous love lies in gravest beauty tamed
And sighs are merely like mere wisps of clouds.

Perchance your ill thoughts of me
Arise from whispers that assail the ear.
Would I might remove the slurs of other's spite
And in this action we then should be
Entwined in all embraces, all lies forfend.
And now I beg that you might cast away all doubts,
To talk of hopes and not besmirch my name.

I know that I am kept at length with cold visage.
My dream is broken, spare your sour notes.

We needs must part and we must break our troth,
All joining in sweet remembrance, though
We are together, tied in past sorrows.
God will judge my heart, e'en though I be not well with you.
My   l   ord
greet   ings
From   Elizabeth
Of   e   ng   land
Our two   states
          ar   e   in grave

Per   il
from the
      might of   sp
A   in   we   should be
al   lies
And   I beg   you
To talk

                    at length with
My   e   m is   s ar y
We   must
      join
    together
God   be   with you

Nathan raised his head and looked at his sister. He smiled. For many months, Marie had been embroidering handkerchiefs and being paid well for them. *And I thought nothing of it,* he reflected, *thinking it woman's work and her business.* Now he looked at his sister with new respect. And Will Shakespeare too, although somehow Nathan was not surprised that Will was involved in secret work. He had always kept his own company and few men knew what went on inside his head and his heart. *But still,* thought Nathan with a flush of realization, *I have been drawn into Sir Francis's web too, and I must learn not to be surprised by anything anymore.*

CHAPTER 2

AT THE FEET OF THE MASTER

ATHAN woke as the first light of dawn filtered through the curtains. He crept silently out of bed and quietly dressed, taking care not to wake Marie. His sister had slept poorly that night. He had tried to reassure her that he would be safe, he would be careful—that he was nearly a man—but he had just made things worse. It had been just the two of them since their father, Samuel Fox, had left them in the care of Mistress Fast and disappeared. Nathan had only been five and barely remembered his father. Marie never spoke of him, except to say that she had sworn to him that she would protect her brother.

Despite John Pearce's reassurances that Nathan would only be away for a few months before he would be back in Shoreditch again, both brother and sister knew that once Nathan had the taste for adventure he would not return to his old life. Nathan's barely contained excitement at the prospect of his new future had filled the room last night, while a very subdued Marie packed her brother's clothes.

Now Nathan resolved to take one last look at Shoreditch and the theater before he left. No one was about. He strode into the middle of the road to avoid being drenched by some early riser emptying a chamber pot out of the window, and made his way through the silent streets to the theater. The air was cold and damp, and Nathan shivered as he pulled his cloak around him. He was more than a little afraid but he was excited too. He opened the back door of the theater and fumbled his way through the gloom until he found himself on the wooden stage, half-lit by the breaking dawn. He walked up and down, remembering all the parts he had played, all the plays he had performed in since he was eight years old. He realized, with a pang, that he would miss the theater life, more than he had thought. Apart from Marie, the men in the Burbage company had been the only family he had known for the last few years. He would miss the kindness of Will Kempe, the patient instruction of Will Shakespeare—even the mercurial temperament of the arrogant Richard Burbage. Tears pricked his eyes.

"How now, Master Fox, it does no good to brood." Will Shakespeare stepped out of the darkness and Nathan jumped with surprise.

"Will! You frightened me. What are you doing here so early?"

Shakespeare smiled sadly. "I sometimes come here, when I can be alone, and watch the characters in my head walk around the stage. It's no matter," he added, seeing Nathan's puzzled expression. "You must be made of sterner stuff than that for the life that you are about to embark on," he said gravely. "Are you sure that you want to do this? I know how persuasive Sir Francis can be."

Nathan nodded firmly. "I am sure, Will. I know that I can do it—and the work is important."

Will looked sad. "You understand that spies live in a shadowy world? You may never be thanked or rewarded for the risks you take."

"I still want to do it."

Shakespeare patted Nathan's back. "Well, then, we'll speak no more of doubts."

Nathan looked at his friend gratefully. "Will . . . there is one thing you could do for me."

"Name it."

"Look after Marie while I am away. She will be lonely now and I fear that she will make herself ill with worry."

Shakespeare smiled. "I shall keep her in my sights all the time."

Nathan suddenly had another thought. "Master Burbage! I am leaving his employ without a word. He will be furious."

Will laughed. "He will certainly have a fit of choler at this new turn of events—but am I not a great inventor of stories? I shall weave our friend Burbage such a story that he will be proud that you once served under him." Will looked intently at Nathan. "Now, Master Fox, there is a service you can do me."

"Of course."

Shakespeare's eyes gleamed. "Remember all your adventures, Nathan—every single detail. I want to know the characters you meet, the devilment, the politics, and the cunning. Keep your eyes and ears open for me, and when you return, seek me out while they are still fresh in your mind. Your life may prove to be a window into other men's souls. Will you do that for me?"

"Gladly, Will. I shall be pleased to have a friend to confide in."

The pair walked home through the awakening streets, reminiscing about their times on the stage. They were laughing so much that Nathan's sides began to ache but when they reached their destination, the laughter stopped as they saw Marie frantically pacing the floor.

"Nathan," she sobbed, flinging herself at him. "I thought you had gone without saying good-bye!" Her embrace was so tight, that her brother could hardly speak.

"Calm yourself, Marie," said Will gently. "He was just saying farewell to the theater, that's all."

Nathan felt torn. He did not want to upset Marie further but he was anxious to begin his adventures. It was a relief when a moment later there was a knock at the door and John Pearce entered.

"Are we ready, young master?" Pearce inquired with a broad smile. His easy and confident manner made Nathan feel not only that they were already friends but that whenever Pearce was around he would be safe. It was with eagerness that Nathan picked up his bag and made toward the door.

Marie sniffed loudly and Nathan stopped, shuffled awkwardly, and mumbled a good-bye. Marie straightened his jerkin, mustered a smile and a nod of encouragement, then gave him a kiss on the cheek. He felt one of her tears trickle into the corner of his mouth and he rubbed it away.

"I'm not leaving forever," he said by way of reassurance, the huskiness of his voice betraying his own uncertainty. He cast a look at Shakespeare, and his friend nodded, remembering his promise to look after Marie.

"I shall guard him with my life, sweet lady," said Pearce. Then he ushered Nathan from the room and they were gone.

Outside the house, two horses waited, heads down to let the fine rain trickle away from their eyes. Pearce unhitched them from the post. "I trust you can ride, Nathan. I never thought to ask."

Nathan snorted. "Gypsies ride horses better than they can walk." He vaulted into the saddle.

Impressed, Pearce swung himself onto the back of the other horse. "I see I was not wrong in choosing you for this work."

Nathan grinned and the new partners made a stately progress toward London.

Shoreditch was a good hour's canter from the walls of the City. The authorities had decreed that playhouses be built away from the City, to avoid the risk of plague from large gatherings. *And yet*, thought Nathan, as their horses entered the City proper, *there can be no greater risk than the sheer mass of humanity surrounding us now.*

The working day was underway. There were peddlers selling wares off their backs—ribbons, paste jewelry, gewgaws of all kinds. Carts vied for space on the muddy street with people, dogs, and horses. Nathan was forced to drop behind John as they picked their way among the throng. People were shouting at one another—some were trying to sell fruit and vegetables, others were just shouting abuse.

Pearce turned his horse's head southward and Nathan followed. Soon the great, wide expanse of the river Thames lay in front of them, and to the left, Nathan saw the forbidding citadel of the Tower of London. An involuntary shiver ran through him as he noticed the faint outlines of some rotting heads on pikes. Pearce followed his gaze and murmured, "Traitors," by way of explanation.

"We're almost there," called John, as the horses negotiated the narrow walkway of London Bridge.

"Where are we going?" Nathan asked, once the two horses were able to walk side by side again.

"Master Robey's School of Defense. There is none better." He slowed his horse to a halt outside a large mansion within the shadow of Saint Savior's Church. As they dismounted, a man appeared and took the horses' reins. He had left the heavy oak door of the house ajar and Pearce led Nathan through the entrance, down a hallway, and into a large room.

Nathan's mouth dropped open as he took in the sight before him. The ceiling was vaulted, like a church's, with windows set up high that allowed pools of light to fall onto the floor below. The right-hand wall was lined with every conceivable weapon: swords, daggers, bucklers, staffs, pikes, and other weapons he had never seen before. The left-hand wall was covered in a curious arrangement of wooden bars, beams, and iron rings.

"What is this place?" he whispered. His voice seemed to echo around the vast space. Suddenly a man's voice rang out from above.

"Master Fox!"

Nathan jerked his gaze upward to see a figure, dressed entirely in black leather, standing on a gallery at the end of the room.

"This, young master, is where you learn to defend yourself in ways that you never dreamed were possible."

The man vaulted over the balustrade and plunged effortlessly, a full eighteen feet, to the floor below. When Nathan caught his breath again he realized that the man had, in fact, slid down a rope so fast that it appeared as though he had jumped.

The man came toward them. *He walks as silently as a cat,* thought Nathan in awe.

"I am Robey," said the man, holding out his hand. Nathan tentatively held his hand out and Robey grasped it. Nathan suspected that Robey might be testing his hand for strength by applying a firm but not painful pressure. He responded. After examining Nathan's other hand, Robey commanded him to shed his boots. Nathan did as he was told and stood in his stockinged feet while they too were examined. Nathan held his breath as Robey produced a dagger but he merely slid the blade of the dagger under the arch of each foot.

"Good, high arches, good," he muttered. Then he placed the dagger flat on the floor. "Clasp your hands behind your back, boy, and pick up that dagger with your foot." Nathan looked puzzled for a moment, then smiled. He pointed one foot out like a dancer, and with his big toe he nudged the hilt of the dagger toward him. It was an Italian stiletto, with a thin, straight hilt. He could easily curl his toes around it and lift it from the floor. But the blade was long and he needed to bring his knee almost up to his waist in order to raise the full length of it off the floor. This he did, without losing his balance or dropping the dagger. He stood motionless for a full fifteen seconds before Robey barked the command, "Drop." Relieved, Nathan released the dagger.

Robey broke into a huge grin and slapped the boy roughly on the shoulder. "Excellent! Excellent!" he exclaimed, well pleased with his new pupil. Nathan felt honored that he had passed this first test and he looked to Pearce for reassurance.

He seemed well pleased too. "Then I may leave you to get on with your work, Master Robey," he said, backing away.

"Oh no!" said Robey sternly. "Sir Francis says that I have only what remains of this month before the boy is pressed into service. Therefore, John Pearce, you must take my place with my other students, so that I may concentrate on the task in hand."

"But I had plans, Master," Pearce moaned. "There is a young lady, who expects my company today . . ." His voice trailed off as Robey merely raised one disapproving eyebrow.

"Orders from Sir Francis," Robey said firmly and Pearce's shoulders dropped in resignation.

Robey strode across to the corner of the room and flung open a door. "In here," he barked and two young men bounded in, like eager puppies. Pearce groaned. "The Silver brothers!"

"John Pearce!" the two brothers chorused enthusiastically, then they leapt off in separate directions, each grabbing a sword and a dagger from the wall of weapons.

"I favor the rapier and dagger today," said George Silver breezily.

"The short sword and dagger for me," said the equally energetic Toby. The brothers stood expectantly, weapons in hand.

"I'll fight with two swords then," said Pearce in a resigned voice and he moved reluctantly to the wall to select weapons.

"Gentlemen," said Robey. "If you will adjourn to the small hall, I shall teach in here." He ushered the three young men through the door and closed it—but not before Nathan heard delighted whoops from the two brothers and John Pearce exclaim in irritation, "NOT BEFORE I'M READY, YOU DOLTS!"

Nathan's grin was wiped off his face when Robey turned back to him and said quietly, "This is where you learn to kill another man or be killed yourself." Nathan grew cold as Robey circled him slowly. "I do not teach Sir Francis's agents to fence like actors in the theater. Nor do I teach them to fence in the elegant Spanish fashion, like young men do at court for the amusement of the ladies. I teach street fighting, in the Italian style, for they have perfected the dirtiest form of brawling in Christendom. Be aware, boy, that there are no rules here. I teach you to survive and you will do that by whatever means possible—with the sword, the dagger, your fists, or a broken piece of glass. Do you understand?"

Nathan nodded. He was unable to speak—his tongue seemed to have stuck itself to the roof of his mouth and he felt stupid. He realized that, in his naïveté, he had viewed the world of spying as an exciting adventure. Robey was painting a very different picture.

Robey came up very close and spoke softly. "This work is a dirty business, and if you value your life you will walk out of here now and never come back. No one will think the worse of you."

Nathan looked at Robey intently and he noticed the deep scar over the man's brow and cheekbone—a line that went almost to his ear. "I am afraid, sir," he confessed. "But I am no coward," he added defiantly.

Robey held his gaze. "Fear is good. It sharpens the senses and musters the will. I promise you, lad, that when I have finished with you, you will be almost the equal of John Pearce in skill. Now..." Robey turned on his heel and strode toward the weapons wall.

"We have work to do. . . . But first let me say this." Robey paused on his way to fetch a sword. "Your most important weapons are your feet."

Nathan laughed. "My feet, sir?"

"Yes." Robey's seriousness made the laugh die in Nathan's throat. "The best and quickest way to save your life is to run and run fast. Never go into a fight if you can avoid it."

"To run away would be cowardly, sir." Nathan was scornful.

"No. You would be alive to do your job—to maybe save other people. There are no cowards amongst clever men. There is no courage in fighting, or dying, needlessly."

Nathan did not respond. He understood the sense of what Robey was saying, but his pride could not allow him to acknowledge that there might be situations where running away was the best option.

Robey selected a rapier and walked back toward his pupil. "This weapon has many purposes," he said, holding it to one side to demonstrate. "It has two very sharp edges, or rather, it should have. Many men do not look after their swords. These edges should be razor sharp, for their job is to slash your opponent and disable him. If you sever the muscle of his sword arm, he can no longer fight." He saw Nathan wince. "Do you have the stomach for this work?" he inquired seriously. "You cannot afford to hesitate if your life, or the life of another, is in danger."

Nathan shook his head. "My stomach is strong enough, Master." He was lying but he felt confident that he could overcome his squeamishness.

Robey strode toward the door of the small hall and flung it

open. "Desist!" he barked and the sound of clashing swords ceased. "I need assistance in here." The Silver brothers and John Pearce entered, flushed from their exertions, swords and daggers in hands.

"Master George, step forward," said Robey. The young man obeyed. "Nathan, watch and listen. Here"—he laid the side of the rapier across the upper part of George Silver's right arm—"is the first point of disablement. Cut deep across this muscle and your opponent will not be able to raise his sword to counterattack. Here"—he laid the rapier across Silver's right thigh—"is the second point of disablement. Sever the muscle of the leg that he uses for balance—which is on the same side as his sword arm—and your opponent will not be able to lunge toward you with his sword. Here"—he laid the rapier across Silver's left thigh—"is the third point of disablement. Cut him on this leg and he will not be able to retreat from your sword. And here"—he laid the rapier across Silver's left upper arm—"is the fourth point of disablement. Cut him here and his left arm is useless. Obviously, if you are confronted by a left-handed sword fighter, the points of disablement are reversed. You go for the left upper arm first, then the left thigh, then the right thigh, then the right upper arm. Got that?"

"Yes, Master Robey." Nathan hoped he sounded more confident than he felt. George Silver grinned as Robey lifted up his arms into a crucifix position and flicked his thighs to make him spread his legs apart. "Now I will show you the slow-death points of attack." He laid the rapier first on one side at the base of Silver's neck and then the other. "Here and here," he continued, "are where the blood flows fastest through the veins of men. Cut him on either side of the neck and your opponent will gush blood so fast that he will drop to the ground unconscious within a very few seconds. Pierce him here . . . ," and he indicated in Silver's armpits, "and he will let blood equally as fast and no doctor will be able to stem the flow. If you pierce him here," and he indicated Silver's groin, "he will also lose blood quickly and be unable to move his legs. Thank you, Master George, you may resume a normal stance now." George Silver sprang to attention and winked at Nathan. Robey continued. "The quick-death points are here," he said, pointing his rapier at Silver's heart, "and here." He pointed at Silver's abdomen below his rib cage. "But you need not worry about those."

Nathan was puzzled. "Why not, sir?"

Robey indicated toward the corner of the hall. "John, bring over King Philip of Spain." Pearce dragged a large man-shaped object across to Nathan. It swung from a wooden frame, like a man hanging from the gallows. "This," said Robey, waving the rapier in its direction, "is your enemy. It is covered in soft leather, which is similar in consistency to a man's skin and it is stuffed with rags, which is like the flesh and sinew beneath the skin. Now I want you to take this rapier and lunge it into King Philip's breast with all your force."

Nathan took the sword gingerly, took a deep breath, and lunged at the stuffed man with a mighty yell. His first thrust bounced clean off the leather and slid to one side, so that his face and body smacked into the dummy and he dropped the sword. He felt his face becoming hot as the two Silver brothers sniggered.

"Try again," said Robey calmly.

Nathan picked up the sword, stepped back several places and lunged again, with all his force. This time the rapier penetrated, but try as he would, he could not pull it out. He struggled to pull it from the hilt and was about to go in close and grasp the blade with his other hand when Robey yanked him back. "Think, Master Nathan! That blade is razor sharp. You will cut your hands to ribbons."

Nathan felt foolish but Robey patted his back.

"You have done well, lad. None of your experience could have done better. Those of us who fight for a living know that to pierce a man with the point of your rapier is a mistake. It takes great strength to pull a blade out of a man's body and you cannot do it at arm's length. The thrust is only employed if your opponent is down and you can finish him off with the point and put your foot on his chest to pull out the blade. Understand?" Nathan nodded.

"Now," said Robey, turning his attention to his older pupils. "Master Nathan will do wrist-strengthening exercises, whilst you brothers do agility training under the tutelage of Master Pearce." The brothers groaned and began to strip off all their sword belts, leather jerkins, chain-mail gloves, and boots. Robey, meanwhile, put his rapier back and selected a longer, heavier sword. He then took a jagged piece of chalk and a leather string from a pouch on his belt. He proceeded to tie the chalk to the end of the sword, in line with the blade. "Come with me," he commanded, leading Nathan down to the wall underneath the gallery. "This is what you are going to do." He raised the chalk-ended rapier in front of him, and extending the full length of his arm, he drew a perfect number eight on the wall. "Now you will do this, without moving your arm—just the wrist—and when you have perfected it to my satisfaction, you will do the same with your other hand."

"But I am right handed," protested Nathan.

Robey smiled. "Not anymore," he replied. "When you fight someone, boy, you'd better be able to do it with either hand or your life will be snuffed out quicker than a candle at bedtime." And with that he turned back to the Silver brothers, who were scaling the curious wooden projections along the long wall.

Nathan raised the heavy rapier and began his task—alleviating his boredom by imagining that he had bested the finest swordsman in Spain and was just humiliating the man by carving a swift number eight on his chest. As his daydream took over, the numbers became more and more extravagant and he began to mutter to himself, *"Take that, you scoundrel! How dare you challenge Nathan Fox—Queen Elizabeth's personal bodyguard!"*

But after about five minutes, the muscles in Nathan's arm and shoulder were so sore that he could barely hold up the sword and all dreams of being the queen's bodyguard evaporated, driven away by the embarrassment of being so weak. Robey's voice in his ear startled him. "Switch to the other arm now, lad, before you seize up altogether." Gratefully Nathan did as he was told, only to find that the wrist of his left hand would not obey him. Nevertheless, Robey seemed pleased.

"Now," said Robey, grasping Nathan by the shoulders and vigorously massaging away his aches and pains. "I hear that you are a wondrous acrobat. So I ask you now to show this pair of fumblers what you are made of."

Nathan's heart lifted and he gladly stripped off his boots, belt, and jerkin. The Silver brothers were now down on the ground. Toby had fallen a third of the wall's height and was busy rubbing his behind. Pearce smirked at his discomfort, then showed his obvious delight when Robey informed them that Nathan was to do some agility training.

"Watch and learn," said Pearce, giving Toby Silver a good-natured cuff around the ear.

All four men watched in respectful silence as Nathan climbed the wall with the speed and ease of a spider.

"That boy has suckers like an ivy plant," said George in wonderment, as Nathan reached the top of the wall.

"Now get yourself to a rope," called Robey, pointing to the ropes that were tied along a ceiling beam some four feet away from the wall. Nathan launched himself, like a cat, toward the nearest rope and clung at beam level, awaiting further instructions. "Up onto the beam and walk its length," came the next command. Nathan swung his legs over his head and up onto the beam. He then hoisted himself up, effortlessly, and stood erect. Nimbly he walked the length of the beam with perfect balance and stopped, looking down at them all.

"He's not troubled by great heights then," murmured Toby enviously.

"Now back onto the ropes," directed Robey. Nathan obliged. "Turn upside down and hang by your feet only." Grasping the rope between his thighs, Nathan arched his back and dropped down like a stone, holding his arms outstretched, to show that he was truly hanging on by his legs only. Only the week before he had performed a similar trick in the theater.

"God's teeth!" exclaimed Toby.

"Come down now, lad," said Robey. "You have put us all to shame."

When Nathan reached the floor, George, Toby, and Pearce surrounded him and expressed their admiration. He flushed with pride and happiness.

That night, after many more grueling exercises, Nathan was plunged into a hot bath, drawn by Robey's servants—then thoroughly scrubbed and rubbed down with a foul-smelling liniment. When he was eating a bowl full of stew, he complained to Robey about the overpowering smell of the liniment.

"You'll thank us in the morning," said Robey, smiling at Nathan's discomfort. "Never go to bed with sore muscles because you will be a cripple the next day. Always find some hot water to soak your bones in and rub yourself down afterward—goose grease or lard will do."

Nathan gratefully sank into what felt like the softest bed ever and began to doze. Pearce jolted him out of his sleep by patting him on the shoulder. "I shall be gone for a few days," he said softly. "I have some apologies to make to a certain lady who will have waited in vain for me this evening." Pearce winked and left, taking the light of the candle with him.

In the darkness Nathan smiled contentedly. Today he had entered a world where men fought hard and lived by their wits. It suited him just fine.

CHAPTER 3

WHAT YOU LEARN
MAY SAVE YOUR LIFE

NATHAN awoke in his attic bedroom, sore but not stiff. He pulled on his clothes but could not find his boots or stockings anywhere, so he padded down the stairs in his bare feet and followed the smell of food. There, around a huge table in the kitchen, sat Robey and three silent men who were eating heartily.

Nathan stood in the doorway awkwardly. Although he felt he had proved himself to be a quick pupil during yesterday's training, the absence of John Pearce made him feel vulnerable and uncertain.

Robey looked up and said encouragingly, "Come in, lad, and fill your stomach," and he motioned to one of the men, who rose and filled a plate from the iron griddle suspended over the fire. A plate piled high with ham, eggs, and warm bread was placed on the table, and Nathan was motioned to sit and eat. The spit-roasted ham was delicious and the juices ran down his fingers as he picked it up in his hands. One of the men slid a spoon across the table so that he could eat his eggs. The glorious mess of it all slid down his throat and hit his grateful stomach with a warm glow. Nathan realized that in the excitement of yesterday he had eaten very little.

"Have some water, lad," said Robey, gently pushing a pewter jug and cup toward him. "We don't drink ale here," he added. "Addles the wits. And people in our business need our wits about us. Remember that."

Nathan nodded and drank the cold water. His mouth clear of food, he was now able to speak. "I cannot find my stockings and boots, Master."

Robey nodded. "From today, you will dress your feet differently. We will show you when you have finished breakfast."

Nathan was curious but carried on eating, at the same time observing the men around the table. They were all powerful, with scars on their arms that betrayed old wounds. One even wore an eye patch. Nathan reflected that if he had met them in an alley in Shoreditch he would have run for his life.

Robey noticed Nathan's eyes flickering from one man to another. "You must excuse my lack of manners, for I have not introduced you to my men. We are professional fighters and we tend to forget the niceties of life. This is Bardolph. . . ." He indicated the man with the eye patch, who nodded his egg-smeared face in greeting. "This is Pistol. . . ." Robey pointed to a man with huge forearms, knotted with muscles, who grunted a greeting. "And this is Nym. . . ." The third man grinned at Nathan, showing the gaps of many lost teeth. "The four of us will be your tutors throughout your time here. You will find us harsh but fair. We will teach you as much as we can before we send you on your way. But, like John

Pearce, you will doubtless come back to us to refine your skills from time to time. Now, Nathan, let us begin our work."

Robey waved his hand toward a bucket in the corner. "First you must wash the grease from your hands. You need to grip swords and knives with confidence. Bardolph will be your tutor this morning."

Robey took some strips of cloth and a pair of new boots from a nearby closet and sat Nathan down on a chair. "I am now going to bind your feet and ankles. You must watch carefully because you will have to do this yourself every day. Why this is necessary will become clear when you put these boots on."

He began to work the strips of cloth in a figure-of-eight shape around Nathan's arches and then around each ankle. The cloth was cut so that it stretched but when Robey had finished one foot and tucked in the last piece of fabric, Nathan's ankle was held quite firmly yet he could still move his foot up and down. Robey made him stand and walk around with one foot bound up. "It must be tight enough to give you support but not so tight that the blood cannot flow through your feet," he explained. Nathan found it uncomfortable but he knew he would have to get used to it.

Robey held up one boot. "In both boots there is a special inner compartment, just large enough to conceal a small flat-bladed dagger on the outside of each ankle. You must wear these boots at all times. Only when you need to climb will you remove the blades. Otherwise, you must always wear these two daggers for your protection."

"But I can fight with a sword," Nathan protested.

"You are a boy and most likely will be playing the part of a servant. You will not be carrying a sword," said Robey firmly. "Bardolph will teach you all you need to know about using the knife. John Pearce will defend you with his sword. You will defend him with your dagger."

Swallowing his disappointment at not being allowed a sword, Nathan let Robey bind up his other foot. Then he put on the boots. It was hard for him to walk with his usual spring and agility. The lengths of steel down each ankle felt awkward but throughout the morning, he became used to the restriction. Nathan soon realized the purpose of the binding, which was to stop the rigid boots from chafing his skin.

His lesson with Bardolph was in the large hall. First he had to learn to retrieve the daggers quickly from their sheaths inside his boots. For the best part of an hour he fumbled through this task, nicking the skin on both legs several times. They were awkward weapons to grasp, since they were designed to fit smoothly down the side of each boot and not be noticed. They were very flat, even the grip was flat, but there was a notch cut in each side of the grip, about halfway down their length. Eventually Nathan worked out a system of hooking the first two fingers of each hand around the notches then whisking the daggers out quite nimbly. Bardolph grunted his approval.

Having mastered the fast retrieval of the daggers, the next lesson was to accurately throw them at a target. This involved whisking them out of his boots, throwing them slightly into the air, and catching them by the blade, ready to throw. Because they were meant to be used in this way, the blades were blunt. Only the tips were sharp to pierce the target. If he missed catching the daggers in midair as he spun them, he would not run the risk of cutting his hands. Nathan thanked God that he was a skilled juggler and when Bardolph examined his hands at the end of the morning, there was only one small nick between his left thumb and forefinger.

The target was a man-shaped piece of wood, hanging from a rope. On the front there was a red circle painted over the heart and another red circle painted over the abdomen. To demonstrate, Bardolph threw two daggers, which clashed together in the heart of the target. Nathan tried to copy but he used too much force and the dagger spun through the air wildly, hit the target hilt first, and bounced back toward Bardolph, who nimbly dived out of the way with a muttered curse. Bardolph taught Nathan to pull back on his strength and use his wrist to greater effect. "Flick the weapon, don't hurl it," he said gruffly and Nathan obeyed. Soon he was sending the daggers straight to the target. Practice would make his aim better but he had mastered the technique.

When Nathan seemed to be doing quite well, Bardolph set the target swinging. "You can't expect a man to stand still while you throw a knife at him, can you?" he said with a grin, winking his one good eye at his pupil. At first the target swung gently but still Nathan missed the wood more times than he hit it. Bardolph taught him to use his eyes to judge where the target *would* be when it had swung one way and was coming back the other way. Still Nathan found it difficult and Bardolph grudgingly admitted that "It is not something easily taught—being more of an instinct, like." Nathan chewed his lip in frustration and then hit upon an idea. He would stop thinking of the dagger as a dagger and think of it as his favorite toy, the diabolo. He could throw a diabolo high into the air, spin round, and catch it on the rope with ease, because his instinct told him how long it would take it to rise and fall. Once he stopped thinking of the knife in his hand as a weapon, he began to relax into the timing of the operation. Soon he was hitting the moving target with every throw, although not always in the red zones.

When Bardolph moved on to throwing leather balls in the air as moving targets, Nathan thought of juggling pins. When he and Will Kempe had juggled together onstage, he had learned to gauge the time it would take a pin to leave his hand and connect with Will's. So, as the leather ball left Bardolph's hand, Nathan would launch the dagger and soon he was bringing down every ball. Impressed by his pupil's growing skill, the old soldier became less gruff as the morning progressed.

At noon, they broke for another feast around the kitchen table. First Nathan had his small wound dressed with lavender oil. It stung like fire but Nathan, determined to show no weakness, just gritted his teeth.

They sat around the table eating thick, hot stew with bread and cheese and the men were more talkative than they were earlier. As they cleared their plates, Robey became serious. "Your next lesson will be outdoors," he declared. The other men laughed and winked at one another. Nathan had an uneasy feeling that he was about to be truly tested.

Bardolph took him out into the backyard and showed him a deep man-made hole with a heavy grille over the top. "This is an oubliette," he said, slapping Nathan on the back. "Invented by them poxy Normans." He spat on the ground to express his disgust. "Most castles 'ave 'em. They throw decent Englishmen down 'em and leave 'em to rot. They forget about 'em. Terrible death it is—dyin' o' starvation." Nathan looked at Bardolph and his blood ran cold. He knew what was coming next.

"Now you, my lad, are going down in that hellhole. Then you are going to figure a way out," said Bardolph, with a deep, wheezing laugh. "Don't you fret, young Nathan. Old Bardolph won't leave you to rot. I'll come back in an hour and see what's what, eh?" And with that, he lifted off the iron grate and pointed at a heavy rope that hung down into the darkness from an iron ring set in the courtyard-stone. "Down you go."

Feeling apprehensive, Nathan grasped the rope and dropped off the side of the hole. His feet touched the brick walls of the oubliette and slithered. The walls were wet and mossy, so he clamped the rope between his feet and inched down to the bottom. It smelled vile. Nathan looked up to see Bardolph's face grinning down at him. "Don't worry, lad, there's no rats down there. I checked afore you got up this morning." He then pulled up the rope and the heavy iron grille clanked into place.

Nathan heard Bardolph's footsteps disappearing. He wanted to take some deep breaths for courage but the smell was so bad that he could barely bring himself to inhale. How many poor wretches had met their deaths in holes like this? Reluctantly he felt the walls around him. The bricks were damp and smooth and the mortar between them was slightly crumbly from the permanent moisture. Nathan racked his brains for a solution to his predicament. *They know that there is a way to escape, or they wouldn't have put me down here.* He felt all around the walls to get an idea of the structure's size. Could there be a secret passage or some hidden footholds in the walls? No, that would be too easy. He traced the walls with his fingers, like a trapped rat, his mind turning and turning. Suddenly he smiled as a solution came to him. Of course! The boots. I can use the daggers.

Carefully Nathan wiped his sweaty hands on his clothes, then removed the two daggers from his boots. Feeling with his fingers, he found a mortar join between two bricks at about knee height and forcefully pushed one of the blades into it, up to the hilt, to form a step. He put one foot on the hilt and levered himself up on it. It took his full weight. Smiling to himself, Nathan took the other dagger and found a second mortar join slightly up and to the left. He pushed the other dagger in. With his left foot he transferred his body weight onto the higher dagger. Now came the business of trying to retrieve the lower dagger from the wall. The walls were slippery and he had no handholds so when he tried to grab the lower dagger, he just fell off—which was fine at such a short distance from the floor of the oubliette but might be fatal near the top.

Frustrated he dropped to the floor again and pulled the daggers out. As he did so, he felt a chunk of mortar come out with the blade. *I'm so stupid!* he thought, with a flash of inspiration, *I need to use the daggers to make holes!* He started to chip the mortar out from between certain bricks so that the toe of his boot would fit into them. He made three such holes up to head height and levered himself into the first one, pushing one dagger into the mortar each time he ascended, while using the other to make a foothold above him. Slowly and painfully he climbed the walls of the oubli-

48

ette, his breath coming in short gasps as he meticulously ascended, a foothold at a time.

Halfway up the wall he was close to tears. His left arm ached so much that he feared he would fall. *Idiot!* he cursed. *Just change hands, for God's sake!* He pushed the right-hand dagger into the wall and transferred his body weight onto it while he let his left arm hang limply at rest. Then he resumed his slow climb.

The circle of light above his head got bigger and bigger, inch by inch, until he could smell sweet, fresh air and the top of his curly hair grazed the iron grille. Just as he was wondering where he would summon the strength to push aside the cover, he heard Bardolph's voice exclaim, "God's teeth, if he 'asn't got to the top already! 'Ere quick, Pistol, give us a hand to grab 'im." The grille was lifted and two strong arms grabbed Nathan under his armpits and hoisted him to safety. Although he was ashamed of himself, tiredness and fear made him cry tears of relief as he was hauled out onto the ground. Hard, calloused hands gently took his boots off and rubbed his sore and aching arms. All the time the men were murmuring to him that he was a brave lad, a strong lad, a clever lad. Nathan could not see them through the tears that streamed down his face. Bardolph rubbed a warm, wet cloth over his sweaty face. "There, lad. It's all over now. You've done a miracle, you 'ave. Better than most of the men who been through this school. We never thought you'd do it. We never thought you'd 'ave the courage and the wit to get yourself up them walls like that."

49

Nathan smiled through his tears and weariness. "Will I have to do it again, Bardolph?" he asked.

"Never, lad. Not unless you're captured by them Spaniards. But *we* won't put you down another one."

Lying in bed that night, Nathan was visited by a solemn Robey. "It was a great feat of strength you performed today."

Nathan nodded. "I was very frightened, sir," he said quietly.

"Only stupid men feel no fear in the face of danger," replied Robey. He paused and looked intently at Nathan. "Listen well. You can walk away from all of this and become an actor again. You could have died today because we underestimated you. We thought we would return to find you sulking in the bottom of the hole. Bardolph was looking forward to showing you how to use your daggers to climb the walls but you denied him that pleasure. We do not mean to be cruel but we have to teach you to survive. Do you understand?"

"Yes, sir." Nathan stirred a little in the bed to ease his aching limbs. "I still want to work for Sir Francis." After his ordeal in the oubliette, he was ready for anything.

Robey nodded and strode to the door. "Well, then sleep now. We shall do brain work tomorrow, to give your body a rest."

"Sir?" Nathan's voice halted Robey at the door. "Did you put John Pearce in the oubliette?"

"Of course," replied Robey.

"Did he get out?"

Robey smiled in the moonlight. "Yes," came the answer, "John Pearce got out."

Nathan smiled too and sunk into a deep sleep, only this time it wasn't dreamless. He dreamed that he was in a deep, black hole and there was no light up above him. The air was foul and he couldn't breathe. He was suffocating and trying to shout for help at the same time. He woke with a start, drenched in sweat—unsure, for a moment, of where he was. The moon hung like a pale orb in the window; then the sound of a cart trundling through the street below reassured him that he was in his bed, safe, at Robey's School of Defense.

CHAPTER 4

THE MEANING OF MESSAGES

AT breakfast the next morning, Bardolph, Pistol, and Nym chatted to Nathan as though he were an old friend. Nathan felt good, as he realized that it was a sign of acceptance. They had judged him to be one of them—to be worthy—and he was elated. Nathan began to learn more about his band of strange tutors—except for Master Robey, who kept his own counsel and remained a mystery.

Bardolph, he discovered, had soldiered all over Europe for whatever country would pay him. His skills with the knife had been learned when fighting as a mercenary for some of the Italian states.

"Dirtiest fighters in the world, the Italians," he said with an approving grin. "What they don't know about slitting a man's throat silently ain't worth knowing." Nathan's pulse quickened when Bardolph talked about Venice. "Greatest place on earth, boy," he said with a wink. "You'll see things there you ain't never dreamt of. The women is beautiful, the men is clever. And they got a head for business, them Venetians. That's how they keep old Philip of Spain at bay, y'know, 'cos he owes them so much money they calls the tune and he dances!" The men around the table roared with laughter. Even Robey's inscrutable face broke into a grin.

Nym was a Welshman and an expert archer. He had taken his bow to the Netherlands on many occasions to fight with the rebels against Spain. Nathan's blood ran cold when Nym removed the leather glove from his left hand to reveal that the first two fingers were missing.

"I got caught by the enemy, see," he explained in his singsong voice, "and the first thing they do with any bowmen they capture is cut off the first two fingers of the bow hand to stop you pulling the string back."

"Yeah," said Pistol in his deep growling voice, "except old Nym 'ere, being a clever bastard, tricks 'em into thinking 'e's a left-'ander, so they cut off the wrong fingers, didn't they?" Everyone chuckled appreciatively.

"How did you do that?" inquired Nathan, turning over Nym's cunningly constructed glove in his hand, which had wooden shams in the first two fingers.

Nym winked. "When you shoot professional-like, you wear a leather brace on your forearm of the hand that holds the bow and you have a leather finger tab on the first two fingers of the hand that pulls the string. I just swapped them over quicklike. So when this Spanish captain grabs each man's hand, places it on a bloody block, and chops off the string fingers with an axe, he just grabbed the hand that had the tabs on." Everyone fell silent for a moment, out of respect for Nym's lost fingers.

"You know what we do, lad, we archers, before a battle?" Nym said with a slow grin, breaking the silence. Nathan shook his head. "Afore the battle starts, all the archers raise the two fingers of their string hand in a kind of salute to the enemy." He raised his right hand and, with a triumphant look on his face, made the insulting V sign with his first two fingers. "That shows 'em we're all fit and ready for work." There was a grim nod of appreciation around the table.

Nathan turned to Pistol. "And what of you, sir?" he inquired. "What adventures have you had?"

Pistol looked a little sheepish. "Not so much as these men, lad," he volunteered. "I was trained as a musketeer but, mostly, I make guns—matchlock, wheellock, and snaphaunce muskets."

"And shoots them too," explained Robey. "Pistol here is an expert with the short handgun, or pistol, hence the name. He will tutor you in this at some point."

"Are these band of rogues entertaining you?" came a voice from behind. Nathan's head whipped around with delight to see his friend and partner, John Pearce, who had silently slipped into the kitchen.

"John," cried Nathan. "Are you staying here today?"

"I am that, lad," said John with a smile. "I am to be your tutor. Master Robey's orders. He dragged me from the arms of a very delightful young lady to come here and teach you the refinements of cryptography."

Nathan's wide grin split his face from ear to ear. He realized that he had sorely missed John Pearce's reassuring presence, although he was relieved that Pearce had not been there to witness his tears after the oubliette incident. He had felt foolish and weak, once he had recovered, even though Robey and his men had praised his courage. He would not have liked John to have thought ill of him or, worse still, shown him pity.

"And now it is time, John," commanded Robey, breaking into Nathan's thoughts, "to take Nathan to my rooms for this work." He raised an eyebrow in exasperation. "We have a fencing tournament in the training hall today." The tone of Robey's voice and the expressions on his men's faces told Nathan that they were not looking forward to the event.

Nathan followed Pearce up a staircase by the kitchen. Halfway up the stairs, he paused to look out of the window onto the street below and he smiled at the sight of the Silver brothers acting as shepherds, driving a flock of young men through the street doors into the School of Defense. All were carrying swords and looking anxious. "Young men of quality," murmured Pearce over his shoulder. "Sent by their fathers to learn the noble art of self-defense at the hands of England's best fencing master."

"Will they be taught what I am learning, John?" asked Nathan.

"No, Nathan. You learn special skills. Those lads only learn how to carry their sword at court without tripping over it." Nathan smiled and followed John up the stairs. It felt good to be special.

Robey's rooms were a shrine to learning and Nathan was filled with awe. The passageway leading to the sitting room was lined with books, and the smell of leather and ink filtered into Nathan's nostrils. The walls in the sitting room were adorned with pictures— scientific drawings, maps of the known world, and charts of the stars in the sky and the seas of the earth. To one side there was a table covered with many instruments—scales, weights, glass tubes. On shelves above the table were bottles of all shapes and sizes.

Some were labeled and some were not. Nathan peered in wonder at the murky colors of the powders and potions.

"Master Robey is probably one of the cleverest men in the country," explained Pearce, "if not the world. As you can see, he has many interests. He loves literature, art, and all forms of science. He knows many things. You would do well to learn from him as much as you can. I am still learning and shall continue to do so for the rest of my life."

Pearce indicated an empty table by a window. "We shall sit here and do our work today."

Nathan sat down while Pearce began to fill the table with sheaves of paper, ink pots, blotters, and books. His shoulders and neck were so stiff and sore from scaling the wall of the oubliette that he had a slight headache. He hoped that he would be able to concentrate on this "brain work."

Pearce sat down and looked at him. "Are you recovered from yesterday, Nathan?" he inquired gently. "So far, you have exceeded even my high expectations of you. You are remarkably talented and brave. I could not have a better partner."

"Thank you, John," said Nathan with pride.

"Now. To work," said Pearce, opening a book. "You know that we work in secret and often in dangerous circumstances. We need to be able to send and receive messages to our employers and allies, without the enemy intercepting them. So we must master the art of cryptography: the science of codes and ciphers."

"I know something of that," Nathan interrupted eagerly, and he proceeded to tell Pearce about his sister embroidering handkerchiefs to lay over the coded messages hidden in Will Shakespeare's verses. Pearce listened, while sharpening two quills with a knife then placing them by the ink pots.

He nodded. "Yes, that is one part of cryptography. But those messages that Will and Marie concoct can only be used when you know in advance what message you need to send, because it takes some time for Will to write a verse and for Marie to embroider a cloth. When you and I need to send a message quickly, to ask for help, or to relay some vital piece of information, we have to learn codes that we can use at any time. Let me give you the simplest example."

Pearce pushed a piece of paper across the table to Nathan. On it was written:

A B C D E F G H I J K L M N O P Q R S T U V W X Y Z

"Now, underneath that, I want you to write the alphabet backward, so that each letter is directly under the letter above."

Nathan took up his own pen and completed the task. The paper now read:

A B C D E F G H I J K L M N O P Q R S T U V W X Y Z
Z Y X W V U T S R Q P O N M L K J I H G F E D C B A

"I shall write you a message and you must decode it—using this simple substitution cipher." Pearce scribbled for a moment, pressed and rocked the blotter across his writing, then passed it to Nathan. It read:

RU BMF XZM WVXRKSVI GSRH XLWV

GSVM BMF SZEV WLMV DVOO

Nathan looked at the jumbled letters and took his quill. By substituting the letters of the alphabet on the top line for the letters below he was able to write back to John:

IF YOU CAN DECIPHER THIS CODE

THEN YOU HAVE DONE WELL

"It's easy," said Nathan, laughing.

"Of course it is," agreed Pearce, "*too* easy. That's why we would never use such a simple code. Even a thirteen-year-old boy could decipher this." He gave a sly wink. "No, I merely show you this to start you off on the complex science of cryptography. We have to be more cunning in our correspondence systems. Walsingham has the best intellects in the country coding and decoding messages all day long. Some of them have even invented ciphers that will never be known to anyone else, save those who work for Sir Francis. For most of our work now we use a Vigenère Square. It's a recent French invention and the Spanish do not yet use it."

Pearce reached into his leather jerkin and produced a folded-up square of linen. On it, written in ink, was the following:

	a	b	c	d	e	f	g	h	i	j	k	l	m	n	o	p	q	r	s	t	u	v	w	x	y	z
1	B	C	D	E	F	G	H	I	J	K	L	M	N	O	P	Q	R	S	T	U	V	W	X	Y	Z	A
2	C	D	E	F	G	H	I	J	K	L	M	N	O	P	Q	R	S	T	U	V	W	X	Y	Z	A	B
3	D	E	F	G	H	I	J	K	L	M	N	O	P	Q	R	S	T	U	V	W	X	Y	Z	A	B	C
4	E	F	G	H	I	J	K	L	M	N	O	P	Q	R	S	T	U	V	W	X	Y	Z	A	B	C	D
5	F	G	H	I	J	K	L	M	N	O	P	Q	R	S	T	U	V	W	X	Y	Z	A	B	C	D	E
6	G	H	I	J	K	L	M	N	O	P	Q	R	S	T	U	V	W	X	Y	Z	A	B	C	D	E	F
7	H	I	J	K	L	M	N	O	P	Q	R	S	T	U	V	W	X	Y	Z	A	B	C	D	E	F	G
8	I	J	K	L	M	N	O	P	Q	R	S	T	U	V	W	X	Y	Z	A	B	C	D	E	F	G	H
9	J	K	L	M	N	O	P	Q	R	S	T	U	V	W	X	Y	Z	A	B	C	D	E	F	G	H	I
10	K	L	M	N	O	P	Q	R	S	T	U	V	W	X	Y	Z	A	B	C	D	E	F	G	H	I	J
11	L	M	N	O	P	Q	R	S	T	U	V	W	X	Y	Z	A	B	C	D	E	F	G	H	I	J	K
12	M	N	O	P	Q	R	S	T	U	V	W	X	Y	Z	A	B	C	D	E	F	G	H	I	J	K	L
13	N	O	P	Q	R	S	T	U	V	W	X	Y	Z	A	B	C	D	E	F	G	H	I	J	K	L	M
14	O	P	Q	R	S	T	U	V	W	X	Y	Z	A	B	C	D	E	F	G	H	I	J	K	L	M	N
15	P	Q	R	S	T	U	V	W	X	Y	Z	A	B	C	D	E	F	G	H	I	J	K	L	M	N	O
16	Q	R	S	T	U	V	W	X	Y	Z	A	B	C	D	E	F	G	H	I	J	K	L	M	N	O	P
17	R	S	T	U	V	W	X	Y	Z	A	B	C	D	E	F	G	H	I	J	K	L	M	N	O	P	Q
18	S	T	U	V	W	X	Y	Z	A	B	C	D	E	F	G	H	I	J	K	L	M	N	O	P	Q	R
19	T	U	V	W	X	Y	Z	A	B	C	D	E	F	G	H	I	J	K	L	M	N	O	P	Q	R	S
20	U	V	W	X	Y	Z	A	B	C	D	E	F	G	H	I	J	K	L	M	N	O	P	Q	R	S	T
21	V	W	X	Y	Z	A	B	C	D	E	F	G	H	I	J	K	L	M	N	O	P	Q	R	S	T	U
22	W	X	Y	Z	A	B	C	D	E	F	G	H	I	J	K	L	M	N	O	P	Q	R	S	T	U	V
23	X	Y	Z	A	B	C	D	E	F	G	H	I	J	K	L	M	N	O	P	Q	R	S	T	U	V	W
24	Y	Z	A	B	C	D	E	F	G	H	I	J	K	L	M	N	O	P	Q	R	S	T	U	V	W	X
25	Z	A	B	C	D	E	F	G	H	I	J	K	L	M	N	O	P	Q	R	S	T	U	V	W	X	Y
26	A	B	C	D	E	F	G	H	I	J	K	L	M	N	O	P	Q	R	S	T	U	V	W	X	Y	Z

Nathan's eyes widened in horror at the sea of letters. *How do I understand this!* he thought in panic.

"I know it looks daunting, Nathan, but it is merely a system to be learnt. Once you understand it, you will find it comes easily, and you will always have a Vigenère Square of your own to carry with you."

Slowly and patiently, Pearce explained how the system worked.

"The beauty of this cipher is that it uses a different line for each letter, so that no one, unless they have one of these squares in their possession, can decipher your message. Even if they have a square, if they do not have your personal password, then they still cannot decipher the message. Look at each of these numbered lines of letters." He pointed at the left-hand side of the square. "We use the first letter of each line to tell the person receiving the message which lines are to be used to break the code." Nathan still felt confused but Pearce continued, "Let us say that your personal password is your name: Nathan. That's simple enough, isn't it?" Nathan nodded. "The person you are communicating with will know your password and you will both use that to code and decode your message. Look...."

Pearce wrote on a piece of paper:

NATHAN

THEN HE WROTE BELOW IT:

LINE 13 BEGINS WITH N

LINE 26 BEGINS WITH A

LINE 19 BEGINS WITH T

LINE 7 BEGINS WITH H

"Look at the square," he said, "and look at the top line, which has no number. That is the decoded line. We concoct a message from the decoded line, in plain English. A simple message..."

He wrote on the paper:

THE QUEEN IS GOOD

"Now," he continued, "using your password 'Nathan'—which we use over and over again to tell the receiver of the message where to look—follow down with your finger from the letter T in the decoder line until it meets line thirteen, which begins with the letter N, the first letter in your password. What do you find?"

Nathan traced his finger down from the top letter T until it bisected line thirteen and he stopped on a letter G. He looked up at John and said, "G."

"Good," said Pearce. "So that means that the code letter you use for the letter T is G. Now do the same with H on the top line—trace it down with your finger until it meets line twenty-six, which starts with the letter A, which is the second letter of your password...."

Nathan did the same and found another letter H. "Now do the same with the letter E, tracing it down to line nineteen, which starts with the letter T and is the third letter of your password...."

Nathan duly traced down to the letter X.

"So," explained Pearce. "Do you see that by you and the receiver of the message using your password over and over again," . . . he wrote on the paper:

NATHANNATHANNATHANNATHAN

"The message 'The queen is good' would be encoded as GHX XURRN BZ GBBD."

Nathan was still unsure so John Pearce wrote him out a further explanation, again using the password NATHAN:

PASSWORD: N A T H A N N A T H A N N A
LINES: 13 26 19 7 26 13 13 26 19 7 26
13 13 26
CODED MESSAGE: T O W Z A I R E G N L N
A D
PLAIN ENGLISH: G O D S A V E E N G L A
N D

Nathan studied the lines and began to double-check them against the Vigenère Square. Then with the suddenness of a candle flame igniting from a taper—he understood. He wrote back to John Pearce:

EOULYVFMTZTRE

Pearce looked at the message, then the square. He laughed. "He certainly is, lad, he certainly is!" as he passed over a sheet of paper with the encoded message

ROBEY IS MASTER

After that it became a game between the two of them. When Nathan speeded up coding and decoding the messages, John changed the password. This he did several times and when Nathan became proficient at coping with the changes, Pearce began to write messages in Italian.

Nathan's mind was buzzing with numbers and letters when a knock sounded at the door and Pistol entered with a tray of food and two mugs of water.

"Is it noon already?" inquired Pearce with surprise.

"Aye, Master Pearce," replied Pistol. "The master asks you to excuse the lack of hot food but we 've our 'ands full downstairs with a pretty passel of poltroons."

Pearce laughed. "Worse than usual, is it?"

Pistol shook his head and rolled his eyes. "Never seed such sore lack of grace. Still," he said over his shoulder as he turned to leave, "pays the wages, don't it?"

"What is he talking about?" asked Nathan, rubbing his stiff neck and flexing his cramped fingers.

"The gentlemen of quality, fencing below," relied Pearce. He motioned with his head toward a curtain in the corner of the room. "Behind there is a door and if you would care to open it for me we could take our food and be entertained whilst we eat."

Nathan pulled back the heavy curtain, turned the key in the lock, and opened the door. A mighty din hit his ears—the sound of shouting, swords clashing, yelling.

He stepped through the door and found himself on the gallery from which Master Robey had made his spectacular descent on his first day of training. It stretched the full width of the hall, and below, England's finest young gentlemen were making a complete pig's ear of themselves in combat.

There were six pairs of swordsmen dueling. Robey strode down the hall, unconcerned by any danger he may be in from flailing and undisciplined swords, shouting insults and critiques at the flushed and sweating young men.

"By all that's holy, keep your backside in, Master Throckmorton," roared Robey. "You look like a Michaelmas goose!"

"You should be dead by now, young Tylney," he roared at another. "You have not parried one single thrust all morning."

Nathan sniggered as Robey continued to belittle the hapless students below, and he considered himself fortunate that Robey had never employed such withering remarks during his training. A broad wink from Pearce made Nathan feel as though he was part of a privileged elite. *I am one of Walsingham's agents,* he thought to himself with a trace of smugness, *and that sets me apart from Robey's other students.*

The perpetual clamor of steel against steel, grunts, and curses rang out. Now and then, a duelist would give up, shout, "I yield!" and be taken to one side by one of Robey's men, then doused in cold water to cool him down. All around the hall were buckets of cold water and wooden ladles so that the exhausted pupils could quench their thirst. When one of the men was forced back at great speed by a superior opponent, then tripped and sat down with great force in one of the buckets, Nathan thought he would laugh until he cried.

It was Pearce's loud guffaw that made Robey glare disapprovingly at the gallery, sending Nathan and John scuttling back to their lessons as fast as they could move.

When the light began to fade and they ventured downstairs to the kitchen, all was quiet. Bardolph, Pistol, and Nym were slumped around the table, looking worn out. "The master's gone a-visiting," said Bardolph, with a weak smile.

"Don't blame 'im neither," added Pistol. "God save us from the bleedin' gentry and their sons." He paused and then apologized. "There's no grub, me lads. We've all been too busy."

Pearce smiled. "Seems to me like we could all do with an outing to a tavern."

The men's eyes lit up. "I reckon you're right, John," said Bardolph, perking up.

So they stepped out into the night air, five unlikely companions, and took a deep breath before heading to the nearest inn to spend an evening of warmth and cheer, tall stories and jokes, roast pork and ale.

CHAPTER 5

A DISHONOURABLE WEAPON

Uring his second week at Robey's school, Nathan found himself facing a day of archery training. He cursed himself that he had not, like many actors, been scrupulous in attending weekly practice at the butts, as was demanded by law. Most actors found a way to avoid archery training, even though, since the dim and distant days of the wars with France, successive rulers had placed great emphasis on the English skill with the longbow. He hoped that his natural hand-eye coordination would see him through.

Nym took Nathan to some public training butts in the marshy outlands of Southwark, near where the tanners plied their stinking trade of scraping and curing leather hides. Nathan hardly dared breathe as they passed by the tanneries with their great vats of urine in which they dipped the steaming animal skins. No wonder tanners are forbidden by law to practice their trade within the City walls, he thought, as the bile rose in his throat.

Nym had brought along six yew bows, wrapped in oiled cloth,

which he lovingly unwrapped and strung with hemp strings that he produced from a pouch at his belt. "Always keep your strings dry, lad," he advised patiently. "A wet string is no good to man or beast."

Nathan acquitted himself well at straightforward shooting but then Nym rigged up a target on wooden wheels, which he pulled from one side of the field to the other. Nathan found himself retrieving more arrows from the grass than from the straw butt. Nym grinned a toothless grin. "Now, young Master. Bardolph tells me that you mastered the art of throwing knives at a moving target. Just fix your mind in the same way for the arrow, see. It's easier with an arrow, 'cos you has it in your eye line from the start." He drew his own bow up to his cheekbone, as if to reinforce the point. "With an arrow you can be much more accurate—even at long distances. A knife starts dropping to the floor after twenty feet. An arrow only starts falling after fifty."

Nathan steeled himself and tried again. He was not ready to give up. Eventually he began to gauge the timing of the arrow from leaving the bow to arriving at the target but just as he was mastering the technique and successfully hitting the mark, Nym changed him to a heavier and faster bow and he had to start over.

"You got to be prepared to use any bow," Nym said, with a twinkle in his eye. "You might pick someone else's bow up in a battle and you've got to be able to compensate, like, for the different weight and speed."

With a sigh, Nathan resumed the practice and each time he became at ease with a bow, Nym would change it for another. On and on they practiced, until Nathan's shoulder blades felt as though they had been pried away from his body with a meat hook. Nym had paused only to allow his pupil the occasional gulp of water and a mouthful of bread and cheese. But, as the light began to fade, Nym announced that they would stop and Nathan slumped gratefully down onto the cool grass.

"You've done well today, lad. And with practice you'll improve more. I'd not be worried to have you at my side in a battle, that's for sure."

Nathan gave an exhausted smile of pleasure. They then set about collecting their precious arrows, carefully wiping down each one, noting whether any fletchings needed replacing and whether all nocks and tips were in good order. "Always check your equipment afore you put it away, lad. And if it needs repair, do it as soon as you can. Never forget, otherwise, when you really need it, you'll find it wanting and your life will be forfeit."

On the journey back to Robey's school, Nathan noticed, for the first time, the massive bulk of the archer's shoulders as he sat hunched over the horse's reins.

"Will I develop shoulders like yours, Nym?" he asked.

Nym cackled with great amusement. "Nay, lad. I've spent a lifetime shooting a hundred-and-thirty-pound bow. I'm fit for nothing else. You have to be agile. You have to fight with a sword, climb a castle wall—in fact you have to be a jack of all bleedin' trades. You don't want shoulders like sides of beef now, do you?"

Nathan laughed and then coughed and spluttered as the odors of the tanneries smacked him full in the face.

The next day was bright and crisp, and Nathan felt chirpy as he sat down for breakfast.

"What's today's lesson?" he asked. Pistol shifted a little in his chair and cast a look at Robey, who made a small encouraging movement of his head. "You are to accompany me, young sir, to the ordnance stores in Woolwich," said Pistol.

Nathan opened his eyes wide with excitement. "Guns?" he asked enthusiastically.

Pistol nodded.

"Not just guns," Robey interjected. "Other weaponry too. Last year, the queen's advisors ordered the storehouses by the dockyard at Woolwich to be repaired, so that they could store weaponry there in readiness for the Spanish invasion." He looked thoughtful for a moment and then motioned to the men to leave the room. Swiftly and silently Bardolph, Pistol, and Nym obeyed.

"Nathan," Robey said gravely, "Pistol is taking you to a place where the full horror of war can be seen—for those who can see it properly."

Nathan frowned. "I'm sorry, sir, I don't understand."

Robey looked distracted for a moment. "No, of course you don't. Come with me." He left the kitchen and headed toward his private apartments. Once inside his room, Robey unlocked a small wooden cabinet and took out a snaphaunce pistol. *It's beautiful*, Nathan thought.

"I've never seen a handgun before," he said breathlessly, as he traced a finger over the iron stock and barrel of the gun. The handle was covered in silver tracery, a web of flowers and leaves and there were small creamy white insets of horn. The mechanism for firing the gun gleamed tantalizingly in the early morning light that was edging through the window.

Nathan looked up at Robey excitedly and felt the enthusiasm

drain from his face as he met the master's eyes. "It is a beautiful thing," said Robey quietly, and he sat down opposite Nathan, the gun in his hands. "Pistol made it about five years ago. He is a great craftsman and he loves his work—but he knows that these guns are the most dangerous weapons ever created."

"Surely all weapons are dangerous, sir?" asked Nathan.

Robey smiled ruefully. "So they are, my lad, so they are. But this requires no skill. Anyone—a child even—can pick up a loaded pistol and explode it in a man's face, and that man would have no face left."

Nathan winced.

"All of these exploding weapons could blow apart humanity with ease. The killing is indiscriminate. With hand-to-hand fighting, a man can only kill one at a time. And there is some skill in such combat: the will to survive allied with the knowledge of how to handle a weapon. So if the generals cry, 'Halt,' then many lives are spared. Those who have fought bravely and survived will carry on with their lives. But fifty men can be killed at once by firing a cannon. Twenty-five of those men could have been skilled enough to survive a battle fought in the traditional way. Each cannon shot needlessly takes lives." He sighed and looked dissatisfied with himself. "I know that I am just resisting the march of time. I know that I am a mass of contradictions. I have lost count of how many men I have killed with the sword but, somehow, there was honor in that. I faced a man and he faced me. We knew why we were there; that we both had to fight for a chance to survive. When you fight a man, face-to-face, you have a great respect for the other man's right to live—if he can. There is no honor in these handguns. You can wipe out a life without even looking into a man's face. Besides . . . I fear them."

Nathan was startled at this admission from Robey, whom he regarded as invincible.

"I fear that these weapons may move away from the battlefield and on to the streets. They are easy to carry. Like the stiletto knife, they are an assassin's weapon. This is why, apart from that one in front of you, which is never loaded, I do not keep guns here. Can you imagine such a thing in the hands of some drunken fool in the Southwark byways? I could disarm a man with a sword or dagger but I could not disarm a man with a pistol."

Robey stared out of the window for a while, lost in his own thoughts. Then he turned to Nathan with a more positive air. "Nevertheless, Pistol is a craftsman and he should be honored as such. Today, he will take you to the ordnance stores and show you all the weaponry stored there. It is a secret place and you must say nothing at all, to anyone, about what lies at Woolwich. England is storing up her arms in many unlikely places. God forbid the Spanish should find them out."

Nathan swore that he would be silent. "You are a good lad, Nathan," said Robey. "You must make your own mind up about this weaponry but I felt that I should give you my thoughts."

As Nathan climbed into the horse and cart beside Pistol, he could not banish from his mind the image of a man's face being destroyed by a gun. Pistol looked at him sideways. "Did he give you the talk?"

Nathan nodded.

"Master Robey is a great man," said Pistol, as the horse pulled out of the yard and into the street, "but he's too much of a philosopher. Don't do for a soldier to think too much, lad. It makes 'em nervouslike. Me—I don't think about nothing. I just make the guns.

It may be wrong of me, but that's the way I am. But Master Robey is torn between the old and the new. He would like everything to stay as it was but he knows that you can't stop change. He employs me because he needs someone who understands firearms. He don't have no choice."

They sat in silence as the horse and cart plodded its determined way through the morning bustle of the streets. Nathan was lost in his thoughts and Pistol was silent. He knew the boy had been influenced by Robey and he was uncertain of what to say or do to remove this sudden awkwardness between them. Nathan finally snapped out of his reverie and pointed off into the distance at the barely visible masts of a great ship.

"Look, Pistol!" he cried. "That ship! Is it the queen's?"

Pistol grinned. "It is now. Her Majesty bought it yesterday off Sir Walter Raleigh. Building that ship was one of his grand ambitions. It was going to be called the *Ark Raleigh*. But Sir Walter ran out of money. Now, the queen is renaming it the *Ark Royal* and it's going to be a flagship of the Royal Navy. Would you like to see her up close, lad?"

Nathan's eyes widened. "Really?"

"Of course. I know some of the lads a-building her. We'll have a good look at this ship that's bankrupted Sir Walter, shall we?" As he turned the horse toward the river, Nathan could hardly contain his excitement.

"She's a galleon," said Pistol. "A new type of warship, invented by the Portuguese. And there's my mate John." Pistol pointed to a man standing on the quayside.

"'Hoy there, John Bates." Pistol stopped the cart and jumped down. The man on the quayside squinted, and then broke into a big grin.

"Pistol, me old mate!" he boomed. Pistol introduced the boy to his large, loud friend.

"Come to see the *Ark,* have you?" bellowed John Bates, looking at Nathan. "Come on then. But keep your wits about you. There's a right mess on deck and no mistake."

Nathan followed the two men up the gangplank and looked down into the curious dock where the ship lay. It was a hollowed-out basin, with no water in it. The mighty ship seemed to be balancing in the air, though, in fact, he saw it was held upright by an elaborate network of wooden props that were placed between the ship's flanks and the walls of the basin. The sides of the basin were lined with wood and stone. Nathan craned over the side of the ship to see more.

The smell of burned wood and tar hung in the air. There were men hanging over the side of the ship on ropes, caulking—stuffing hemp in the cracks between the planks of wood and sealing them with boiling hot tar. There were two men up the mainmast, attaching rigging to the spars. The deck was indeed a mess of coiled ropes that slithered slowly in all directions, as the men worked with them. The deck seemed alive, like a barrel of snakes.

"She's a hundred feet long on the keel by thirty-seven feet beam," shouted Bates proudly, "and she'll carry a total of forty-four guns. Aye, she's a fast and weatherly ship, that's for sure. Come down below, lad. See the innards of the beast."

They descended down a short flight of stairs and Bates showed them various cabins.

"How many men will sail in this ship?" asked Nathan.

"About one hundred eighty mariners, thirty gunners, and one hundred fifty soldiers."

"Where do they all sleep?"

Bates laughed loudly. "Mariners sleep in shifts boy, so three men can share one bed. The gunners sleep by their guns and the soldiers sleep either down in the hold in hammocks or up on the deck, ready to fight."

Nathan looked around and tried to imagine the ship crammed with more than 350 souls, and for one brief moment, he felt a sense of panic as his imagination summoned up the scene at the height of battle.

"Had any cannon delivered yet?" Pistol asked.

"Just the one so far," said Bates. "A thirty pounder on the main deck. Came up from the foundry in Sussex two days ago. She's a beauty, come and see."

It was gloomy on the gun deck because all the gun ports were closed, but they could just make out the long shape of a cannon mounted on a wooden carriage. Bates opened up two of the gun ports and the light came streaming in. Nathan ran his hand over the gun and looked at the embellishments—the queen's crest and various heraldic animals had been cast into the iron.

"This is a breach loader," Pistol told Nathan. "Which means the gunner loads the powder and ball from the rear. He doesn't have to pull the gun back from the gun port to reload. Saves time. It doesn't shoot as far as the muzzle loaders but this beauty is fast and lethal in close sea battle. Are they all to be breech, John?"

"No. All different. The navy wants to hedge its bets. Them

Spanish ships are bigger and slower than ours, I hear. The admiral will want some long-range muzzle loaders as well."

Pistol seemed well pleased but now he was anxious to leave. They had a few miles to go to Woolwich and this detour had been unscheduled. Nathan and Pistol took their leave of John Bates and set off again toward the bustling port of Greenwich and beyond that to Woolwich. Their conversation along the way was animated. Nathan had been impressed by the *Ark Royal* and Pistol found himself endlessly plied with questions.

The road to their final destination was desolate. The river lay, steely gray and calm, on their left. Nathan could see the far bank. There were a couple of small fishing boats bobbing about on the water but no movement in the forests. On their side, all was marshy, strange, and wild. Reeds grew in abundance, a flock of mallards circled in the air, and here and there, black moorhens were strutting about their business. It was an isolated spot but Nathan observed that the cart track was well used and that trees had been felled recently. As they rounded a bend, he saw the masts of two ships above the trees.

Pistol slowed the horse down and the cart came to a standstill before a high palisade with wooden towers either side of huge, solid timber gates. A musketeer stood in either tower and as the cart came to a stop, one of them shouted out, "Ho there! Is it Pistol, you old vagabond? Be you friend or foe?"

Pistol grinned. "I'll give you foe, you clapperdudgeon! A pox on you. Open the gates, I've got a terrible thirst on."

The gates slowly rumbled open and the cart eased through. Inside the palisade, Nathan was amazed by the fever of activity. Men were unloading large cannon from the two ships berthed at the dock. In a thatched, open-fronted building, five or six blacksmiths were pumping fires, heating iron, and soldering metal.

"There's much to see," said Pistol, leading Nathan into one of the big storehouses. Nathan was completely unprepared for the sight that met his eyes when he stepped inside the building. Rack upon rack of gleaming metal glittered in the light coming through the open doors.

"The daggers and swords you're familiar with," Pistol began. "There are rapiers—standard length, mind—short swords, two-handed swords, daggers, parrying daggers (for use with rapiers), battle axes, black bills...." He took the long staff, with its chopping blade at the end, and turned it around in his hands. "I used to fight with one of these," he said, suddenly roaring into life, hacking and slashing an imaginary tide of infantrymen. Nathan laughed hysterically. Pistol returned the black bill to its rest and picked out a halberd. "I used to fight with one of these too," he said, thrusting its metal spike forward and up, into an imaginary mounted cavalryman. "Oh, you need a lot of strength to be an infantryman," he puffed. "Trying to unhorse an armored rider takes muscle." He put the halberd back in its place and continued down the serried ranks of weapons, naming as he went. "There's the short staff or half pike, the forest bill—sometimes called the Welsh hook—the partisan, the long staff, morris pike, javelin...." On he went, touching all the weapons with apparent reverence and yet Nathan sensed some contempt in his expression.

"What is it, Pistol?" he asked.

Pistol smiled ruefully and shook his head. "Look at this," he said, taking a staff from a bundle. "A piece of wood. Granted a strong piece of wood and a good weapon if you have nothing else to hand. But, in a battle, what use would this piece of wood be if I am being rained upon from above by arrows, or being slashed by the steel of swords from mounted cavalry? One blow of a short sword and this piece of wood is broken in two and I am defenseless." He warmed to his subject and grabbed a morris pike. "A pike can defend me from both horse and man—if I have room in the crush of battle to move it through its length. But a man who is swinging around a sword or axe will have a better chance of life."

Pistol brought his face close to Nathan's and spoke passionately. "Anyone who has ever been an infantryman in battle will tell you that to survive, you need the best, the strongest, the most powerful weapon at your disposal, otherwise you are just meat for the crows, boy, meat for the crows. This is what Robey does not understand. He's a great swordsman but he's never walked on his own two feet into the thick of battle. Robey's a fine horseman and has looked down on the likes of me, sweating and dying at his horse's feet, with only my pike or halberd between meself and oblivion. But he has never felt the terror of being knocked to the ground, of wondering if you will be killed by a man or trampled to death by a horse. If he had, Robey would understand why an infantryman needs a gun—to give ourselves a chance, Nathan."

Nathan saw the years of battle fear in Pistol's eyes and he could hear the note of vengeance in his voice when he spoke of guns. Pistol held Nathan's gaze for a moment and then patted his shoulder reassuringly. "Don't pay no mind to me, boy. I get above meself sometimes. Come, let me show you the armor warehouse, then the artillery."

The next warehouse was filled with cannon, gleaming dully in the half-light, their cannonballs piled beside them.

Another warehouse was filled with long and short guns. Pistol lifted one of the long guns. "These are such beauties," he breathed. "See the barrel is fire-blued to give it that dark. Protect it from corrosion. The barrel's reinforced by something we call 'damascene.' Strips of metal, size of my finger, are wound around the barrel, down the whole length, then heated, welded, hammered, and forged. Makes it strong. You can pack the whole length of this barrel with gunpowder and fire it. Other gun barrels would burst open if they had just a quarter of that amount of gunpowder in 'em."

"What happens if a gun barrel bursts?" asked Nathan, fearing the answer.

"You might get your head blown off but most certainly you'd lose your hands," said Pistol matter-of-factly. He held on to the musket and moved on to the short guns.

"See, a flint is attached to a spring-loaded arm. When the trigger is pressed, the cover slides off the flash pan, then the arm snaps forward, striking the flint against a metal plate over the flash pan, producing sparks that set fire to the powder. That's the idea, anyhow." Then he added, "But it don't always work. You have to pull the arm back and reset it—have another go."

Nathan nodded dubiously.

Pistol suggested that they go to the proving ground to try out a pistol and a musket. He led the way enthusiastically. Some distance away from the storehouses was a target range. There were four thick wooden targets set about thirty feet away from the firing line. Farther along, some men were positioning a cannon.

"They're going to prove her, see if she works," said Pistol. "Let's wait."

In the distance Nathan could see a massive wall of wood, like a castle gate or the side of a ship. He assumed that this was the cannon's target. One of the gunners came over to them.

"Keep back," he warned loudly, putting his hands over his ears.

Nathan and Pistol followed suit. The gunners stood to the side of the cannon and the main gunner touched the breech with a red-hot piece of coal. There was a moment's silence, then a mighty boom. The cannon recoiled several yards and smoke billowed from its muzzle. There was a crack, and as the smoke cleared, Nathan saw that the wooden target wall had been smashed in half by the cannonball. The gunners made appreciative sounds and went to retrieve the ball.

"Do they do that all day?" asked Nathan.

Pistol nodded. "That's why most of them is deaf."

Pistol then moved on to showing Nathan how to arm and fire a musket.

"You need one pound of fine powder to two pounds of lead shot, and a good musketeer should be able to fire two, even three, shots in a minute," he explained. "At thirty yards, a musket ball will go clean through a man, even if he's wearing breast and back plate armor. Heavy musket balls can penetrate and wound at one hundred yards."

He then took Nathan through the twenty-seven steps for loading and firing a musket, demonstrating the moves as he did so.

"Open your pan; clear your pan; prime your pan; shut your pan; cast off your loose powder; blow off your loose powder; cast about your musket; open your charge; charge with powder; charge with bullet; draw forth your scouring stick; shorten your scouring stick; ram home; withdraw your scouring stick; shorten your scouring stick; return your scouring stick; recover your musket; draw forth your match; blow your coal; cock your match; try your match; guard your pan and blow; open your pan; present arms; give fire."

At that he pressed the trigger, and with an almighty crack and a puff of smoke, the ball smacked through the wooden target, leaving a clear hole.

"Uncock your match, return your match," Pistol finished his list of instructions.

"Not exactly a fast weapon then, is it?" Nathan said dryly.

Pistol grinned. "No. It takes some getting used to. But the snaphaunce now. That's a fast weapon, so to speak. No fire needed, 'cos it has the flint. You can wear this gun on your belt and prime it on the move."

He went through a shorter version of the maneuvers required to shoot the handgun and the resounding crack achieved the same result as the musket. Nathan was allowed to try the snaphaunce but he only had limited success. He found it difficult to aim—he was used to a bow, where he could line the arrow up along his cheekbone and get his eye in. Bringing a pistol up close to your face was not recommended. But the thrill of trying the new weapon compensated for its shortcomings and, eventually, Nathan was able to hit the target.

"I could never be accurate with this, like I could with a knife or an arrow," observed Nathan.

"It doesn't matter," said Pistol. "You don't need accuracy in battle. The musketeer's job is to cut down the enemy and thin out his ranks before the hand-to-hand fighting starts. Mostly, you're firing at a wall of men, not one man on his own."

But echoing in Nathan's mind were Robey's words about the gun being an assassin's weapon. He wondered whether Robey could see the future more clearly than Pistol.

On the way back from Woolwich, Pistol was in good humor after spending the day in an atmosphere of hot furnaces, gunpowder, and grease. He talked long and lively about his former regiment, the Honorable Artillery Company, set up by the queen's father, old King Henry. His stories were filled with blood and guts, humor and tragedy. He did not seem to notice that Nathan was silent, or if he did, he probably assumed that the boy was tired after such an adventure. In fact, Nathan barely heard Pistol's stories—all he could hear, in his head, was Robey's voice: *This requires no skill. Anyone—a child even—can pick up a loaded pistol and explode it in a man's face, and that man would have no face left.... There is no honor in these handguns.... Besides ... I fear that these weapons may move away from the battlefield and on to the streets.* Nathan knew, after all he had seen today, that Robey was right. But he looked into the face of Pistol, his animated face and shining eyes quite different from the look of fear and anger that had consumed him earlier when he had explained to Nathan the lot of the infantryman in battle—and he knew that handguns would be the preferred weapon of the future.

CHAPTER 6

SHARP WITS ARE
MORE IMPORTANT THAN
A SHARP SWORD

T H E next two days were a blur of activity.

Dueling with John Pearce was a joy for Nathan. Pearce was generous in his maneuvers, and although he made Nathan do all the running about and thrusting, he did not try to humiliate him, although Nathan suspected that Pearce could disarm him with a simple flick of the wrist at any time, if he had chosen to do so.

Robey watched them and, occasionally, would interject and take over Nathan's role and fight Pearce, to demonstrate a point. Nathan would watch, breathless, at the consummate skill with which Robey overcame Pearce. Nathan recalled his very first impression of Robey—that he moved like a cat—for indeed, when he had a sword in his hand he displayed such grace and agility that he seemed almost weightless. Nathan also dueled with both of the Silver brothers and found himself working very much harder than he had with Robey or Pearce. George Silver, in particular, gave no quarter when he fought and Nathan was soon panting hard as he parried each aggressive attack.

"Don't they ever stop?" Nathan gasped during a brief interlude.

Pearce smiled and shook his head. "They do not have a cupful of wit between them but there are no men that I would rather have behind me in a fight than those two," he commented. "But all men have different talents, Nathan. Your sharp wits and physical dexterity mean that can you do things poor George and Toby will never be able to manage. I doubt that either of them would be able to learn the Vigenère Square in one day or scale a high wall like a spider."

His knife work continued with Bardolph, who now upped the stakes by making Nathan throw his knives not only at swinging targets, but also from various vantage points—halfway up a rope, or upside down, hanging by his legs from a beam.

There were more lessons from Pistol, and Nathan had to recite the twenty-seven moves for priming and firing a musket. Robey allowed him to handle his snaphaunce to practice, without ammunition, the firing and aiming of a handgun.

"Why am I taught to do this, Master Robey? John Pearce does not carry a pistol and neither will I."

"No, lad, but you are to travel on a ship where the mariners carry them. If there was a battle at sea, you must know how to use one of these weapons, should one come into your possession. Also the Italians are greatly in love with artillery and I hear that guns have begun to find their way onto the streets of Venice. It is best that you know how to handle yourself in any situation."

Pearce took Nathan to Robey's rooms again for more cryptography work. They went over the use of the Vigenère Square again, this time with longer and more complicated messages. "You must be able to send Sir Francis as much detail as you can," insisted Pearce. "I may not be there to send the message for you."

Nathan felt a chill of fear. He had not thought of the possibility that John Pearce could be separated from him or even killed, leaving him alone in a foreign land. He pushed the thought from his head, but it resurfaced in his next session with Robey.

Master Robey had decided to test Nathan's memory. First, a table was laid out with forty objects on it. They were small objects such as a spoon, a pewter cup, a stirrup, and other such items. Nathan was given several minutes to memorize them, before turning his back while some objects were taken away. He then had to tell Robey what items were missing. Nathan had some success but not enough for Robey's exacting standards. After several attempts with the objects, he was asked to memorize the number of books on one of the shelves as well as the colors of the bindings. Some of the books were taken away while he turned his back and it was Nathan's task to remember how many books, and of which color, were missing.

Robey explained the importance of these games. "You must notice everything. When you go into a room, you must make a note of all that is there. When you look at a man, you must observe what he is wearing and where he carries or conceals his weapons. When you look at a horse, you must observe how he is bridled, saddled, and how he is tied up. Any small detail could be important."

Nathan understood the importance of noticing details. Will Shakespeare had always stressed that when acting in a play, the actors should remember not only words, but also where they should be onstage and what they should be carrying.

Robey continued, "Most important of all is your survival. When you go to a strange place, you must first find all the doors and windows, all the passages and hiding places, so that, if there is danger, you will know the quickest exit or the best place to conceal yourself."

Robey sat him down and spoke quietly but firmly. "Above all, you must think only of yourself. Even though you are partnered with John Pearce, you must take care of Nathan Fox first. If it means leaving John to his fate, this is what you must do."

Nathan shook his head vigorously. "I would never desert John, Master Robey. Never."

"Listen to me, lad. John is a highly trained agent. He has survived longer in this work than many others. He knows what to do if he is in trouble and he should not have to worry about you. This is important. You must understand."

"Yes, sir," Nathan conceded but he privately swore to himself that he would never leave Pearce, if he could help him.

"There is another matter, Nathan, and then I have finished my work with you."

Nathan looked at him expectantly.

"My men and I have taught you to defend yourself but the greatest defense of all cannot be learnt at the hands of a fencing master or a gunsmith or an archer...."

Nathan was puzzled. "What is it, sir? What is the greatest defense of all?"

"As I have told you before—to run. Fight only if there is no way out. Your intelligence is your most valuable asset, not your skill with a weapon. Sir Francis needs agents who can think, observe, negotiate, plan, and thwart the plans of others. He can pick up any soldier in the street to fight for him. He cannot find another John Pearce or Nathan Fox so easily. Don't hold yourself cheap, boy. Realize your value and draw back from any unnecessary brawling."

For the first time since studying with Robey, Nathan saw the sense in this advice. He remembered when Robey had first told him that the best defense was to run, and he had scorned it as cowardice. Now he was wiser. He had seen what the new weapons could do and now he understood that pointless bravery would serve no one.

Robey drew a deep breath and stood up. "Now, Master Fox. You are to leave my school and visit your employer. May God watch over you."

He held out his hand and Nathan shook it firmly. "Thank you, Master Robey, for all you have taught me."

"You must come back here, before your next mission. There will be new skills to learn. All my best pupils return whenever they can. They are the best because they know the importance of constant training."

Nathan bade a sad farewell to Bardolph, Pistol, and Nym. He knew that the three grizzled soldiers had grown fond of him in the short time he had been with them, but they tried to make light of his departure.

"Wish I was coming with you to Venice, me lad," said Bardolph, with a wink. "I could do with an eyeful of them Venetian beauties. You'd better make sure to keep old John here on the straight and narrow."

Nathan was now well aware of his partner's reputation as a ladies' man and he joined in their bawdy laughter.

Out in the street, two horses were waiting and Nathan's bag was already tied to one of the saddles. "Where are we going, John?" he inquired.

"To Westminster," came the reply. "Walsingham needs to talk to us before we leave for Plymouth."

Westminster! The queen's palace! Nathan could hardly contain his excitement, and as the horses picked their way through the crowds entering London Bridge, he called happily to Pearce, "Is that where we join Drake's ship?"

Pearce shot Nathan a warning glance and pressed his finger to his lips. "Do not talk of such things in the open. No more questions now."

Nathan subsided into remorse, feeling foolish that, in the first hour of possibly his first mission, he had so forgotten himself as to be indiscreet in public. Nevertheless, he could not completely calm his rapid pulse and the simmering tension as he thought about the fact that his training had come to an end, for now, and he was about to put it all into practice.

They rode slowly and silently through the busy streets. *When shall I be in London again?* wondered Nathan. It was then that he felt his first pang of homesickness for his sister, for Shoreditch, and for the theater.

When they arrived at Westminster Palace, their horses were taken away by grooms, and Nathan followed Pearce along many corridors, marveling at the sights as he went. The paneling and ornamentation of the walls was so rich, the tapestries so fine, the paintings so breathtaking. Several times, Pearce had to retrieve Nathan as he stood openmouthed and transfixed by a huge portrait of the queen or some other royal.

"We shall never see Sir Francis if you stop every ten seconds," said Pearce, impatiently dragging the boy along by his sleeve.

"It's just so wondrous," Nathan breathed. He had stopped again, this time to stare at the glittering figure of a woman gliding toward them. "Is that the queen?" he whispered in shock.

"No!" said Pearce scornfully. "It is one of her ladies. Good day to you, Lady Anne." Pearce swept down into a reverent bow.

The lady before them sunk into a low curtsy. "Why, Master Pearce, how honored we are to see you twice in one week."

"The honor is mine, lady." Pearce took her hand, raised her up, and pressed his lips to her long, white, bejeweled fingers.

As he spoke, a man appeared. *A nobleman*, thought Nathan, judging by his clothes and manner. He was short and stocky with a face creased into a permanent scowl. Nathan decided at once that he did not like the look of him.

"And who is this creature, gaping at my wife like a codfish?" inquired the nobleman, surveying Nathan with amusement.

"My servant, my lord," Pearce replied briskly. "New to my service and overcome by Lady Anne's beauty. Where are your manners, boy?" Pearce swiftly cuffed Nathan around the ear and glared at him. Nathan realized his mistake and quickly made an awkward bow. Lady Anne smiled in appreciation and her husband's narrow eyes flickered over Nathan's face.

"I have only once before seen eyes that color," the man said curtly, staring intently at Nathan. "What is your name?"

"Nathan Fox, my lord," Nathan mumbled.

"Ha! And is your father's name Samuel Fox?"

Nathan's look of astonishment caused the nobleman's eyes to glitter. John Pearce's face set hard with suspicion.

"My . . . my father is dead, my lord, for many years. But . . . yes . . . his name was Samuel. Did you know him?"

The man nodded but then waved his hand dismissively. "It is of no importance. Your home is in Clerkenwell, is it not?" he said, his voice assuming a softer tone.

Nathan, caught off guard, spoke before John's restraining hand reached his arm. "No, sir, Shoreditch."

The man's mouth twitched a little at the corners. "Ah, Shoreditch. I must be mistaken." Then, as if bored with this social interchange, he snapped at his wife. "Come, my dear, we have duties to attend to. Good day to you, Master Pearce."

"Lord Harcourt, Lady Anne," Pearce murmured as he swept into a deep bow. Nathan followed suit, sure that he had committed some folly.

As the lord and his lady disappeared from view, John turned to Nathan. "Too much information. You must never tell a stranger so much." He looked concerned. "We must speak to Sir Francis about this."

Nathan was bewildered. "Why would such a noble lord know my father? Why would he care where I live?"

John looked steadily at Nathan. "Exactly. Harcourt would never normally engage in conversation with a servant. Added to

89

which, he is one of the most dangerous men at court. . . ." Pearce trailed off, leaving the sentence unfinished, then turned on his heel. Nathan scurried after him at a respectful distance until they reached Walsingham's rooms.

Walsingham was dictating to his secretary as they entered and he motioned them to sit while he finished. When the secretary was dispatched about his business, Walsingham turned his full attention to his two agents.

"Well, Nathan, your time with Master Robey was not too arduous I hope?"

"No, I loved it, sir," replied Nathan with a smile.

Walsingham sat down behind his desk and motioned them to sit before him.

Straightaway Pearce relayed to Walsingham the incident with Lord Harcourt in the corridor. The spymaster pursed his lips in concern. Before he could speak, Nathan stammered an apology but Walsingham waved him aside. "You were not to know the reputation of this man."

"There are certain courtiers whom we suspect of having Spanish sympathies and of passing information to the enemy by secret means. Lord Harcourt is one such man. He is a ruthless individual with an unsavory past. You met his wife, Lady Anne?"

Nathan nodded.

"She is his second wife and much younger than he, as you will have observed. His first wife died in mysterious circumstances and so have other people who have had dealings with him. He is someone that we watch very carefully." He looked at Pearce before speaking again. "I share John's concern that Harcourt appeared to have knowledge of your father. Why, it is a mystery—but I think I shall send someone to watch over your sister for a while, just to be safe."

Nathan could not bear the thought that whatever had passed between him and Lord Harcourt had put Marie in danger. His anxiety did not go unnoticed by Walsingham.

"Do not worry, Nathan. Your sister shall be protected."

He then quickly assumed a businesslike air. "So, now, I will give you your assignment." He lowered his voice and spoke confidentially. "You are to proceed to Plymouth, where you will meet Sir Francis Drake. He has gathered a small fleet of privateers and is also on a mission for Her Majesty. One of the ships will take you to Venice. John, you are to pose as Michael Cassio, a soldier from Florence. You will present yourself to the doge of Venice and give him this." From a drawer in his desk, Walsingham produced a sheaf of papers and a linen cloth. Nathan recognized it at once as the cloth that his sister had embroidered with strawberries, flowers, and leaves.

"This collection of verses is a gift for him. It contains the code, which requires the handkerchief to decipher. The message is from the queen, requesting an alliance between Venice and England against Spain. You will be guided by the doge as to whether he will make an alliance with us and what support he will give us in the event of war. Venice has a sizeable fleet of ships, which could keep the Mediterranean open for us, if the Spaniards decide to attack us in the English Channel. Needless to say, we would not wish the Spaniards to learn of these negotiations, otherwise they would take steps to blockade the Venetian fleet, making them useless to us as allies.

"The ship that takes you to Venice will remain there to bring your message back to me, but you are not to contact the captain yourself. Any messages must be sent through a man named Mordecai Luzzatto. He is a prominent member of the Jewish community and you will find him in the Jewish quarter of Venice. He is a moneylender and you will visit him on the pretext of borrowing money. If you are successful on your first meeting with the doge, then you will return with the ship to England. If the doge requires more persuasion, then you will remain and the ship will return for you as soon as it can. Any questions?"

Nathan cleared his throat and looked at Pearce for permission to speak. Although he had absorbed, with precision, all the details of the mission and even kept his excitement under control at the thought of traveling to the exotic city of Venice, there was one thought that nagged at him.

Pearce and Walsingham looked at Nathan expectantly. "Yes?" said Pearce by way of gentle encouragement.

"What am _I_ to be called, sir?" asked Nathan.

Sir Francis smiled. "Well, of course you must have a name. You shall choose it yourself. What shall it be?"

Nathan's mind raced through the plays he had performed in Shoreditch. "Marco," he said, remembering one play in which there had been a reference to Marco Polo, "Marco . . ." He struggled to think of a family name.

"Pignatti?" suggested Pearce, plucking a name out of the air.

"Yes, I like it," said Nathan. "Marco Pignatti."

"Marco Pignatti, servant to Michael Cassio, it shall be, then . . ." Before Walsingham could speak further, the door was flung open and there, to Nathan's astonishment, stood the magnificent Queen Elizabeth—Gloriana herself.

Walsingham and Pearce leapt out their chairs in haste and bowed deeply. Nathan, a fraction behind them, bowed so low that his head almost touched his knees.

"Begone," the Queen commanded to the courtiers who were trailing behind her. "BEGONE!" A flurry of brocades and velvets beat a hasty retreat down the corridor. Only two men at arms remained, for they were always at her side. The queen closed the door behind her and walked into the room. She moved quite unlike the lady-in-waiting Nathan and John had met earlier. That woman had glided. The queen strode, thought Nathan, like a purposeful man. She was tall, deathly white, thin faced, with bright red hair. Her mouth was painted in a crimson slash and her cheeks were rouged red. Her gown was white and silver and covered with so many jewels that Nathan marveled at its brilliance. When she moved, a thousand lights flashed. *She is not young*, thought Nathan, *but I could not say how old she is*. The queen stared at the trio with a dissatisfied air.

"So, you are plotting to send Master Pearce away from us again, are you, Sir Francis?"

Walsingham knew from experience that he should not attempt to answer. The queen's eyes now flickered over to Nathan, who felt his breath becoming more shallow and rapid.

"Who is this?" she inquired.

"A young boy actor, with many talents, who is to serve Master Pearce, Your Majesty," Sir Francis explained in a deferent tone.

The queen's eyes flashed. "God's teeth, Sir Francis! Are we

sending children out now to do our dirty work?" She was not pleased. Nathan suddenly felt afraid that all his training would be for nothing if the queen forbade his mission.

"Your Majesty." His voice sounded high and weak and he saw the anxiety leap into Sir Francis's eyes, but he persisted. "Forgive me..." He bowed again, then straightened up. The queen was waiting to hear what he had to say and he took some comfort from that. "If the Spaniards invade England, then it is the children who will suffer the most, who will have their future and their liberty taken from them. So is it not right that a child should help to save other children? If he can." He was trembling now, afraid that he had gone too far, but the queen's face softened and she held out her hand imperiously for him to kiss.

"Out of the mouths of babes...," she murmured. "You are a brave boy and doubtless an intelligent one or Sir Francis would not have singled you out. And if you are to serve with John Pearce, then I am satisfied that you will be in the best care. What is your name?"

"Nathan Fox, Your Majesty."

"Then, Nathan Fox, be of service to England but take care. I shall expect to see you grow up to be a handsome man at my court before long, then you shall spend your days flattering your old queen, as Master Pearce does now."

Nathan smiled with relief. "Your Majesty," he replied, "I intend to be *exactly* like John Pearce."

The queen laughed at the thought but then turned to Walsingham and her face grew hard. "Take heed of my words, Sir Francis, and you too, John Pearce. If this child comes to any harm, I shall part both your heads from your bodies, do you understand?"

Both mumbled an affirmative answer and with that the queen flung open the doors and strode off out of sight. The men at arms closed the doors and hastened after her, leaving two visibly shaken men and an ecstatic Nathan behind.

Today I met the queen! I spoke with her! I kissed her hand, thought Nathan. His life was changing so fast, that he could barely keep up.

Minutes later, as Nathan and Pearce rode out of Westminster Palace, the joy of the royal encounter was still singing in Nathan's brain. Pearce was too amused by the besotted boy to notice that, in the far corner of the courtyard, Lord Harcourt was lingering in the deep shadows of a doorway. Neither did he notice the two men who mounted their horses, after a brief consultation with Harcourt. One began to follow John and Nathan, and the other, once through the palace gates, turned his horse left toward Shoreditch.

But high up at the window of his office, Sir Francis Walsingham, noted well what was taking place and once Harcourt had turned his back on his business, he gave an imperceptible nod, a signal that caused yet another man to mount his horse and make speedily for Shoreditch.

CHAPTER 7

A HERO IS NOT ALWAYS
WHAT HE SEEMS

HE journey to Plymouth was long and hard.

"We must get there within the week," said John Pearce during one of their overnight stays at a wayside inn. "Drake wants to up-anchor soon. He fears that Her Majesty will change her mind about his mission."

"What *is* his mission?" asked Nathan.

Pearce shrugged. "I have no idea. He has been gathering men and ships for some weeks now. Whatever it is, it is important, and knowing Drake, it will be spectacular."

"Is Drake a friend of yours, then?"

Pearce sighed. "No, not a friend—but I respect him. He is a great sailor—perhaps the greatest in England. But he is a ruthless, brutal man and I do not like him. But these are dangerous times and it is men like Drake who stand between us and the Spanish Empire. But never forget that Drake is an adventurer, a privateer. He wants only the money and treasure from the towns he plunders or the cargoes he can extract from the ships he sinks. He says that he does it for England but would he do it if there was no promise of riches?"

Nathan was shocked by Pearce's reply. He had always thought of Drake as a hero. Like many boys of his age, Nathan had been brought up on tales of Drake's daring and ingenuity. Drake was invincible—the man who had sailed completely around the world, the man who was more pirate than courtier. Obviously Pearce thought otherwise, and maybe others did too.

It had been a hard day's riding and both Nathan and Pearce were hungry. The inn was packed with traders staying overnight for a nearby cattle market tomorrow. Pearce managed to find two spaces on a bench and Nathan pressed through the crowd to ask for two bowls of stew and some bread. As he shouted his order to the innkeeper, he caught the eye of a man on the other side of the tavern. The man quickly looked away but not before Nathan felt a hot pang of recognition. He had seen the same man in the last inn they had stayed at. His instincts told him that the man was watching him. As he pushed his way back to John, he felt anxious. But he could not just bawl out his fears to Pearce. He would have to wait until they were back in the room. The stew arrived and Nathan ate as fast as he could, all the while scanning the crowd for the watchful stranger. The man had disappeared.

Nathan made a sign to John that he was going outside. He picked his way through the crowds and went out into the cold night air. There were a few men relieving themselves in the bushes but he could see that none of them were the man he was looking for. Making his way silently to the stables, he climbed up onto a barrel and peered through a crack in the wood. There was his man, lounging against a bale of hay, in the shadows. He was eating food from the saddlebags beside him.

Nathan made his way back into the tavern and finished his stew. Later, once they were safely in the room, he told Pearce of his suspicions. His partner took the news calmly, without displaying any surprise.

"I have had my suspicions too, for the last thirty miles. There has been a rider following us who has matched our every pace. When we have slowed, so has he. When we have galloped hard, so has he."

Nathan was astonished. "I saw no one!" John smiled and shook his head.

"Nor would you, the man is good at his job. But we shall fool him tomorrow. I know his tactics. He leaves the tavern early, before we rise and he waits, hidden, on the road. Then when we pass, he follows. Except tomorrow, we shall cut across country and take another route. It will add a day to our journey, but we must hope that Drake does not leave without us. Sleep now."

As they drifted off to sleep, Nathan kept wondering who their pursuer might be. Unable to contain himself, he voiced the question. In the darkness, Pearce replied, stifling a yawn, "You will learn, Nathan, that Walsingham's world is filled with shadows. There will always be someone watching his agents. Whatever moves we make, King Philip's spies will match them. Now get some sleep."

The next morning, it was as John had predicted. The man and his horse had gone. Once mounted, Pearce turned his horse off, then rode into the dense forest. "We must pick our way through this forest until it comes out on the Salisbury road. Then we shall ride hell for leather to the south and approach Plymouth from the west. Let us hope our shadow waits overlong before he realizes that we have taken another route. No doubt he will resurface in Plymouth."

No further conversation was possible for many hours, as the two agents ducked and dived through thick woodland, their sure-footed horses moving patiently through unfamiliar territory. Now and then they would startle some deer, or the horses would stop at a brook for a drink. Always Pearce would motion silence as he listened intently for the sounds of another rider following. But their journey continued peacefully until they emerged onto the main track that led to their destination.

PLYMOUTH was a bustling port. The sea wind smacked Nathan in the face as they turned the horses down the road toward the docks. He had never seen so many ships. There were thirty or forty at the docksides—a great forest of masts, as far as the eye could see—and more ships at anchor farther out. The docksides were swarming with people. Bales were swinging in the air on the end of ropes, barrels were being rolled up and down gangplanks. On the larger ships, there were continuous streams of men that looked like soldiers, walking on and off the vessels. On the quayside, there were open-fronted warehouses and workshops. The noise of iron being hammered and wood being sawed mingled with the din of people shouting.

"We must find stabling for the horses and a bed for the night," Pearce shouted. "Drake's ship, thank God, is still here." He pointed to the largest of the vessels at the quayside, the *Elizabeth Bonaventure*.

Pearce turned his horse toward the backstreets of the dock area and Nathan followed. Within minutes, they had found a livery stable that would take their horses for an unspecified period, and for a considerable amount of money. They then picked their way through the crowds on the quayside.

As they were walking toward the *Elizabeth Bonaventure*, Pearce stopped short and nudged Nathan. "Drake," he said, and pointed to a richly dressed, stocky man, who was, it seemed, being given some bad news by one of his mariners. Nathan reflected that Drake, in a temper, looked terrifying. The face beneath the dark hair had flushed red—all except for a scar beneath his right eye, which shone white against the choleric skin around it. *That must be where Drake took an arrow from savages in the New World.* Nathan remembered the story of how Drake and his men, badly wounded—Drake himself by three separate arrows— had fought their way back to their ship off the island of Mocha. As Nathan followed Pearce up the gangplank of the ship, he could see that Drake was trembling with rage—so much so that the long pearl earring he wore was dancing in his ear. *So this is the legend.* Nathan was filled with awe as he approached. This was the man who, for the last seventeen years, had harried and plundered Spanish ships to such a degree, the word was, he had thrown almost one million gold ducats and countless jewels at Her Majesty's feet.

"We'll have to take on more men," Drake roared at no one in particular. He then swore a terrible oath and muttered something about "poxy deserters." As he turned, his eye lighted upon Pearce and like brilliant sun after a thunderstorm, his face broke into a beaming smile. "John Pearce!" he shouted. "Well, there's a sight for a blind man's eyes. How are you, you popinjay?"

After much handshaking and backslapping, the effusive Drake was introduced to Nathan. "Ah, I've heard a whisper about you in Walsingham's circles . . . ," he said, his eyes alight with humor. "I hear you're a fine boy. Skilled and shrewd, they say. I've a mind to steal you myself, for a cabin boy. How would you like that, lad?"

Nathan was torn between pride at seeming to have a reputation and terror that Drake would, indeed, press him into service on his ship. His conflicting emotions must have shown on his face because Drake roared with laughter, amused that he could strike fear in the young lad's heart.

Pearce interrupted to ask whether they would be sailing on the morning tide. Drake's face darkened as suddenly as it had brightened a moment before, and Nathan saw a savagery there that chilled him to the bone.

"Some of the crews have deserted. They didn't turn up in London, so the ships have sailed without them. This is the work of my enemies at court, you can be sure of that." He raised his head defiantly and his bearded chin stuck out above his lace ruff. "Well, a pox on them!" He spat on the ground. "I'll recruit more men here in Plymouth. Good West Countrymen, like me. I'll not sail without a full complement." Nathan could see that Drake would have his way, no matter what others did to make his life more difficult.

Nathan took stock of the activity around him. The men, having finished hauling in and tying off the boat, had assembled on the deck for inspection. They were a fearsome bunch. Barefooted, sweat soaked, well muscled, and tattooed, they presented to Nathan the perfect picture of a mob of bloodthirsty pirates. He stared at them in fascination. Some were so brown and weather-beaten that they looked like foreign natives. Others had fearsome scars all over their arms. Some were stripped to the waist and displayed the white lines of old whippings on their backs. One man had strange tattoos that covered his face. Several had shaved heads. All stared ahead, respectfully, at Admiral Drake, who surveyed them in silence.

He spoke to his men, "Those scum who deserted these ships shall hang, I promise you that. You men, who have honored your contracts with me, will share in all the riches that this voyage brings. Those who have sailed with me before know that I am fair. But I say to you now, I will not tolerate desertion or cowardice. I will go where you go. When we fight, I fight with you. I expect no more of any man than I expect of myself. But if you do not do as you are commanded, I will kill you. You have my word on that. Is it understood?"

"Aye, aye, sir," shouted the men in unison.

Drake looked satisfied and raised his voice again. "Good. When we have a full complement of men, we shall go and stick a rapier up the King of Spain's ass!" A loud cheer went up, then the men turned back to their work.

Drake led Pearce and Nathan down into his cabin. "Now, let us discuss business," he said, tearing the starched ruff from his neck. "I am authorized by Her Majesty to raid Spanish and Portuguese harbors and do what damage I can to their fighting ships. You have to get to Venice. I cannot take my ships into the Mediterranean or I risk them being trapped by the Spanish fleet. I must stay out in the Atlantic, where I can make a fast retreat, if need be. So it has been arranged that you will travel on a small merchant ship due to arrive here tomorrow. It will take you to Venice and be at your bidding when you wish to return. Is that satisfactory?"

"Perfectly," replied Pearce.

A shout from on deck distracted Drake. "I must away," he said. "I've a ship to run. Come up on deck, Nathan, and you shall see a ship rigged out for heavy weather. A lad like you needs to see real men at work, you'll learn nothing from a fancy man like John Pearce." With a laugh of satisfaction, Drake left the cabin.

"Do you have the measure of the man, now, Nathan?" Pearce inquired softly.

Nathan smiled. "I think he is a great man, who likes to be in command. He likes flattery and he does not like to be crossed."

"Well observed," said Pearce admiringly. "You are a good judge of character, Nathan, which will serve you well in our business. Drake is a great man, but he is also a braggart and a bully. And, from my point of view, I think it is well that we are not sailing with him. I should find it hard to hold my tongue."

CHAPTER 8

THE SECRET

HE next day was spent idling around the port. To Nathan, Plymouth was more exciting than London. He saw more exotic sights here than he had ever seen in Shoreditch or Southwark. Many of the people were foreigners— dark skinned, wearing strange clothes. There was a ship in port whose whole crew had unusual slanted eyes and spoke to one another in an incomprehensible, singsong tongue.

The ship smelled strongly of spices. So strongly, that it was almost impossible to pass by without choking on the pungent sweet odor.

People in Plymouth knew a lot about Drake, their local hero, and many of them had spun yarns to Nathan, in the tavern where he and Pearce were staying.

"He's a wizard is Drake. A man possessed of the magical arts, when he chooses to use them," said one old man knowingly. When pressed by Nathan he told him the story of Drake's cannonball. "When Drake was sailing around the world, he told his wife to wait for him for seven years, and if he had not returned, she could marry again. So the poor lady waited, and at the end of the time, she agreed to become another man's wife. But as she was standing at the altar, a great cannonball landed between her and her husband-to-be and she knew that Drake was alive, so she called off the wedding."

Everyone around them nodded wisely. Nathan was captivated, until Pearce took him to one side. "Don't believe this nonsense. This local legend is the measure of how much they hold the man in awe, nothing more."

On the quayside, Drake's senior captain, William Burroughs, had set up shop to hire more men. Word had got around and men had gathered from all over the West Country, anxious to be part of Drake's latest adventure. Nathan watched as Burroughs inspected the would-be mariners for signs of weakness or disease. *He treats them as though they are horses,* thought Nathan, as Burroughs made each man open his mouth, so that he could inspect their teeth.

"He's looking for signs of scurvy," explained Pearce. "It shows in puffed and bleeding gums. Drake works his ships hard and fast," he added, "the men need to be sound in wind and limb."

Just then, Nathan heard raised voices. There was a dispute among the men. Burroughs stepped back, sensing trouble, and his hand strayed to his sword in readiness. Pearce tensed and did likewise, pushing Nathan behind him.

"What did you open your mouth for?" raged a huge man wearing a large felt hat.

"You ain't taking a job away from a good Protestant seaman, you scum!" retaliated a much smaller man, with several missing teeth.

"It ain't none of your business."

105

"Drake don't like Catholics aboard his ships," yelled the smaller man, baring his gapped teeth and landing a punch square on the other man's jaw.

The crowd of men erupted into an all-out brawl that sent several of them flying backward. As Nathan got pushed to the floor, a hand reached out from nowhere and yanked him back. He looked up from the ground and found himself staring into the face of a curiously dressed man. He wore a long flowing robe, like a doctor's or apothecary's, and it was covered with odd symbols—stars, moons, and spheres. He wore a black mask, which covered the top part of his face, and he had long, dark, curly hair, with streaks of gray that hung in an unruly mass about his face and neck.

"Best to stay back now, young sir," he said. His voice was soft and slightly accented. He smiled gratefully and looked toward the fighting, which had escalated into such violence that Pearce and Burroughs were being forced to punch their way out of the center of the crowd.

"Such nonsense," the man murmured, and he smiled at Nathan. "And all over a man's religion. I must put a stop to this." With that, he drew a glass bottle from the sleeve of his gown. It was shaped like a ball but had a cork stopper in the top and Nathan saw that it was filled with some yellow liquid. Swiftly the man threw the glass bottle into the center of the crowd, where it smashed on the ground. A vile odor and thick smoke emanated from the spilled liquid. Soon the men were reeling and staggering away, eyes streaming and mouths muttering curses. Nathan stared in astonishment but the man merely smiled back at him, his blue eyes glittering, framed in the black mask.

Pearce came spluttering back to where Nathan was standing. "What in God's name was that?" he wheezed, hardly able to catch his breath.

Nathan pointed to his companion. "He threw it. . . . I'm sorry, I don't know your name, sir."

The masked man smiled again. "Stefan," he replied with a bow. As he straightened he produced, again from his sleeve, a wet square of linen that he offered to Pearce. "It will relieve the effects."

Pearce gratefully took the cloth and rubbed it around his eyes and face. He blinked several times and shook his head. The cloth seemed to have done its work. "Thank you, sir."

"Are you a magician?" Nathan asked.

"Among other things," came the enigmatic reply. "My people are over there." Nathan and Pearce followed Stefan's pointed finger and saw a group of acrobats and jugglers performing for a growing crowd. "Come and watch."

There were six men, all dressed in the Italian fashion of brilliantly colored, tight doublet and hose. They were forming a human pyramid as Nathan approached. As the smallest and lightest man ascended to the top, he balanced briefly and then launched himself into the air, somersaulting midflight and landing perfectly upright. The assembled crowd applauded and cheered. The pyramid broke up and the performers dived for the ground, picking up various objects to juggle, balance, and throw. One man was using a diabolo and Nathan excitedly clapped at the sight of his favorite toy.

"Would you care to try?" asked Stefan gently. Nathan nodded

eagerly and Stefan pushed him forward. "Graco," he said. "Let the boy have a turn." The performer stopped the diabolo's spinning and handed it, and two sticks joined by string, to Nathan. Graco winked at Stefan and prepared to be amused by the fumblings of an eager boy. Nathan, however, astonished the performer by moving into a space and immediately setting the diabolo spinning furiously. He then went through a series of tricks—clockwise suns, counterclockwise suns, trapezes, and over-arm orbits. He did it with such ease that Graco put his finger and thumb in his mouth and blew a series of appreciative whistles. But Nathan had noticed something in the moments when his eye left the diabolo: Stefan's face bore a strange, sad look. When Nathan had finished, Pearce applauded heartily and slapped him on the back with pride. "You never cease to amaze me!" A look of pain fleetingly crossed Stefan's face and it froze Nathan's smile of flushed pride. *What's wrong with him?* he wondered. There was something about this masked man. . . .

"Sir," said Nathan, clearing his throat. "You seem familiar. Have we met before?"

Stefan shrugged and smiled. "It is possible that we have met at some fair in London, is it not?" he said. Nathan frowned. *How does he know I come from London?* he wondered, feeling even more uneasy. Robey's training had taught him to be aware of the careless comment that could give away a Spanish agent. Nathan felt he needed to ask more questions. "Are you traveling around England?" he asked Stefan.

"Yes. We are forever traveling," was the enigmatic and unsatisfactory reply.

The performers were now passing bowls around the crowd and being rewarded by the satisfying chink of money. "Come and meet my people," Stefan urged. He clapped his hands to summon them and all six men came bounding over, taking the opportunity to praise Nathan for his skill.

"Graco you have met; he has many talents," said Stefan, beginning the introductions. "This is Pepe, who is our fire-eater; Manolo and his brother Pedro, they are our best jugglers. Samson, who performs feats of great strength, like his Bible namesake; and Waldemar, the smallest and nimblest, whose speciality is walking the wire."

"Walking the wire?" asked Nathan. Waldemar grinned from ear to ear. "Show him, my friend," said Stefan, smiling.

Without any hesitation, Waldemar scurried up the gangplank of the *Elizabeth Bonaventure,* and then, like a monkey, he swung himself up onto the forestay. Attached to the forestay was a rope, stretched taut, that led all the way up above the foresail, on the main mast. From top to bottom the rope was at a steep angle but the nimble wire-walker hopped onto it and began to walk up its length. People shouted and pointed as the agile man curled his bare feet around the rope and ascended slowly and surely. William Burroughs, turning to see what the fuss was about, shouted out, "'Hoy, you there! Get down off my ship!"

Waldemar looked at Burroughs, wobbled, and seemed to fall backward. In that split second, Nathan's hand flew up to his mouth but Waldemar fooled them all by grabbing the rope as he dropped and swinging completely around it, like Nathan's diabolo on its string. A collective shout of relief went up from the crowd and Waldemar played to his audience by swinging around the rope again, this time letting go in midair, flipping himself over and catching the rope once more, going back the other way. Burroughs looked ready to explode. "Get down, man, or I will shoot you down!" Waldemar obligingly dropped from his great height, to another gasp from the crowd, and landed perfectly upright on the deck.

Burroughs strode over to Stefan. "You'll oblige me, sir, by taking your band of gypsies and performing elsewhere," he said gruffly. Stefan bowed with a sardonic smile and he and his men turned to leave. Nathan grabbed his long gown.

"You are gypsies?" asked Nathan in an urgent whisper.

Stefan nodded his head. "So am I," said Nathan.

Stefan looked at him long and hard. "I know," he said quietly. "We will talk again, Nathan Fox, you can be sure of that." Then he was gone.

Nathan's mind was racing. *I don't remember telling him my name. Did John say my name?* He couldn't remember and, usually, his memory was so good. Pearce had taught him to be wary of strangers but there was something about the mysterious Stefan— Nathan's instincts told him that the man was *not* a stranger.

Pearce was speaking to him now, but he didn't hear. "Nathan . . . NATHAN." Pearce finally got his attention. "Burroughs says that our ship has arrived. It's a Dutch merchantman, *The Flemish Queen*. We must meet the captain now."

Nathan scanned the crowd for a last time, searching for the gypsy troupe, but they had vanished. He turned back to his friend and tried to focus on the business at hand but while he was walking with Pearce, he kept hearing the words, *We will talk again, Nathan Fox, you can be sure of that.*

PEARCE and Nathan made their way up the gangplank of *The Flemish Queen* and sought out the captain. Finisterre was a bluff, jovial Dutchman and he took the pair belowdecks to show them their sleeping arrangements.

"You shall have this cabin," he said to Pearce, opening the door of a cabin that was little more than a box. "Your servant shall sleep with some other passengers down below. We sail with the morning tide. Please present yourselves at dawn." Then, with another friendly smile, he ushered them back on deck and left them alone.

Pearce stiffened as he surveyed the quayside.

"Our friend from the tavern is back with us, I see."

Nathan followed his gaze and spotted the man they had left behind on the Plymouth road. As Nathan looked, their eyes met.

"He has seen us," Nathan breathed in alarm.

"No matter," John said surprisingly. "He cannot follow us once our voyage begins. We have only tonight to worry about. Whilst we are still on land, we are in danger. Tonight, we must sleep with knives under our pillows."

Nathan grew more uneasy as the day lengthened into night. He had little appetite at dinner and he noted that John ate sparingly too. *This is what it is really like being a spy*, he thought as the tension mounted, *the waiting and the watching and the fear of what is to come.* This, he knew, would be the greatest test for him. He was frightened—not for his personal safety but for whether he would prove a worthy partner for John Pearce.

As they settled down in their room, Pearce unbuckled his sword and laid it under the bed on his right-hand side. Nathan drew the daggers from his boots and placed them under his pillow.

The sounds of the town were beginning to dull as drunken sailors weaved their way back to their ships or slumped, snoring, in nearby gutters. "The candle will not last," John spoke quietly. "No one will come while there is light in the window—better we snuff it out now and hasten the event, whilst we are still awake."

Nathan pinched out the flame with his trembling fingers and they lay, senses heightened, in the semidarkness of the moon's glow.

An hour must have passed and Nathan could feel his limbs becoming heavy as he succumbed to sleep. Then suddenly he heard the door handle being turned. He sensed John quietly feeling for the hilt of his sword beneath the bed. Nathan's temples pounded and his breath grew shallower and faster. The door inched open, without a sound, and Nathan could make out a dark figure standing in the opening. The figure moved slowly forward and Nathan's eyes, aching from the strain, just caught the glimpse of a dull gleam from a weapon, raised at waist height, poised for attack. Then he realized, with a short intake of breath, that the figure was advancing toward *him* and not Pearce. He rolled onto his front, feeling frantically for the daggers under his pillow, when he saw the flash of John's blade as it swung through the air. There was a scream—not one but two—*a man's and a* woman's, thought Nathan—then the room was filled with light. Nathan jumped up only to find himself staring at his sister, Marie, lantern in hand.

"What?" Nathan spluttered as he looked around the room.

Pearce was half raised on one knee, his sword still in midair, waiting to strike the assassin.

It was not he who had struck the fatal blow that saved Nathan. From nowhere strode the masked gypsy, Stefan, who bent down and pulled his knife from the back of the figure lying facedown on the floor. Then he rolled the body over. "Harcourt's man," he pronounced grimly.

There was a silence. So dumbfounded were Pearce and Nathan that they could only look at each other.

It was Marie who spoke first.

"Nathan, I would like you to meet our father, Samuel Fox."

CHAPTER 9

SO MUCH DECEPTION

NATHAN stared at Stefan like an idiot. His mind was a jumble of words—nothing connecting—nothing that he could form into a coherent sentence.

"Holy Jesus," Pearce murmured in disbelief.

Nathan's confusion merged suddenly into two overwhelming emotions—anger and fear. Anger that this man, who claimed to be his father, had walked back into his life without any gentle introduction; anger that his sister had known his father was still alive and had kept it a secret from him; and fear—fear that this man in front of him—his father—was capable of murder.

Pearce spoke again, "I thank you, sir, for saving our lives, but I think that you must explain yourself before I am reassured enough to put my sword away."

Stefan nodded and sat down heavily on the nearest chair. The dead body lay on the floor between them all and Stefan turned his head away. Nathan realized then that his father had not easily knifed this man.

Nathan looked at Stefan closely. He could see now how alike they were. The same dark hair, the same ice blue eyes, and the voice—the familiarity of his voice must have been a faint childhood memory. He felt a fool for not realizing it before.

"Why did you leave?" Nathan blurted out the question that had hung on his lips all his life. He felt his heart beat faster as he waited for an answer.

Stefan took a deep breath. "Because of this man here." He motioned toward the dead body. "Well, the man who employs him." Marie sat beside Nathan and squeezed her brother's hand. Nathan shot her a sullen glance. Until he heard the full story he was not sure that he was ready to forgive her secrecy.

Stefan continued, "When your mother died and you were very small, I made my living as an apothecary. We lived in the City and I prospered. I had many rich and highborn patrons, many lords and ladies from court, who came to me seeking relief from their various agues and ill humors."

Nathan fixed his eyes on Stefan's face and listened.

"One day a lord who was a great favorite of the queen's came to me and told me of his inability to sleep."

"Harcourt," ventured Pearce. Stefan nodded.

"His nights were bad, he said, and he needed a potion. At that time I was not so wise in the ways of the world. I gave him a potion to bring sleep. It was a powerful remedy of herbs, dangerous if taken in any quantity, but I gave him full instructions—a few drops each night, no more. Then, I heard that the lord's wife was found dead and there was a rumor that he had killed her so that he could marry a younger highborn lady. I knew that he had used my potion to do this terrible thing and I sought him out. He denied it, of course, and the next day, I was set upon by three men, armed with swords, who wounded me badly and left me for dead. Mistress Fast found me. She was passing by with her brother and she saw me lying in a ditch. The good woman and her brother lifted me into their cart and took me to Shoreditch, where I lay in a fever, near death, for many days. But Mistress Fast nursed me back to health and when I could talk, I told her of my fears for my family. She and her brother rescued you and Marie from our house in the City. Poor Marie was taking care of you. She was only nine years old and I had disappeared without trace. She assumed I was dead and did not know what to do—except keep both of you alive. By now, Harcourt's men, ordered by their master to bring proof of my death, had returned to the ditch and could find no body. So they continued to look for me, as they have done for the last eight years. When I was fully recovered I decided that I would have to leave. I was putting you both in danger. I knew of his guilt and Harcourt might use my family to get to me. So Samuel Fox the apothecary had to die, and Stefan the magician was born. Mistress Fast, out of pure kindness, agreed to look after you both, although Marie has always taken care of you. I have sent money and kept in touch with her. I told her never to tell you anything. You were too young to understand and it was safer that you did not know. But now things have changed...."

Nathan stared at his father, remembering the times that he had been ushered out of the room when strangers had come to call, the times when Marie would write notes that she kept hidden. He felt foolish. Why had he never suspected anything?

"Why did you never send me a message? What father would not try and see his son?" Nathan asked angrily.

Stefan smiled. "But I did. I have seen many plays at the theater. I have watched you grow up, Nathan, as best as I could, without putting you in danger. I have marveled at your skills and I have swelled with pride every time I have seen you."

Nathan's eyes pricked with tears.

"Why did you not tell me who you were when we met today?" he asked, desperately fighting the urge to cry. He felt shame, but more than anything, he was now afraid that his indiscretion would cost him his place on the mission to Venice.

"It was too dangerous," Stefan confessed and hung his head. "The day that you left London, one of Harcourt's men was asking questions in Shoreditch about the Fox family. He went to your lodging house but Marie was out. How Harcourt knew where to look, I do not know."

Nathan bit his lip and hung his head in guilt. "It was my fault. I told him."

Marie looked appalled. "You told him!" Her voice was a mixture of disbelief and accusation.

"I didn't know who he was!" Nathan's voice rose in indignation. "I met him at court. He remarked on the color of my eyes, asked me my name, and wanted to know if my father was called Samuel. I said yes and he asked me where I lived before going into John's service. I thought he was just being friendly. If you had told me about all of this before, I should not have been so free with my answers!"

Stefan sighed. "Nathan is right. It is not his fault, Marie. We should have told him."

Pearce broke into the family discussion. He pointed at the dead body. "This can't be the same man who was trying to find Marie in Shoreditch. This man has been following us since we left Westminster. So what happened to the man who went to your lodgings?"

Marie let out a great breath of relief. "Thankfully, I do not know. Walsingham's agent got there before him and was waiting in our rooms."

"Of course," said Pearce with a wry smile. "I should have known the old fox would be one step ahead of everyone."

"He whisked me away, with only the clothes I am wearing, and told me that he was taking me to Plymouth and that I should contact my father and tell him to meet us here."

"How Walsingham knew I was still alive, I do not know." Stefan shook his head in amazement.

"England's spymaster general would not employ anyone without finding out everything about them and their family," Pearce said matter-of-factly. "From the moment I suggested Nathan for this work, Walsingham would have had him investigated."

"I forgot—Walsingham sent this for you." Marie fumbled in her bodice and drew out a parchment. She handed it to Pearce.

"Pass me the lantern. I need to decode this." Pearce leapt off the bed and took both lantern and parchment to the table, pulling his Vigenère Square from his jerkin as he sat down.

Father, son, and daughter looked at one another awkwardly, not knowing what to say. Stefan strode over to the window, opened it, and gave a low whistle. Pearce looked at him inquiringly.

"We must dispose of the evidence," said Stefan quietly. Pearce nodded and went back to his decoding.

In a moment the room was silently filled with the gypsy troupe. Stefan made a small movement of his head and the men quickly gathered up the dead body.

"Bury him deep," was all the instruction Stefan gave. The men nodded, then as an afterthought, Graco whispered, "His boots are very fine. Can I have them?"

Stefan laughed. "Begone, you rogues. Meet me later at the usual place." And they were gone.

John had now finished decoding the message and did not look happy.

"It appears that Walsingham wants us to take Marie to Venice. She is to be part of our mission."

There was a collective outburst from everyone in the room. No one but Marie was happy with this change of plan. Pearce was concerned that he would have another person to take care of and Stefan was wary of handing his daughter over to a man he hardly knew. For his part, Nathan was outraged that Marie was spoiling his adventure. *This is my mission! Why does she have to come along?* he thought. He felt a great rage toward his sister, who had kept so many secrets from him and now was ruining everything. When Pearce stated that Marie would have to pretend to be his mistress, Stefan exploded.

"If you touch one hair of her head . . ." His threat was silenced by a contemptuous look from Pearce, who then replied that he had a serious task ahead of him. He clearly resented the fact that Stefan was questioning his professionalism. Marie ignored her father's overprotective outburst. She was determined to be part of the mission.

"I can be your eyes and ears, like Nathan," she said. "Women's gossip is just as valuable as servant's tittle-tattle. And I am skilled, like my father, in preparing healing potions."

John Pearce was forced to agree. He turned to Nathan. "Your sister has proved herself to be discreet. Think of all the years that she has been in contact with your father and how she has helped Will Shakespeare create ciphers." Nathan knew this was the truth but it did not stop him feeling frustrated that Marie would now be sharing *his* adventure. *If she once tries to baby me . . .* , he thought savagely, but he nodded his head in reluctant acceptance.

Stefan took Pearce to one side. "It seems as though my daughter's honor and my son's life are to be in your hands," he said quietly. "Take care that you return them both to England unharmed or you shall suffer for it."

Pearce merely offered his hand to Stefan. "You have no need to threaten me, sir," he replied. "I have sworn to the queen that I will protect Nathan with my life. I swear to you that Marie shall have the same protection."

Satisfied, Stefan shook the offered hand.

There were plans to make. Walsingham had made it quite clear in his message. Marie would take the name Bianca Dandolo, as John Pearce was to become Michael Cassio and Nathan, Marco Pignatti. Pearce tested Marie's grasp of Italian by having a fast and complicated conversation with her. He pronounced himself satisfied.

Stefan beamed. "I have two very talented children, do I not,

Master Pearce?" He was warming to the man who was about to take his family under his wing.

"Where will you go now?" Nathan asked, not able yet to call this man "father."

Stefan smiled sadly. "My friends and I will disappear into the countryside, as we have always done. My only regret is that now we have met, we have no time to get to know each other. That will have to wait until you return from your mission."

"Then we *will* meet? You promise?"

"I promise. You and I shall spend many days together when you return."

Stefan gently kissed Marie and said something to her in a language that Nathan did not understand. Then he left.

"Was that Roma?" Nathan asked his sister.

"Yes," answered Marie. "The language of our people." She wiped away a tear.

"Tell me about our family." Nathan was insistent. There was so much he needed to know.

Marie knew she owed her brother that much, so until the dawn crept in through the small window, the missing parts of Nathan's life were revealed. And the boy who did not realize that he was incomplete became whole again.

PART 2

CHAPTER 10

THE MISSION BEGINS

S o this is Venice," Nathan murmured as the three English spies set foot on the quayside, ready for their diplomatic mission on behalf of Queen Elizabeth. Nathan had never seen so many palaces, or what looked like palaces. Pearce smiled, breathing in the sea air deeply and feeling grateful for the firm land under his feet.

The journey through the English Channel and the Bay of Biscay had been rough, and John Pearce had taken to his bed with seasickness. Marie had been in her element—plunging into her bag of dried herbs and brewing a foul-tasting but efficacious concoction that stopped the vomiting and earned her Pearce's undying gratitude. Nathan, with his perfect sense of balance, was unaffected by the rolling seas and found it slightly amusing that his hero had such an inconvenient weakness.

Before they left the ship, Pearce had told Nathan and Marie that from now on they must only speak in Italian. Nathan soon found himself thinking in Italian. He knew that when he started dreaming in Italian he would be completely immersed in the language.

The captain stood on the quayside beside the trio. He shook Pearce's hand. "I shall be in Venice for two weeks. You must send me a message through your contact as to whether you will take sail with us back to England. If not, then another ship will be here in one month. You must go to your contact for instructions."

The captain went about his business and Pearce turned to his companions. "First we must go to our lodgings, and then we must buy clothes. I fear that we do not look like a prosperous Italian couple and their servant."

Nathan agreed. Their clothes did look drab compared with those worn by the Venetians who were milling about in the huge square ahead of them. Nathan had never seen such colorful garments: rich red velvets, gold silk, and extravagant hats. As they wandered through the Piazza di San Marco, past the tall columns that guarded the waterfront, Nathan gaped at the grandeur and opulence. Beyond the imposing arcades of the buildings surrounding the square, he could see domes and turrets, some gilded and shining brightly in the sun. The people they passed were of all races: Venetians, Turks, Orientals. Marie kept exclaiming at the women— such dresses, such exotic colors, fine materials, and jewels!

Nathan wrinkled his nose as they passed over a small bridge and the full odor of the murky water beneath hit his nostrils. Stinks like marshland, he thought. But mingled with that dank, rotting smell were other odors—Eastern perfumes, spicy food, sweet spices, and the smell of burning candles coming from the open doors of the many churches. It was intoxicating. The whole city bustled with life and laughter. They passed several people wearing strange white masks, and here and there, Nathan saw signs swinging above doors, signaling the house of a *mascherera*. A mask maker, Pearce told him. The masks were worn to carnivals, to private parties, or to gambling casinos. And everywhere was music. The sound of singing filled the air and sometimes they heard a lute playing in the street, or a tune coming from an open window. Nathan was dazzled by it all and would have been happy to walk the streets all day but Pearce had stopped in front of an imposing but faded building.

"This is to be our home," he stated. Brother and sister gawped at the height of the house.

"It must have at least three stories," Nathan breathed.

"These columns are marble," Marie murmured, stroking the hard, smooth multicolored stone.

"It belongs to the Jewish merchant Luzzatto. He keeps it here for other merchants who visit him on business. Come—let us enter," said Pearce firmly as he pushed open the doors and strode into the cool, dark interior. Inside, there were two servants—a woman and a boy—waiting for them. Nathan quickly remembered his own role and dropped back behind his sister and Pearce.

The boy, Nathan saw, was about his own age.

"Greetings, Signor Cassio," said the woman with a curtsy. "I am Graziella. This is my son, Enrico. Your rooms are ready, but Signor Luzzatto did not say that you were bringing the signorina."

"An unexpected turn of events," said Pearce quickly. "Signorina Bianca must have a room made up as soon as possible. Also, the signorina requires the immediate services of a good dressmaker."

Straightaway Pearce had assumed the confident air of a master used to instructing servants. Nathan was impressed.

Graziella surveyed Marie's clothing with amused concern. "I know of a woman who lives near the Basilica of San Marco. I will send Enrico to fetch her. If the signorina would care to rest in your room, Signor, the dressmaker will be here within the hour."

Pearce nodded. "First, have Enrico help my boy up with the baggage. I must find a tailor myself."

Nathan followed Enrico as they carried the baggage up the marble stairs. They set everything down in a large airy room with a view of the sea. Enrico winked at Nathan. "Your master, he has plenty of ladies, yes?"

Nathan grinned. "Plenty." He saw no harm in boosting John Pearce's reputation a little. "I'm Marco," he added, and Enrico nodded happily.

"You sleep downstairs. When your master goes out, come down and have some food. My mother is a good cook."

Pearce and Marie entered the room and Enrico bowed quickly and left on his errand to fetch the dressmaker. Even though they were now alone, Pearce continued to speak in Italian.

"So far, so good. Nathan, you must go down to the servants' quarters and ingratiate yourself with them. Find out whatever gossip you can. Every little detail is important. Marie, order three dresses, and get the dressmaker to have one ready for tomorrow morning. Here is some gold to pay her. I am off to the nearest tailor. Today we will rest. Tomorrow, Nathan, you will accompany me when I visit His Excellency, the doge...."

"What about me? Can I not come as well?" interrupted Marie.

"My meeting with the doge is men's business," Pearce replied matter-of-factly. Marie scowled at his answer and Nathan couldn't help smirking. "But," continued Pearce, "when I become involved in the social niceties of Venice, you will accompany me, as my woman. Suitably dressed, of course."

Marie seemed placated, for now, by the thought of wearing fine clothes and going to grand houses.

When Pearce had left, Nathan went downstairs, ready to act the spy and ferret out what information he could from the housekeeper and her son. He felt like an actor assuming a character and he tried to clear his mind of all thoughts, but as he reached the ground floor, his stomach overwhelmed his good intentions as the delicious smell of food hit his nostrils. Graziella was leaning over a fire and stirring a large, spicy sausage and lentil stew. Nathan's mouth watered. Knowing an appreciative audience when she saw one, Graziella offered him a bowl. It was hot and rich and Nathan ate greedily.

"He is a fine gentleman, your master," said Graziella. "He must be rich, if he is a friend of Luzzatto. He only deals with the finest nobility."

Nathan nodded, his mouth too full to make any comment.

"Does he have a profession?" she continued.

"Soldier," Nathan mumbled through another mouthful of the delicious sausage.

Graziella nodded.

"Signor Luzzatto said that your master is from Florence. Do you come from there too?" Nathan sensed the doubt in her voice and he shook his head.

"Ah. From your accent and your skin, I would have said more Naples way?" Nathan sensed that Graziella expected to be right.

"Roughly," he said.

She looked at him and smiled. "Eat up. A big, strong boy like you needs his food. So tell me, have you been to Venice before, Marco?" she added.

"No. Never."

Graziella sighed. "It is not what it was."

Nathan continued eating and listened to Graziella chattering. Mostly, it was local gossip—who was courting whom, who was the richest and the poorest. When she began to talk about the "stocking" groups, Nathan became more interested. Apparently the young men of Venice formed themselves into gangs that each wore different colored stockings. It was the job of the stocking gangs to prepare the entertainment for the various carnivals, but recently they had become more than masters of ceremony. They had begun fighting and causing trouble.

"Now the Ortelani are feuding with the Cortesi gang. Last night there was such a commotion in the streets. A Cortesi was killed, they say. The Council of Ten will have to pass a law to put a stop to this, they really will. Already there is talk of a law forbidding people to wear masks in the street unless it is carnival time. These young men should be whipped for all the trouble they cause." Graziella rolled her eyes heavenward. "It's getting so that it's not safe to walk the streets at night."

THAT night, Nathan listened to Enrico snoring in the next bed. He was too excited to sleep. Pearce had organized some new clothes for him too and tomorrow his work as an agent for Sir Francis Walsingham would really begin.

He looked out of the window into the street. Everywhere there were lighted torches in sconces and the streets were bathed in a flickering glow. The house overlooked one of the many canals that crisscrossed the city like a spider's web and there was a constant traffic of gondolas. Each boat was lit by a torch and one man rowed from a standing position. Nathan thought of the riverboats in London—flat and broad and drab brown wood—where a seated rower, with arms and shoulders like haunches of beef, would take you from one side of the Thames to the other.

Nathan smiled as a group of swaggering youths came around the corner. They wore half-masks, hats with sweeping feathers in them, and multicolored stockings. Nathan could not quite make out the colors by the light of the torches but one leg appeared to be red and the other green. His smile faded as he noticed that the young men wore chain-mail gauntlets and were holding glinting rapiers. *A stocking gang*, he thought, *looking for a fight.*

"Enrico, Enrico, wake up," he hissed, shaking the sleeping boy.

"What . . . what is it?" Enrico yawned.

"There's going to be a fight. Come and look."

Enrico rubbed the sleep from his eyes and reluctantly tumbled out of bed to the half-open window. By now, the gang was calling out insults.

"Hey, Moscato, you turd . . . show your face!"

"Come on, Moscato, chick . . . chick . . . chicken!"

"Where are you, Alimpato . . . the coward!"

They were laughing but there was menace in their faces.

"Go away, you louts!" screamed an old woman from some high window. "Decent people are trying to sleep!" This was met with a torrent of abuse from the youths in the street. "God will punish you!" shouted the old woman before slamming her window shut to the night.

Just then another group of youths rounded the corner, wearing stockings with flowers embroidered on them. "The Ortelani have come to deal with the Cortesi scum," shouted a young man who appeared to be the leader. "Prepare to defend yourselves, you sons of whores!"

The two groups circled one another, like animals. The young men smiled, rapiers and daggers in their hands. Nathan held his breath as the two leaders began to fight, to the catcalls of the others. Their skirmish was brief. The Ortelani leader was the superior swordsman and he swiftly disarmed his opponent. The others then began to fight. Soon, the entire street was filled with young men leaping and ducking as their swords and daggers flashed and clashed in the torchlight. Everyone in the area was now awake, peering into the street to see what was happening. It was difficult to watch so many pairs fighting, so Nathan concentrated on the duel between the Ortelani leader and his opponent. The others were pathetic. *Robey would call this brawling, not dueling*, thought Nathan. *There is little skill here.*

Then, from nowhere, a knife flashed through the air and hit the Ortelani leader between the shoulder blades. He fell forward into the canal, dead. The fighting stopped. There was a shocked silence and everyone looked at a tall, pimply Cortesi gang member. There was no doubt, from the triumphant look on his face, that he had thrown the knife. He then turned and ran, the Cortesi gang close behind him, leaving the Ortelani scouring the water for the body of their leader.

The onlookers watched in pity as the young man was hauled from the canal with the dagger still in his back. Two of his comrades were weeping as they carried him away.

Nathan was shocked. "Have you seen a fight like that before?" he asked.

Enrico shrugged. "Yes," he answered sleepily, "but not often. Anyway, Giacomo Ortelani asked for it. The Ortelani are scum."

Nathan looked at the boy in surprise. "You know these men?"

Enrico smirked. "I am a member of the Cortesi gang, of course I know them." He held his head high but to Nathan he looked ridiculous—a boy in a nightshirt, pretending to be a part of a gang.

"What does your mother think of you being in the gang?" Nathan's question cut into the swagger like a hot knife and Enrico grew sullen. "It's nothing to do with her. I will soon be a man and then I shall please myself." He turned and climbed into his bed, his back to Nathan.

Moments later a small voice came out of the darkness. "You won't say anything to my mother, will you?"

Nathan smiled to himself. "No. It's none of my business." Enrico grunted by way of reply and soon fell into the heavy breathing of a deep sleep.

As Nathan lay there, he knew that he must not relax too much under the spell of Venetian splendor. This was a dangerous place and from now on he would be on his guard.

CHAPTER 11

THE PRICE OF COOPERATION

N the morning there was no sign of the previous night's bloodshed. Someone had washed the cobbles and the passersby were going about their business as usual. Graziella was muttering about her disturbed sleep and the disgrace of it all. She was ashamed for Venice, she said, that visitors should witness such things.

All thoughts of stocking gang feuds were pushed out of Nathan's mind by the arrival of the new clothes. Both the tailor and the dressmaker had worked through the night and Nathan was summoned upstairs to change. Pearce looked every inch the Italian nobleman in a gold-and-black doublet with a high collar, trimmed with lace, and slashed sleeves that allowed his shirt to be pulled through into fashionable puffs along the length of his arms. Nathan was to be dressed completely in dark red, with a red cap, set with a brown feather. It was quite the best outfit he had ever owned, and for the first time in his life, he felt handsome—but the realization of it made him blush. The tailor seemed pleased with his work and assured Pearce that two further outfits would be delivered by the end of the week.

When Marie appeared, Nathan's mouth dropped open. She looked extraordinary. Her dress was made of purple silk, and the underskirt and sleeves were white and gold. A stiff white ruff stood up from her shoulders and encircled the back of her neck and her dark curls were dressed in an elaborate style.

"You look like . . . like . . . ," Nathan struggled to find the words.

"Like a highborn Italian lady should," Pearce said with an appreciative smile and he bowed deeply to honor her.

Nathan was amazed by his sister's appearance. She did, indeed, look highborn. She reminded him of the few ladies he had seen at Queen Elizabeth's court, except Marie's face was not painted. Now that he had seen her in fine clothes, he could see that his sister was truly beautiful. *The sort of woman that would turn men's heads and loosen their tongues,* he thought, remembering the lines from a play he had once seen. *And I suppose that could have its advantages for a spy.*

Marie was ecstatic. She had been promised more dresses by tomorrow, but for the moment, this one was enough for her.

The weather was warm and humid as Pearce and Nathan stepped outside. Despite last night's violence, the city's energy filled him with excitement.

When they arrived at the doge's palace, he gazed in awe at the jumble of massive buildings. Everywhere there were statues— knights, lions, mythical creatures. Nathan later discovered they had all been looted from Constantinople during the Crusades. Next to the doge's palace was the great Basilica of Saint Mark and, on its gallery, glistening as though with golden sweat, stood four massive gilded statues of powerful horses. They were mounted on pillars, each with one foreleg raised, as if they were about to jump down on the city below.

John was tugging at his sleeve and, reluctantly, Nathan followed him. There were guards at the main entrance of the palace and John stated his business before being allowed to pass. Inside the massive vaulted entrance hall were paintings unlike any Nathan had ever seen before. His face flushed a little as he found himself staring at a pantheon of naked breasts. He remembered the formal paintings he had admired in Westminster Palace. Somehow he could not imagine the queen of England filling her palace with the decadence he saw before him now.

Surrounded by such opulence, Nathan felt almost as though he were dreaming. It was just a short time ago—*was it really only a few weeks?*—that his life had consisted of one large, cluttered room in Shoreditch, overlooking the fields, and a walk each day, along the muddy track that passed for a street, to the dingy theater. He had never imagined that he would, so smoothly, enter the world of wealth, privilege, and intrigue.

The large doors facing them opened, and a man entered. He looked like a priest and was dressed in a magnificent gold floor-length robe, with a red skullcap.

"Signor Cassio?" he inquired of Pearce, who removed his hat and bowed. "I am Monsignor Stephano, the doge's private secretary. He will see you now." Nathan followed at a respectful distance as they walked down a long corridor. The monsignor said nothing, he merely smiled and indicated with his hand when they needed to turn a corner or go through a door. At last, they reached a set of doors, flanked by two guards, who opened them at the monsignor's signal. Inside was the doge. He was seated in a grand chair at the end of a huge table scattered with many papers. This was a man of business. The doge offered his hand and Pearce knelt to kiss his ring, as though he were the pope, while the monsignor motioned Nathan to sit in a chair by the door.

Pasquale Cicogna had been elected doge two years ago, and according to John Pearce, he was notoriously mean. During the traditional procession, which took place when an election was made, the doge was supposed to throw gold ducats to the crowd. Cicogna had chosen to throw small silver coins instead, which the people of Venice now referred to contemptuously as *cicognini*.

Luzzatto had set up the meeting, and the doge knew that Michael Cassio was not what he seemed. Pearce handed him the gift, put together by Walsingham, and drew his attention to the special verse and the handkerchief. The doge smiled and motioned to the monsignor to read the message.

"Monsignor Stephano is my eyes," he said to reassure Pearce. "All matters remain secret with him, have no fear."

The monsignor read the message from the queen of England and whispered it into his employer's ear.

The doge looked steadily at Pearce. He then rose and looked out of the window.

"You understand," he began, "that in Venice we occupy a unique position. We tread a delicate line through our commercial transactions and we manage to preserve our neutrality. But no one likes us—the pope is angry with us because we give sanctuary to heretics and Spain is ambitious to get her hands on our territories. But we have been allies of the Spaniards in the past and our independence is the price they pay for that past help. England, Signor Cassio, has very little to offer Venice. It is a great country but a small one. Great but small."

Pearce showed no emotion on his face, although Nathan knew he must be feeling disappointed.

"Excellency, you would have our help," Pearce countered, "if you should need it, against any of your enemies. You know that in recent years, England has sent troops to assist the Netherlands in their struggle against Spain. Her Majesty would do the same for Venice, I am assured of that."

The doge sat down and smiled. He was silent for several minutes. "Perhaps there is a way," he said, leaning forward. "You may be able to help us solve a problem we have been debating in council all week." Pearce waited for the doge to continue. "For many years, the islands around Greece belonged to Venice. One island in particular, Cyprus, was prized above all others. We would like to get that island back. I propose to send an expeditionary force, led by our greatest general, Othello, to try and regain that island for the Venetian Empire. I wish to send you as his second in command. If we are successful in taking the island back from the Turks, then the English could help us defend that island against any future invasion. Your queen could put a small force on Cyprus—soldiers and ships—and keep it safe for us."

Pearce nodded and a small but uncomfortable smile played around his lips.

"Excellency, if this assault on Cyprus is successful, presumably the cost of keeping an English force on that island would fall to England?"

The doge beamed. Here was a man who understood economics.

Nathan could see that Pearce was in the difficult position of representing a queen who did not like to part with money—and asking for help from a man who was equally tightfisted.

"I am sure you are aware that I shall have to relay your terms to Her Majesty," said Pearce carefully. "It will take some weeks to get a reply. When do you plan your expedition?"

The doge spread his hands apologetically. "As soon as possible, I'm afraid. The heat becomes unbearable in the Aegean in the summer. We must attack before the end of this month."

Pearce looked tense. "Excellency," he replied, "I would be willing to assist in the expedition but you understand that I cannot speak for my country."

The doge narrowed his eyes. "It is enough, for the moment. English reinforcements can be sent later, if the mission is successful. There is one further matter you should know. . . ."

Pearce waited as the wily doge continued.

"General Othello must know nothing of this possible alliance. He hopes to be made governor of Cyprus if the assault is successful. This may not be possible if your queen comes to our aid. It may be politic to make the governor an Englishman, do you not think?" He continued without waiting for an answer, "And the people of Venice must not know of this mission. We do not wish to give information of our intentions to the many Turkish spies in the city. So as not to arouse suspicion, the expeditionary force will sail first for the island of Crete, ostensibly to rebuild our fortifications there. Is this understood?"

Nathan was struck by the deviousness of the doge. Even Sir Francis Walsingham might meet his match in this man.

The business concluded, the doge returned the verses and the handkerchief to Pearce. "I have no need of them now. May God speed your endeavors, Signor Cassio. My prayers go with you."

As they stepped out into the bright noon sun, Pearce grimly buckled his sword belt on and swore an oath under his breath.

"Is it not as you hoped?" Nathan inquired. He could see that Pearce was not altogether happy.

Pearce shook his head. "We will talk later. Now we must go and visit Luzzatto in the ghetto."

Nathan was curious. "Tell me more about this man Luzzatto," he asked.

Pearce smiled. "He is a great man. Very powerful in Venice, where the size of a man's fortune and his influence over others is everything. I suspect that half the nobility in Venice owes money to Mordecai Luzzatto. He certainly owns a great deal of property in the city."

"And why does he work for the English?"

"Because he is a Jew and has no love for the Spaniards. I hear he has lost relatives to the Inquisition. He knows that if the Spaniards extend their empire even more, then all Jews, no matter how wealthy and influential, will be rounded up like cattle and forced to convert or be burnt at the stake. Walsingham has a talent for sniffing out men with a vested interest in seeing England safe from the Spanish yoke. He has spies all over the known world. If Philip of Spain sneezes, Walsingham knows about it."

"It was good of Luzzatto to vacate his house for us to live in," Nathan commented.

"Oh, he doesn't live there—he's not allowed to. He owns many houses but he is only allowed to live in the Jewish ghetto," was Pearce's reply.

Nathan found this reply astonishing, and as he followed Pearce down narrow lanes and over bridges, he asked for more information about the ghetto. Pearce's explanation perturbed him.

"In Venice, they have had a separate place for Jews to live since 1516. It's a walled city of its own, where the Jews can do all their business. They may come out into the city center during the day, but they have to be back behind their gates at night."

"But why?" Nathan was puzzled.

Pearce shrugged. "Because they are not Christians, I assume."

Nathan was shocked that people were being confined behind walls and gates just because of their religion. Then he thought about how the mayor of London had prohibited all theaters from the City of London, forcing actors to live and work outside the City walls, and weren't the tanners forced by law to ply their stinking trade outside the City's boundaries? But it did not seem quite the same.

When they turned in through the gates of the ghetto, Nathan saw that it was a city within a city. Cramped houses and shops flanked either side of the street. Most of the dark-skinned, dark-haired men had full beards and their hair in ringlets. They wore black, flowing clothes and skullcaps. He noted that there were no women around. The more brightly dressed Venetians were milling about too, buying cloth, food, musical instruments, medicines, and many other goods. Tailors and shoemakers sat cross-legged in open windows, patiently sewing or measuring up clients. Everywhere, Nathan saw evidence of the Venetians' contempt for the Jews, who were making their clothes or lending them money.

He winced as he heard one young man speak arrogantly to a shoemaker. "I want the best leather for these boots, don't try to palm me off with some inferior material. I know how crafty you Jews are."

They arrived at a wrought-iron gate, set in a small wall. Through the gate was a charming courtyard with a fountain. Pearce pulled a chain, which rang a bell. A servant quickly appeared.

"Please," said Pearce, "tell Signor Luzzatto that Signor Cassio has come to pay him a visit."

The servant disappeared then came back and ushered Nathan and Pearce through the tranquil courtyard.

The house beyond was sparse compared with the doge's palace. There were no statues or paintings but the furniture was of fine, dark wood, beautifully carved. The floors were cool marble made of intricately patterned tiles. They were admitted into a room and, seated at a desk reading a large book, was the man they had come to see—Mordecai Luzzatto.

He looked up from his book and his face creased into a hundred lines of warmth and greeting. "Welcome, welcome, Signor Cassio. Welcome to the house of Luzzatto." He turned to Nathan. "And welcome, young sir. What is your name?"

"Marco," Nathan replied with a bow.

"It is almost noon," said Luzzatto. "You must break bread with me and we shall talk in private. Come." He led the way into a small private dining room where small dishes of food were laid out. There were couches around the table and Luzzatto bade them sit.

"We are honored by your generosity," said Pearce as they began to eat. While they dipped in and out of the spicy and savory dishes, Pearce explained what had happened at his meeting with the doge. Nathan followed the conversation closely, anxious to further understand the complicated politics. Luzzatto nodded sagely.

"Do you think that Queen Elizabeth will agree to pay for a permanent English garrison on Cyprus?" he inquired.

Pearce shrugged. "I doubt it. It is up to Sir Francis Walsingham to convince Her Majesty that such an expense would be worthwhile. It is difficult to see how it would benefit England. It all seems a great gamble to me."

Luzatto smiled. "The Venetians love to gamble. But I think that the doge is gambling with your life, my friend. You are to join Othello's army and fight the Turks. Whatever your queen decides, you may be the loser."

Pearce dismissed the danger. "I am well trained, as you know. I am not concerned about fighting; I am only concerned about the plotting behind all of this. I do not trust the doge."

"You are wise not to trust Cicogna or indeed any man in this city. They would sell their own wives if it made them a profit. So, you wish to send a message to the Dutch captain?" Luzzatto brought the conversation back to the reason for their visit.

"Yes, I shall prepare a cipher today, to send to Walsingham. You must tell Captain Finisterre that I am detained and he must leave as soon as he can. Urge him to make fast passage to England. I must have a reply from Walsingham soon."

"It shall be done. You can write your messages in my library. No one will disturb you. The boy can spend some time with me. I should enjoy the company."

John was installed in the library with pens, ink, and paper, and Nathan was taken through another tranquil courtyard. Luzzatto proudly pointed out many of the architectural details of his house.

But Nathan wanted to know more about the ghetto. "Can I ask you something?" he said suddenly. Luzzatto looked surprised at the urgency of Nathan's tone and nodded.

"What I've seen and heard in the streets here has disturbed me."

"How so?" Luzzatto asked casually.

Nathan scowled. "The way I've heard men speak to Jews; the fact that you are locked in this place at night. I don't understand it."

Luzzatto's eyes glittered but his voice betrayed no emotion. "Don't try to understand it," he said simply. "Only know that in most countries of the world Jews are despised as the killers of Christ—and much more. They hate us because we are good men of business, they hate us because we are different and we will not change to be like them—there are so many reasons. People just hate someone who is different, that's all. Sometimes our men get very angry but there is nothing they can do. We do not have the same rights as Christians. If we were to harm a Christian in the city of Venice, the law decrees that all our lands and property would be confiscated and we would be exiled. That is why you see our men turn away when they are cursed and reviled. That is why we keep our women indoors, or send them away to relatives in the country, where they cannot be insulted."

Luzzatto's face was a little flushed now, although he had spoken the words calmly. Nathan apologized for his inquisitiveness.

"No, Marco, you have shown an interest. You have questioned the order of things. Never lose that desire, young man." Luzzatto paused momentarily. "You will always be welcome in my house." He gave Nathan a long, hard look. "So, tell me," he said thoughtfully, "how do you find Enrico?"

Nathan was a little confused by this change of subject, "I hardly know him, sir, but we seem to get along with each other."

Luzzatto took a deep breath. "When my wife died, Graziella was my housekeeper. I owe her a great debt.... Enrico was brought up in this house. His father left when he was a baby and never returned. Now I fear the boy is in trouble, or soon will be. I hear stories of him following the Cortesi gang around like a little dog. The trouble with little dogs, Marco, is that they are taught bad tricks by their masters, is that not so?"

Nathan agreed. "Last night . . . there was a fight . . . a man died."

Luzzatto looked grave. "I would not have Graziella hurt for all the world, Marco. I do not want her little boy brought home dead on a bier one night because he has been so foolish as to be killed in some street brawl. Enrico will not listen to his mother, nor to me, but he might listen to a boy of his own age. What do you think?"

Luzzatto's eyes held a plea in them that Nathan found impossible to ignore.

"I will try, sir," he answered.

Luzzatto lowered his voice. "Michael Cassio has told me that you are well trained and can fend for yourself. If you cannot persuade Enrico, would you be prepared to protect him? I know this is a lot to ask of one so young."

Nathan was flattered that John Pearce had spoken so well of him to Luzzatto.

"I will do what I can while I am in Venice," he said firmly. Luzzatto's face showed great satisfaction.

"Let this be our secret for the moment, Marco," and he offered his hand to shake, to seal the bargain. Nathan took the hand and smiled. He was excited to be given some private responsibility. He would not tell John of his task until he had accomplished it. Then Pearce would see that Nathan was well and truly ready for any work that Walsingham might throw his way.

CHAPTER 12

A CITY OF DOUBLE STANDARDS

HEN Pearce and Nathan returned to the house, there was a fever of excitement. A formal invitation had arrived from the doge to attend a banquet and Graziella had taken it straight to Marie. The two women were now devoting themselves to lengthy preparations.

In the kitchen Enrico was tucking into some of his mother's pigeon pie, and Nathan and Pearce gladly joined him. In between mouthfuls, Pearce asked Enrico about General Othello. Enrico's eyes lit up and he became quite animated. "He is a mighty warrior, sir," he said with breathless admiration, and he went on to describe the many battles Othello had fought on behalf of the Venetian state. He told of how Othello had once come down off his horse and single-handedly killed thirty men with his sword, and of how he had fought and won another battle with his arm almost severed. Pearce and Nathan raised their eyebrows in astonishment.

Enrico carried on, babbling enthusiastically, ". . . and the most remarkable thing is that he has become such a great general when he was born a slave. . . ."

"What?" Pearce interrupted. "A slave?"

Enrico nodded and looked from Pearce to Nathan, amazed that they did not know the most basic facts about the great general.

"You did not know that he is a Moor—a black man, sir?"

Nathan's eyes widened and he looked at Pearce.

"No, Enrico, I did not know." Pearce shook his head and smiled.

"I'll never understand this city!" Nathan exclaimed. "Jews are locked away—but all the noble families of Venice borrow money from them. And slaves are sold in the marketplace—but one of them becomes the greatest general of the state?"

"It is a city of double standards." Pearce smiled again. "Venetians are men of business. If someone is useful to them, it matters not whether he is slave or freeman, Jew or Turk."

"And if they are not useful to them?" asked Nathan.

Pearce shrugged and pulled a resigned face. "Then they probably don't matter at all. It is the way of the world, I am afraid."

Nathan pursed his lips in disgust.

The sun was beginning to set and it would soon be time for them to leave for the doge's palace.

Marie looked beautiful. She wore the same purple gown, but her hair was dressed in the Italian fashion, long and flowing, and decorated with pearls, flowers, and jewels. Her eyes sparkled from belladonna eyedrops and her cheeks and lips were delicately rouged. Nathan was stunned by her appearance. She looked so different.

But when she inclined her head graciously toward him and murmured, "Good evening, Marco," she overdid the playacting and it made him snigger.

Pearce bowed low in genuine admiration.

"You look very beautiful, my lady. But Venice is a dangerous city," he said, assuming a more businesslike manner, "and I swore to your father that I would protect you. . . ."

Marie smiled disdainfully. "My father forgets that I have looked after myself since I was nine years old. You are not the only one who carries a concealed weapon, you know." Then, to Nathan's astonishment, Marie drew a small, fine stiletto blade from the front of her bodice.

Pearce smiled and bowed again. "Forgive me for underestimating you, Signorina."

Nathan shook his head in disbelief. How many more surprises would his sister produce before this mission was over?

The party of three descended to the street and stepped into a waiting gondola.

There were grand gondolas in front and behind them, and each boat carried a cargo of exquisitely dressed passengers. *Perhaps they are going to the palace, like us,* thought Nathan.

Slowly the boats turned and glided under a bridge, then through an archway. They were now in a queue, as each gondola stopped at the broad steps ahead of them and its passengers disembarked and entered the blazing light of the doge's palace. The great and powerful families of Venice were gathering in the doorway and greeting one another enthusiastically. Nathan, Pearce, and Marie edged their way through the crowd and Nathan noticed that many of the Venetians' eyes flickered over them, registering the presence of strangers at the banquet.

The throng of guests, all murmuring happily, moved forward into the hall and, beyond that, the reception room. Young, black-skinned servants were circulating with trays of wine.

Just then, the large bronze doors at the end of the room opened and Monsignor Stephano, the doge's aide, appeared. "My lords and ladies, prelates and gentlemen—the doge will receive you now," he announced.

As the crowd of guests filed into the next room, John Pearce whispered into Nathan's ear. "Wait until we are seated, then place yourself near us." Nathan nodded and began to ease himself through the throng. There were servants' benches all along the walls of the dining room and he sat in a corner to observe the scene.

The doge was seated upon a dais, and every guest kissed his hand and exchanged a few words of greeting. They then milled around the tables, looking for the name cards that indicated where they were to sit.

It was soon Marie and Pearce's turn to present themselves to the doge and it caused some comment from other guests when the un-known couple were seated at the top table, near the doge. Nathan noted one guest in particular, a powerfully built man with a scarred face, who looked livid with anger.

Nathan's eyes then fell on a couple who had taken their seats to the left of Pearce and Marie. They looked like father and daughter. The man was old and gray haired and she—Nathan's breath caught in his throat—was like some kind of spirit being. Her hair was the palest gold Nathan had ever seen. Her skin was like white marble and she was dressed in a gold-and-white dress, which made her look even more ethereal. This lady seemed to be much admired by the men, judging by the number of them who came to pay their respects and kiss her hand. She smiled sweetly and politely at each of them, but seemed more interested in giving her full attention to her father.

Suddenly there was a shout from the other end of the hall.

"Your Excellency, a thousand pardons for my lateness!"

All eyes turned toward the owner of the booming voice. General Othello had arrived, like an explosion of gunpowder. His teeth flashed white in his black face and the mood of the room lifted in appreciation. *His lateness is deliberate,* thought Nathan. *This is a man who knows how to play an audience.*

Othello moved swiftly along the tables, shaking hands here and there. Finally he approached the doge with his arms outstretched as though to a friend. Nathan instantly admired him. The man's personality was magnetic.

Othello and the doge took their places, side by side, at the top table and Nathan watched as introductions were instantly made between the general and Pearce. Othello seemed genuinely friendly and attentive. Then Nathan caught a glance that shot between the General and the beautiful blond lady. There was no mistaking the intimacy of that glance, especially as the lady's cheeks flushed. Nathan smiled wryly. It appeared that Othello was a lover as well as a warrior. *It is this sort of detail that I must remember and pass to John later,* he thought to himself, pleased he had not forgotten all that Robey had taught him.

A moment later, musicians appeared in a gallery above and began to serenade the guests. The banquet had begun.

Nathan, excited to be part of such a majestic evening, edged his way around the room so he could sit nearer to Othello. Unfortunately that meant he was now directly behind the man who had shown such anger when Pearce and Marie were seated at the top table.

As the dinner progressed, Nathan listened to the man's bitter conversation. His nervous wife kept entreating him to calm down.

"Iago, my lord, it means nothing. It doesn't matter where we sit. It is enough that we were invited."

"I should be up there," he spat. "I am Othello's ensign. This is a deliberate slight to me."

"No, my lord, you are wrong, I'm sure."

Iago snorted in disgust and drained his goblet while his wife picked at her food halfheartedly. Nathan took an immediate and intense dislike to this Iago.

The doge rose and addressed his guests. "My friends, I thank you all for attending tonight. As usual it has been a pleasure. Doubtless you have been wondering about the guest at my side. May I introduce Signor Michael Cassio of Florence. He is here, at my invitation, to bring his professional skills to the aid of our illustrious General Othello. Signor Cassio will be General Othello's second in command for the foreseeable future."

There was a loud crash as the now-drunk Iago stumbled and fell on the floor, breaking a chair as he did so. He lay almost at Nathan's feet and for a brief moment, he stared into Nathan's eyes.

His wife blushed as the doge fixed a baleful glare on Iago. He continued, "Now, I am an old man and must take my leave. Please continue to enjoy yourselves for as long as you wish."

The guests broke into appreciative applause as the doge left the room, leaning on Monsignor Stephano's arm.

Wanting to save Iago's wife further shame, Nathan decided to try and raise her husband from the floor. He was struggling with the dead weight of the man when he heard a deep voice above him.

"This drunken soldier is too much for a young boy to handle."

Nathan looked up. A smiling Othello bent over and hoisted Iago to his feet.

"You shame yourself, man," he muttered to his ensign.

Iago looked at him and tried to focus. "Should have been my job," he slurred venomously, "not some poxy Florentine's."

Othello's wide grin disappeared instantly and Nathan saw the power of the mighty general flex in every muscle of his face. His expression was grim.

"Emilia, take your man home and throw a bucket of cold water over him. Then tell him I want to see him in the morning."

"Yes, my lord." Emilia's face crumpled and a tear escaped down one cheek. Othello's face softened.

"He is a good soldier, my lady. Every good soldier disgraces himself with drink now and then."

Emilia nodded, grateful for the kind words, as servants appeared to remove her husband.

Othello then turned the full force of his charm on Nathan. For

153

a moment, Nathan felt as though he were the general's greatest friend, such was the warmth of the man's smile.

"I thank you, young man, for trying to save the honor of my ensign's lady. May I know your name?"

"M . . . Marco . . . Marco Pignatti," Nathan stuttered. "I serve Signor Cassio."

"Ah." Othello nodded approvingly. "Well done, boy," he murmured before returning to the top table.

On the way home from the banquet, the water lapped around the gondola and the sounds of Venice were reduced to the occasional reveler singing in the back streets. Nathan listened as Marie relayed her conversations with the beautiful lady who had sat next to her. Her name was Desdemona; she was nineteen years of age, unmarried but with many suitors. Her father, Brabantio, had been a member of the Council of Venice, and his wife was dead. Desdemona was his only child. Marie looked satisfied that she had obtained so much information in so little time.

Back at the house, the three spies reflected on the evening.

"I like this Othello," said Pearce. "He is a good man and, by all accounts, a great soldier. But I am uneasy. I sensed that he has some involvement with the girl Desdemona. . . ."

"Don't be foolish." Marie was astonished. "He's twenty years older than her, and a black man—a former slave. She's a Venetian noblewoman."

Nathan disagreed with his sister. "I saw a look that passed between them. Besides, he is so impressive."

Pearce sighed. "Nathan is right. Othello has great charm. But no matter—it is none of our business. What of this man who was drunk tonight—the general's ensign?"

Nathan felt a degree of satisfaction, as he was able to provide the information Pearce wanted. "A nasty piece of work called Iago," he said grimly. "He was bitter because he was not seated at the top table with the general. And he was furious when the doge announced your appointment as second in command. His wife fears him, that was obvious to me. I would watch your back when he is near, John."

Pearce slapped Nathan on the shoulder. "I thank you for that advice, my young friend. Now, Othello has summoned me to army headquarters tomorrow. Nathan, you shall accompany me."

Marie made an exasperated face. She was not happy about being left out of the adventure quite so much. Nathan could not resist giving her a look of amused pity that he knew would annoy her even more.

Nathan went happily to bed, his head bursting with the images of the evening's grandeur and the intrigue that might lie ahead. He would enjoy meeting General Othello again. Now he could understand why Enrico seemed to worship the man. Nathan's candle flickered soft light around the walls and wavered in the gentle breeze from the open window. He glanced at the sleeping Enrico, huddled down among the blankets—but something caused him to look more closely. There was no movement at all. No sound of breathing or snoring. Nathan pulled back the blankets. There was no Enrico—only a carefully contrived sausage of bolsters and blankets. Nathan stared at the open window. Had Enrico gone to meet the Cortesi gang? He remembered his promise to Luzzatto and knew that he must try and find boy.

Candle in hand, he made his way silently up from the servant's quarters to the front hallway. In the room to the side of the front door was Pearce's locked weapons case. Nathan slid the wood-and-leather box toward him and then he listened, holding his breath, for any sounds from the sleeping household. He felt guilty about betraying Pearce's trust, but it could not be helped. He had promised Luzzatto that he would look after Enrico. Nathan took a knife from his boot and regretfully contemplated his next action. Under his breath he thanked Nym who had taught him, on one idle evening at Robey's school, how to pick locks with the point of a knife. It took some fiddling but at last the box was open and Nathan stared at a veritable arsenal of swords and knives, neatly cushioned in velvet depressions. One weapon was missing though for Pearce slept with his best sword under his bed at all times.

Nathan chose the lightest rapier, deciding to carry the sword bare and conceal it under a long cloak, which he grabbed from the hallway as he swiftly but silently left through the front door.

He ran through the streets, not knowing where he should look for Enrico. Venice was like a maze. The moon was almost full and illuminated Nathan's way. Every now and then he would pause to listen for sounds. If he heard a raised voice or laughter, he would change direction and head toward it. Eventually he turned a corner into a square and there he saw the Cortesi gang, huddled together, drinking wine from a flagon and trading insults. Enrico loitered on the edge of the group, looking desperate to be included.

Nathan kept to the shadows and stealthily advanced toward the group, never taking his eyes off Enrico.

"This wine is good," the gang leader said. "Where did you get it, little chicken?"

Enrico stiffened as another youth started making clucking noises.

"I stole it," Enrico replied, trying to sound arrogant. Nathan knew that the wine had probably come from Graziella's stores by the kitchen.

"And what do you want in return?" the leader asked teasingly.

"This baby wants to belong to the Cortesi gang, Mercutio," crowed a straggle-haired youth with uneven teeth.

Enrico's head flew back in a temper and from his sleeve he drew a dagger. "Don't call me a baby!" he shouted. "I can fight as well as any of you!"

Enrico's outburst provoked laughter and mock horror from the gang. Nathan waited in the darkness, poised to move.

"Put your stickpin away, little chicken," said Mercutio. "We shall let you join our gang, if you pass the test."

"What test?" Enrico asked in a trembling voice.

Mercutio looked at his followers and smiled.

"If you want to join the Cortesi gang, then you have to steal some money from the offertory box in the cathedral."

There was a low whistle of appreciation from the youth with the straggly hair.

Enrico stood like a statue in the middle of the square, his knife shaking in his hand. Everyone knew that stealing from the church was a crime punishable by death, whether you were twelve or twenty years old. Nathan decided it was time to stir from the shadows.

"Leave him be." His voice was firm and strong and took everyone by surprise, even Nathan himself. The gang moved, with animal instinct, into a defensive formation. Mercutio grinned again—not with pleasure, but with malice.

"So little chicken has a mother hen to watch out for him, eh?"

Enrico looked appalled. "Go away, Marco!" he spat defiantly. "This is none of your business!"

"I'm making it my business. Why do you want to hang around with scum like this?" Nathan did not take his eyes off Mercutio as he asked the question. The insult drew a warning murmur of displeasure from the gang.

Enrico said nothing.

"Is this your idea of being a man?" Nathan continued. "Stealing wine to buy your way into a gang of fools?" Still Enrico did not answer and Mercutio began to advance slowly.

"Who are you?" he asked Nathan scornfully.

"I am Marco Pignatti from Naples."

Mercutio's face broke into a wide, derisory grin. "Pignatti from Naples. I hear that they don't wash in Naples. Is that true? That all Neapolitans smell worse than a pig sty?"

Nathan smiled grimly. He imagined he were onstage once more in Shoreditch, playing the part of a soldier. He knew that if he held that fantasy in his mind he would not lose courage.

"Nothing smells as bad as the stocking gangs in this city," he retaliated. Mercutio's grin disappeared.

"You insult me and my cousins—but can you fight?"

"I know more about fighting than you can imagine." Nathan felt a surge of excitement.

"Then show me." Mercutio drew his rapier and the blade gleamed in the moonlight.

Nathan's mind raced, turning over all the advice that Robey had given him during his training. *Before you fight an opponent, take the measure of him. Observe how long his reach is. See how he moves. Find his weakness and target it. A man's weakness may not be physical but in his mind. If he is a braggart, then encourage him to show off and he will leave himself open to your blade. If he lacks confidence, then come at him hard and bruise his confidence still more. The art of dueling lies in the intelligence that you put behind your sword. Any man can flail a piece of metal about. The true swordsman thinks as much as he acts.*

Mercutio's reach was certainly longer than Nathan's, and he was at least five inches taller. But as a wispy cloud cleared the moon and threw Mercutio's face into its full light, Nathan saw his opponent's weakness. He was beautiful. Nathan smiled. *This man is in love with himself,* he thought. *If I mark his pretty face, he will be finished.*

Nathan threw off the cloak and revealed his sword. Castilian steel, sharp as a razor, with a needle point.

There was a murmur of appreciation from the gang and Mercutio's face darkened.

"Where did you steal that . . . peasant?" Nathan could detect that an edge of concern had crept into Mercutio's voice.

Out of the corner of his eye, Nathan saw Enrico looking on, amazed. He would have some explaining to do afterward.

"Come, sir, your passado." Mercutio made a derogatory salute with the rapier and crouched, ready. Nathan responded and the two blades stroked each other in the white light of the moon.

Instantly Mercutio pulled back and lunged, his sword heading for his opponent's chest, but it was swiftly parried by Nathan's lightning reaction. Then began the fight in earnest. Swords whipped through the air with the sound of wet ropes. Sparks flew as the blades met. Mercutio's sword was slightly thicker and heavier and he had the longer reach but this was of no advantage to him against someone so nimble and with such quick reflexes. Nathan ducked and weaved, his superior weapon fending off every blow. Several times they crashed into a huddle, swords locked at the hilts. Mercutio tried to use his greater strength to push the boy to the ground but Nathan was always ready with some vicious play; biting Mercutio's hand or kneeing him in the groin.

After one such clash, Mercutio staggered back in a fury and drew a knife from a sheath at his belt. Nathan laughed. He knew now that he was besting his opponent. Robey had always said that if a man resorts to drawing a second weapon, he is feeling defeat. Then you must redouble your efforts with the sword and finish him off. Nathan swung around, slashing his rapier in a wide arc, aimed at Mercutio's dagger hand. Nathan's blade cut deep and Mercutio dropped his knife with a cry of pain. As Mercutio's body caved in at the solar plexus, Nathan brought his sword up swiftly and slashed his opponent's left cheek. Mercutio was forced to drop his sword to bring his right hand up to the wound. He was defeated.

Nathan stood with his sword aimed at Mercutio's chest, as if to finish him off.

No one moved or spoke.

Nathan raised his sword and pointed it at the Cortesi gang, who made a small movement backward.

"I am willing to fight any one of you, now that your leader is down."

No one came forward and Nathan spoke to Enrico without taking his gaze off the gang in front of him.

"Enrico, it is time for you to go home. Direct your gaze toward some real men in the future." He raised his voice a notch and addressed the Cortesi. "Do not think that you can later ambush me or my friend here in some dark alley. I am in Venice on the doge's business and you shall hang from the rafters of his palace if you harm either of us. Is that understood?"

There was no response but it was obvious from their faces that the gang feared him. He backed away, dragging Enrico. "Run!" Nathan hissed as they rounded the corner. "Run, as you have never run before!" And the two boys raced through the dark streets.

When they came to the house, they darted down the side street and in through the open window of their room. As they collapsed, exhausted, on their beds Nathan realized that his legs were trembling uncontrollably.

"Enrico," he said solemnly, when they had both got their breath back. "You were a fool to follow such a band of lickspittles. And you stole from your mother to buy favor with them."

There was a silence and then Nathan heard a muffled sob in the darkness. He felt a wave of pity. It was a hard thing to grow up without a father, Nathan knew that only too well. He could have been like Enrico, roaming the streets and being attracted to trouble, if it hadn't been for the watchful eye of his sister and the companionship of the theater.

"Well, no matter," he said consolingly. "You have learnt your lesson. Let us keep this our secret."

"Yes," came the muffled reply and the two boys lay there in silence. Nathan could feel his muscles aching from the duel. He longed for sleep but he had to return Pearce's sword to its box. He felt his way in the dark to the ground floor. He wiped the rapier as best he could with the cloak and returned it to the box, which he then locked. Everything was as it had been before. Except for Nathan himself. That night he had fought a man and won. It was a great achievement but he was too tired to be proud and, besides, he had to swallow the bitter pill of secrecy—for if he ever told Pearce about this night's work, he risked being sent back home for endangering the mission.

CHAPTER 13

"'TIS THE CURSE OF SERVICE— PREFERMENT GOES BY LETTER AND AFFECTION"

T HIS was just how Nathan liked it—him and Pearce, on men's business. They were heading to the east of the city in a gondola—to the great arsenal, the seat of all military power in Venice.

As the boat rounded the headland, the gondolier struggled to keep his craft stable. The open sea loomed on the horizon and the approach to the arsenal was choppy. Pearce and Nathan climbed out of the gondola in front of the huge gates.

Once inside the gates, Pearce and Nathan stopped in their tracks. The vast enclosure held three massive deepwater docks and row upon row of army barracks and navy warehouses, chandleries, forges, and carpenter shops. There were men and warships everywhere. *For a state supposedly at peace, Venice keeps a mighty military presence*, thought Nathan.

The general's office was tucked into a corner and as they approached, Nathan heard the unmistakable timber of Othello's voice, raised in anger. The door opened and Pearce and Nathan found themselves face-to-face with a livid Iago.

There was a moment's pause before the scar-faced ensign forced a bow.

"Lieutenant Cassio, I am Iago, sir. Ensign to the general. At your service. May I congratulate you on your appointment as second in command."

"Thank you, Iago," Pearce replied coolly.

Iago's eyes flashed but he continued to smile coldly as he made another small bow and marched away.

With some relief, Nathan realized that being ignored by Iago probably meant the ensign had no memory of the boy who tried to raise him up from the floor when he was drunk. But Othello had not forgotten. His mood lifted when he saw his visitors.

"Ah, Michael, you are most welcome. And I see you have brought the gallant young Marco with you—the courteous lad who tried to assist my ensign up from his lowly place on the floor." The general tried to make light of the episode, but Nathan could tell from the tone of his voice that he was still angry.

"Forgive me, sir," Pearce answered, "but the boy is besotted with all things military and he begged to accompany me today."

Othello beamed. "That is good, very good. A man may advance himself through soldiering. Look at me. I was once a slave, now I am a general. All things are possible."

While touring the arsenal, Nathan could see that all the men, whether soldiers, sailors, or artisans, clearly loved the general. Othello had a knack of remembering every man's name and, often, the names of their wives and children.

Pearce took Nathan to one side, while Othello was busy talking to a soldier.

"I'm going to send you back to the house." Nathan opened his mouth to protest, but John held up his hand. "The general wants me to accompany him on some personal business and I need you to do some work for me."

Nathan's disappointment at being sent away evaporated when John mentioned work.

"What do you want me to do?" he asked eagerly.

"Go with Marie to visit Iago's wife. Perhaps if the women exchange pleasantries, it will soften the husband."

Nathan's face fell. He was being asked to escort his sister to a woman's gossip session!

"Now listen to me," John said. "You remember the purpose for which you were employed? To be my eyes and ears in places I cannot go?"

Nathan nodded reluctantly.

"When you get to Iago's house, you will be sent to the kitchen, as all servants are. There you will learn more about the master and mistress. Find out what manner of man this Iago truly is and you will do me a great service."

Nathan had to admit he could see the sense in this.

Pearce continued, "When you get back, explain all to Marie. She must ask Enrico to take a letter to Iago's wife. The house is 20 Via Pellegrino. In the letter Marie must ask if she may call and pay her respects late afternoon. Enrico is to wait for a reply. If the answer is yes, then you will accompany your sister."

Back at the house, Marie was briefed; pen, ink, and paper were summoned; and Enrico was dispatched with the letter. He soon returned with a note saying that Signora Emilia would be delighted to receive Signorina Bianca at four o'clock that afternoon.

There was a watery sun shining when Nathan and Marie set out with Enrico as their guide. He had errands to run for his mother but would return to Iago's house after one hour to escort them home again.

As they turned the corner into Via Pellegrino, Nathan's stomach flipped as he saw a grim-faced Iago walk into the street. He was accompanied by a young man who Nathan recognized but could not place.

The two parties arrived together at the door of number 20 and Iago looked questioningly, and not altogether respectfully, at Marie.

"What does such a lovely young lady want at my house?" he leered with a bow.

Marie spoke quietly, "I am Signor Michael Cassio's lady, Signorina Bianca. I have come to pay a call on Signora Emilia."

Iago's eyes widened and then a cold smile played about his mouth.

"Signor Cassio and his lady do my house much honor." Nathan did not miss the tinge of sarcasm in Iago's words. "Come, no doubt my wife will be eager for the latest gossip from Florence." He pushed open the door and stood back to let Marie enter. Nathan hung back to allow the two men to pass ahead of him. As Iago stepped forward, he stared hard at the boy. Nathan knew that Iago had only seen him briefly, as he lay drunk on the floor of the doge's palace. He didn't remember him and the icy stare flickered away.

"Emilia! You have a guest," Iago shouted out coarsely.

In a moment, Emilia appeared, looking flustered.

"My lord, I had not expected you—"

"The general had no need of my services today." The interruption was sharp and bitter. Iago looked at his friend. "Roderigo and I have matters to discuss. We shall leave you two ladies to your feminine matters. Signorina, you will excuse me." He then bowed curtly and the two men disappeared down the hallway.

Emilia recovered her composure sufficiently to become a gracious hostess. "Signorina Bianca, you are most welcome to our house. Please, come this way and we shall take refreshment."

Emilia smiled at Nathan and pointed along a corridor. "Go to the kitchen, boy, and tell my cook that she is to feed you."

Nathan nodded and followed the direction of her hand. He could smell the kitchen. It was not the warm bread smell of Graziella's kitchen but a sour, boiled-cabbage odor, which seemed to reflect the atmosphere of the house. The cook was a pale, thin-lipped woman. Seated at the table was an old man who Nathan presumed was her husband. He had the look of a soldier about him—that grizzled, combat-worn look that Nathan had seen in Bardolph, Pistol, and Nym.

"Your mistress said you were to be so kind as to feed me, while I wait for my mistress."

The cook grunted and pulled a piece of bread from a round, flat loaf in the center of the table and placed it on a pewter plate with some goat cheese. Nathan sat. The bread was pleasant enough. It was warm and freshly baked but the cheese stank, its ripeness making it run over the plate. Nathan tore off a piece of bread and gingerly dipped it in the cheese. It tasted vile and he decided to eat only the bread.

"This seems like a good place to serve," he said, desperate to make conversation and find out any information that might be useful to Pearce.

"We keep our master's house and mind our own business," came the unfriendly reply from the husband, who promptly got up from the table, glared at Nathan, and left. Nathan looked at the cook.

"Don't mind him," she said wearily, "his bones ache today. It's this house—it's damp."

"Was he a soldier?" Nathan asked her. "He looks like one."

"Aye. Twenty years. A good one too."

"My master's a soldier."

"Oh yes? And who is your master?"

"Signor Michael Cassio."

"Oh, is he, now?" Something approaching a smile appeared on her face.

"You know him?"

"I know *of* him. Heard nothing but his name all last night. My master was shouting it, and a good few cusses, when they brought him home. Your Michael Cassio has a talent for causing a great rage and that's a fact."

Nathan shifted slightly on the bench.

"What did he say about my master?"

168

"Nay, I'm sure I couldn't tell. I may be married to a soldier these many years but I'm still enough of a lady to shrink from saying the sort of words that Master Iago used." She leaned over to Nathan and lowered her voice. "Anybody who crosses my master whips him up into a fury. But it ain't the fury that folks have to worry about...." She looked meaningfully at him.

"What do you mean?" Nathan whispered back.

"It's when the rage is passed and the cold reason comes into his heart, you have to watch him. He's a clever one." She straightened suddenly, as though she had heard a noise. "I've said enough." She looked fearful. "Be off with you, you'll get me into trouble with all your questions. Take your plate out into the yard and eat there."

Nathan obeyed, glad for the opportunity to dispose of the awful cheese. Out in the yard, he stepped toward a low wall and looking carefully around, he dropped the cheese discreetly into the canal. As he turned away he could hear men's voices coming from an upstairs window. It was Iago and his friend, Roderigo. There was a tree growing near the canal's edge and Nathan saw that if he climbed up, he could swing across to the balcony of Iago's room. From there he would be able to overhear the men's conversation and, hopefully, would make Pearce pleased at his intelligence-gathering initiative.

Climbing the tree was simple. It was firm and strong and the bough did not creak when Nathan swung along it on his hands. When he reached a point along the branch where it began to sag, he started to swing the lower half of his body, building the momentum to launch himself toward the balcony. As he let go of the branch and flew toward the ironwork, there was a movement at the windows. Nathan grabbed the iron railings and hung there, his breath coming in short, sharp gasps, while a man's voice spoke above him.

"I thought I heard something." It was Roderigo.

"Pigeons," said Iago. "Back of the house is infested with them.

I'm going to get the servant to chop down that damn tree. Come back in and have another drink. We have plans to make." Iago sounded as though he'd had plenty of wine already.

The footsteps retreated inside and Nathan breathed more easily. Now he had to find a way onto the balcony without being seen or heard. He swung around to the side of the railings and then he slowly pulled himself up so that his chin was level with his hands. There was a large pot containing a bay tree between him and the windows. Nathan swung his left leg up until his foot found the edge of the balcony. Then with great difficulty, he levered himself up until he could climb over the railings and drop into a crouching position behind the pot. Trying to control his heavy breathing, he concentrated on the conversation.

"I'm sorry for your recent disappointment, Iago, but..." Roderigo seemed impatient.

Iago exploded and Nathan heard a taste of what life must be like for his wife.

" 'Sorry'! Sorry is not a word that will do. I have served the black devil, man and boy. I've proved my worth as a soldier. That job should be mine...was mine...until this *Cassio* came along. But then that is the curse of service—preferment goes by letter and affection—Cassio is recommended by those on high, and Othello, to advance himself, takes Cassio as his second in command."

"So why continue to serve him?"

Iago muttered an oath. "I serve no one but myself. I continue to serve Othello because from that position I can take my revenge upon him."

"But what of our contract?" Roderigo was insistent. "I gave you the money to arrange the marriage—now where is Desdemona? I must have her."

Suddenly Nathan remembered where he had seen Roderigo before. He had been one of the young men who had paid court to Desdemona at the doge's banquet. So he planned to marry her in secret? Would she be willing?

"You shall have your pale-faced wench." Iago was slurring his words. "I have paid the priest and named the time. All you have to do is capture the woman. But you should know that there are those more powerful who are interested in her."

"Who?" cried Roderigo in alarm.

Iago let out a deep malicious laugh. "Why, did you not know that the thick-lipped Moor himself has taken a fancy to her?"

"Othello? Then we must act quickly, Iago." There was an edge of panic in Roderigo's voice.

"Yes, we must, for we are to be sent to Crete in two days' time."

Nathan's blood froze. Iago, in his drunken state, was now surely about to reveal military secrets to his friend.

"Crete? Why Crete?" Roderigo asked.

"Ach! Rebuilding some poxy fort. Who cares?"

Nathan relaxed. Obviously Iago knew nothing of the real purpose of the mission, which was just as well. As the doge had said, there were many spies in Venice and the plan to attack the Turks must be kept secret.

Iago was speaking again. "The priest will be waiting at noon tomorrow at the Church of Saint Remigius. Get your woman and do the deed. Now bother me no more, my friend. Be about your business and leave me to mine."

Nathan realized it was also time he left, so he silently vaulted over the railings, hanging by his hands and nimbly dropping to the ground below.

He took the empty plate back into the kitchen and the cook grunted an acknowledgment. He then made his way down the hallway just as Roderigo was leaving by the front door. Nathan knocked at the room where Emilia and Marie were talking and entered.

"My lady, forgive me but our escort is here and we must return home."

Marie looked a little startled. "Has it been an hour already? Such a brief visit. Emilia, you must forgive my departure but Signor Cassio will be returning soon."

Emilia smiled. The formalities of "signora" and "signorina" had been dropped and now she was embracing Marie as an old friend.

Outside in the street, Enrico was lounging by a wall, his errands all done. They set off silently. Marie and Nathan were full of news but they both knew that they must save their intelligence for John Pearce.

Graziella was sweeping the front steps when they arrived and she informed them that the master had returned home about ten minutes ago.

Upstairs Pearce was pacing the floor, a strange look on his face. Marie and Nathan were talking over each other, in an attempt to be first with their news. Pearce held a hand up to silence them.

"Please, please, one at a time!"

Nathan asserted himself. "I eavesdropped on a conversation between Iago and his friend, Roderigo."

Pearce raised an eyebrow. "And how did you manage that?"

Nathan explained how he had climbed up to the balcony, then he told Pearce of Iago's venomous hatred toward Othello, in part fueled by the general appointing Pearce as his second in command. But Nathan warned that Iago's hatred was of long standing, mostly due to a dislike of being commanded by a black man, and he had vowed revenge.

"And what was Roderigo's part in this?" Pearce inquired.

"None. All he seemed to care about was Desdemona and that he had paid Iago to arrange a priest and a church. Roderigo is going to abduct Desdemona and marry her at noon tomorrow."

"No!" cried Marie.

Pearce's frowned and took a deep breath.

"I'm afraid he is too late," he announced carefully. "I myself was a witness at the marriage of Desdemona and General Othello this very afternoon."

CHAPTER 14

"SHE . . . IS STOL'N . . . BY SPELLS AND MEDICINES"

MARIE and Nathan were stunned by the news that Othello had married Desdemona. Would this affect their mission? Pearce was convinced that no good would come of it and he refused to be optimistic about the forthcoming expedition to Crete.

Within the hour, a guard arrived from the doge's palace, with a summons for Lieutenant Cassio to attend an emergency meeting. Pearce looked grim as he buckled on his sword.

Nathan and Marie waited anxiously for several hours but still Pearce did not return. Eventually Marie gave in to sleep. Nathan left her and crept downstairs into the open air.

It was the dead time of night—the early hours of the morning when frail souls give up their fight for life and only the beasts prowl the street. Nathan alleviated his boredom and edginess by throwing stones into the canal. He wondered if news of the general's marriage had filtered through the city yet. It would probably explode onto the piazza with the start of the morning trade.

A growing light from a single torch, and the slap of the pole in the water, alerted Nathan to an approaching gondola. He realized, with a jolt, that Pearce was accompanied by General Othello and the Lady Desdemona.

Within a few moments, the house was ablaze with lights. Fresh torches and candles had been lit and Graziella was running about, flustered and bewildered. "Such scandals, such troubles," she whispered to Nathan as she swept into the kitchen. "The general has married the Lady Desdemona."

"I know," Nathan whispered back but Graziella only had time to widen her eyes in surprise before she swept out again, holding a red-hot warming pan at arm's length.

The general had announced that he would be returning to the arsenal, but not before he had drunk some of Graziella's hot, spiced wine. She pressed it into Nathan's hand and told him to deliver it upstairs.

"No doubt this night's work has brought him many enemies," she muttered grimly. "He will need all the strength he can muster."

Up in Pearce's room, Nathan found a tearful Desdemona being comforted by Marie, who had been woken by the commotion. Othello stood, stony faced, by the fireplace and stared into the flames. He took a large swig of the wine.

"I must thank you again, Cassio, for the hospitality you have offered to my lady."

"It was nothing, sir," Pearce replied.

"Yes, Signor Cassio," Desdemona said through her tears. "It was good of you to give me refuge when my father closed his doors against me." Her voice faltered at this point and Nathan saw that this was the first unhappy consequence of her marriage—and he pitied her. "Oh, Othello," she wailed. "I have no clothes. Nothing. What am I to do?"

"I shall buy you whatever you need," said Othello tersely.

"There is no time, General. You forget we set sail tomorrow," Pearce reminded Othello.

"Tomorrow!" Marie exclaimed. "But, my lord, I thought that you were not to set sail for at least a week."

Othello smiled weakly. "My lady Bianca, it seems that the Turks have other plans. Michael and I were called to the palace tonight because intelligence reports have arrived stating that the Turkish fleet has gathered to attack Crete. Our fleet must leave on tomorrow's tide."

"So the summons was nothing to do with your marriage?" asked Marie thoughtlessly.

His sister's comment made Nathan blush and Pearce raised his eyes to the heavens. Marie caught both reactions and stammered a swift apology, which Othello silenced with a dismissive wave of the hand.

"No, Signorina, we were not summoned because of my marriage. Although my wife's father did interrupt the meeting to accuse me of witchcraft."

Desdemona started quietly sobbing once more.

Othello grew angry. " 'My daughter is abused,' were Brabantio's words, 'stolen from me and corrupted by spells and medicines....'"

"He is an old man...." Desdemona sought to make excuses for her father. "This thing has been beyond his understanding." But Othello would have none of it.

"He called me a beast—a Moor—and questioned why a maiden of such a sweet and delicate nature should fall in love with me." *It must be a long time since others have abused him*, thought Nathan. *He is so used to being feted as a great warrior.*

"I tried to explain to him, my lord," said Desdemona softly. "I tried to make him understand our love. . . ."

Finally Desdemona's words pierced through Othello's self-absorption and he seemed to notice her great distress. Crossing the room, he lifted her from the bed and embraced her.

Pearce spoke decisively. "I shall go to Brabantio's house and retrieve Desdemona's belongings."

Desdemona broke free from her husband's embrace and took Pearce's hand in gratitude. "And you must take my father a note from me, as well." With a brief stroke of her husband's arm, she went to another room to write.

Marie cleared her throat. "General Othello . . . is the lady Desdemona to stay with us while you are away? I should be glad of her company."

"You shall indeed keep my lady company, Mistress Bianca, for it has been agreed that you and she shall accompany us to Crete—along with the lady Emilia, my ensign's wife. You shall be sisters together for this adventure."

Nathan's heart sank to his boots. He looked at Pearce, pleading with his eyes for this not to be true but John responded with a resigned shrug. Marie looked like the cat who had just got the cream and Nathan wanted to strangle her for, yet again, worming her way into *his* adventure.

"But I must take my leave now. There is much to be done at the arsenal before the morning tide." Othello had found his sense of purpose again. "I thank you once again, Michael, for all your assistance. And thank you, Signorina." He gave Pearce's arm a hearty slap, kissed Marie's hand, and gave Nathan's head a pat as he passed. There was a lingering farewell to his wife and then he was gone, in a flurry of regained confidence.

"This next task is one that I do not relish," muttered Pearce as he strode down the stairs. "If you could have seen Brabantio tonight . . . the man was beside himself with anger. He could not have been more grief stricken than if his daughter had died."

"Shall I come with you?" asked Nathan.

Pearce nodded gratefully. "I would be glad of the company and the strength of another pair of arms. I suspect that Desdemona keeps a large wardrobe."

When they arrived at Brabantio's palatial home, it was to be confronted by the sad sight of the old man surrounded by bags and trunks. He had anticipated that his daughter would send for them. He was not unpleasant toward Pearce and Nathan, merely shambling. Nathan felt a great sadness that the vigorous nobleman of yesterday's banquet had quickly become a shrunken, frail old man. *It is as though his daughter had suddenly died,* Nathan thought to himself. *Can a marriage between Desdemona and a black man almost twice her age really be that bad?* But he knew that, to Brabantio, it was.

As the servants were taking the baggage out into the street, a commotion started up. A drunken voice was raised in anger and Brabantio, who had reached the street first, was answering back. Pearce grabbed his sword, drawing it as he ran to the old man's aid.

Nathan was close behind him and immediately recognized the drunk as the embittered Roderigo.

"So, old man. Your white ewe is married to the old black ram!" Roderigo could barely stand and Brabantio grabbed the drunken youth by the throat.

"How many times have I told you not to haunt me, fool. Even if my daughter were unmarried, I would not give her to you—you drunken, worthless waster!"

Pearce intervened, parting the two men. "Have a care, sir," he warned Brabantio. "This drunk is armed." And, with that, he swiftly knocked a concealed knife from Roderigo's sleeve. Although Nathan had overheard the conversation between Roderigo and Iago, and he knew the passion that the younger man felt for Desdemona, he nevertheless was shocked. *Would Roderigo really have stabbed Brabantio?* Beautiful as the pale Desdemona was, Nathan could not comprehend how one woman could cause so much misery.

Roderigo, too inebriated to resist Pearce's firm grasp on his wrist, began to laugh hysterically.

Brabantio lunged for him again, but Pearce held him back.

"Be still, sir," he cautioned the old man. "I care not for this scum of the streets, but you must not fight him or you may harm yourself. Go into your house, sir, to your grief."

Brabantio grunted and took a final look around at his daughter's belongings being loaded into the gondolas. The spirit seemed to leave him once more and he shuffled back inside.

Pearce shook Roderigo. "Who are you, villain? Speak. Give me your name."

"He is Captain Roderigo," said a voice from the shadows. Out stepped Iago. *No doubt he put Roderigo up to this bit of mischief,* thought Nathan. *And hid himself, like the coward he is, to watch Brabantio's murder.*

Iago grabbed on to his drunken friend. "He is one of our soldiers, Lieutenant Cassio. He means no harm. He has been sick with love for the lady Desdemona for many months and the news that she has married the general has addled his wits."

Pearce let Roderigo fall to the ground and the drunk crawled away and began vomiting into the canal.

"I leave him to your care." Pearce curled his lip in distaste. "Sober him up before we set sail tomorrow."

"Yes, sir." There was a sarcastic edge to Iago's voice that made Pearce look twice at him.

"Careful, Iago," Pearce lowered his voice menacingly. "Remember your place."

Iago's eyes flashed with insolence but he said nothing.

Pearce came back to the gondolas and took Nathan to one side. "Follow them," he whispered quietly. "Do not let them see you and be very careful. Venice is dangerous at night."

Nathan nodded and slipped quietly into the shadows.

It was not difficult to follow the two men. Roderigo had sobered up a little but he was still staggering. Their progress was slow and there were many doorways and openings for Nathan to dodge into. Roderigo was also talking loudly, despite Iago's attempts to shut him up.

"I shall drown myself—to live is a torment," he wailed.

"That's stupidity," Iago snapped impatiently. "Come on, be a man. This marriage will not last."

Roderigo stopped in mid-stagger and stared at his friend. "Is there hope then?"

Iago laughed. In the darkness it sounded like pure evil and Nathan shuddered. "These black men are like children. They have their fancies and then they change their minds." Nathan winced at Iago's arrogance toward an entire race of people. "When he has tired of her, he will cast her off."

Roderigo shook his head. "No, Desdemona must love him truly."

"Love," Iago spat out the word. "When she has been with him for some time, she will see the error of her ways. She will long for a man like you—a fine-formed youth of her own society. Just bide your time. I have a plan that may work in your favor."

Roderigo began to walk again. "What plan?"

Nathan craned to hear Iago's next words.

"The general is full of doubts. He thinks to fool them all, the council and the like, with his boldness and bluster. But in truth, he is a former slave who knows that he treads a fine line of acceptance in Venetian society."

Nathan found himself surprised that Iago knew the general so well. A large part of Othello's outwardly confident personality was an act—Nathan had realized that the moment he had seen him at the banquet. *It takes an actor to know an actor,* he had thought at the time. Now he saw that, while he had got the measure of Othello, he had completely underestimated Iago.

"Now he has a wife from the top rank of Venetian nobility," Iago continued. "The council may accept it because they need Othello to do a good job for them, but no one else in Venice will approve. The aristocracy doesn't like it when one of their own marries someone unsuitable."

Iago gave a low, satisfied laugh. "Othello will worry that Desdemona will be persuaded to abandon him—or that she might run off with someone more suitable. . . ."

"Like me?" Roderigo sounded hopeful.

"No." Iago was brutal in his frankness. "You are not a big enough fish to worry the general. If I can persuade Othello that Desdemona is attracted to someone important and more *suitable* to be her husband, then he will fall apart."

"You would do this for me?"

Roderigo really is a fool, Nathan thought, *if he thinks Iago does anything for anyone but himself. This man plans to destroy his master's marriage and reputation, but he will do it by stealth so that it seems to be the work of someone else.*

"What?" Iago was so lost in his plotting that he had momentarily forgotten his friend. "Yes, yes, of course. For you, Roderigo. Together we shall pay back the general for all his arrogance. He shall see that black men should not rise above their stations in life and treat white people as their inferiors." Nathan's loathing for the twisted Iago intensified with every second.

Roderigo was delivered to his lodgings and Nathan watched from the darkness as Iago strode out toward his own house. Once he was satisfied that the man had no intention of venturing out again that night, he melted into the gloom of the back alleys and headed for his own home to report the conversation to Pearce.

Nathan told him angrily of the conversation between the two men and of Iago's despicable plan to break up the general's marriage.

"I fear that it will not prove too difficult a task for the ensign." Pearce sighed. "The marriage is beset on all sides by disapproval. Still, no more of hasty marriages, I have news for you. For my sins, I am to be commanding the ship that will transport the ladies to Crete. Whereas you, my young friend, are to sail with General Othello in his flagship."

"Me?" Nathan was astounded. "I am to go into battle?" He was both terrified and thrilled at the prospect.

Pearce looked grim. "The general would have it no other way, despite my protests. He will trust no other man but me to look after his precious young wife and he remembered that I said you have a fancy to be a soldier. You have made a good impression on him and he wants you for his companion."

Nathan nodded. A great surge of excitement had blotted out all his senses momentarily. He was not listening to Pearce. In his mind's eye, he was already crouching by a cannon, ready to fire on the Turkish ships.

"Nathan!" John's urgent whisper brought him back to reality. "To be on a ship in the thick of battle is fraught with danger."

"Othello will look after me. Everyone says he is a great soldier." *But a poor judge of men*, thought Nathan, remembering the threat that Iago posed to the general. *If I am there*, he thought, *perhaps I can thwart Iago's plans.* "Besides, I can be more useful to you in gathering intelligence if I am on the flagship."

Pearce nodded reluctantly. "You will need all your quick wits for the task ahead. Now come away to your bed, young man. You have done well tonight. Rest."

Nathan made his way down the dark corridor and climbed into

his bed. *I am to be in a sea battle.* His mind raced and he found it impossible to sleep. *This is what Robey's men trained me for. This is the real business of being an agent of the queen.* He remembered his visit with Pistol to the *Ark Royal* and his heart began to pound as he imagined himself in the thick of battle. He could see the cannon roaring and belching smoke. He could hear the screams of wounded men. He could smell the gunpowder and burning wood. But the last thing he thought of, before sleep came to close the visions down, was leaping into the sea from a sinking ship and swimming as hard as he could.

CHAPTER 15

"PRIDE, POMP, AND CIRCUMSTANCE OF GLORIOUS WAR!"

THE next morning Pearce, Nathan, Marie, and Desdemona left for the arsenal. Graziella had grown quite attached to her temporary guests and the farewells were emotional. Nathan had shaken Enrico by the hand and promised that he would bring him back a souvenir of the expedition.

They made slow progress down the winding canals and out into the bay. Venice was awake and bustling, and Nathan was aware that some people were huddling together conspiratorially and looking at Desdemona. The news of her marriage to Othello had obviously spread. One man spat into the water in disgust and another made the sign to ward off the evil eye. *Life for her*, thought Nathan, *will never be the same again.*

Once they were within the gates of the arsenal, Othello appeared and his wife seemed to gather new confidence, a smile finally appearing on her face. Othello whisked her away to his quarters and the rest of them concentrated on embarkation.

The arsenal was packed with large warships and the activity was intense. All ships were scheduled to set sail within the hour.

Pearce escorted Marie aboard their vessel and Nathan followed out of curiosity. It was an oared galley with twenty pairs of great oars, to be manned by the sailors when the winds were low.

Marie was to share a large cabin with Desdemona and Emilia. Pearce would sleep on the gun deck. There was no sign of the others yet, so Pearce ran through a few last-minute instructions.

"Say little and hear everything. Do you understand, my lady? And be kind to Desdemona. There is no guarantee that her husband will survive the battle, and she has few friends now."

Marie solemnly promised that she would be a true friend to the lady. She pressed a bottle of herbal medicine into Pearce's hand.

"I guarantee it will keep away the seasickness," she said, and Pearce lightly kissed her hand in gratitude.

He then took a deep breath and undertook the unpleasant task of telling Marie that her little brother would be joining the general on the flagship. Nathan stared fixedly at the floor as Marie's face turned ashen.

"Mother of God," she murmured, as the full force of the news sank in. "You can't let him do this." She kept her voice low, aware that they were in the middle of a bustling ship. "To send a boy into the thick of battle . . . it's insane!"

Pearce tried to be patient. "I am as unhappy about this turn of events as you are, but the general ordered it to be so. You must respect that Nathan has been trained for this work and he has more skills than most men twice his age. I cannot protect him from acts of God but I know he can protect himself against most acts of men."

Nathan shifted his weight from one foot to the other. "I am almost a man, Marie," he said, with a stubborn note in his voice. "I can do this."

Marie looked at Nathan and her mouth wobbled a little. "You take care of yourself, do you hear me?" she whispered. "If . . . if . . . if anything should happen to you . . . I'll kill you."

All three of them stifled a laugh and Nathan, feeling guilty, stroked his sister's hand to say farewell.

"I will pray for you, brother," she whispered.

Pearce ushered Nathan out of the cabin and left Marie to compose herself. He gazed solemnly at the boy. "Take no unnecessary chances, my friend. Stay close to the general but away from the action, if possible. I need you to return safe and sound and report to me all that you have heard."

"Have faith in me, John." Nathan tried to sound calm and reassuring, although his stomach was fluttering with excitement. "You and Robey have trained me well."

Satisfied with Nathan's reply, Pearce continued, "Our ship and two supply vessels will take a direct course to Crete. There we will meet up with the rest of the fleet when you have done battle with the Turks."

Pearce now escorted Nathan to the general's flagship. It was a towering four-masted warship with a formidable armament. It loomed above them, and on its topgallant masts fluttered the Venetian sea flags: the gold-winged and haloed lion of Saint Mark with his paw on an open book.

187

"Is the general's flagship not a very obvious target for Turkish guns?" asked Nathan.

Pearce smiled. "Yes, but a flagship must be obvious to the rest of the fleet. When the battle rages they look to the flagship for instructions. If she turns away from the battle, then the others must follow. But have no fear. The flagship will stay back from the main action. It is the galleasses that will be placed forward of the fleet to engage the enemy." Pearce waved toward a row of six broad-beamed and flat ships. "They are the most powerful ships in the fleet," he explained, "and little more than floating gun platforms."

Nathan studied them with interest. Compared with the flagship, the galleasses looked rather unimpressive. He would look forward to seeing how they performed in the thick of battle.

It was soon time for Pearce to take his leave and Nathan pressed on up the flagship's gangplank. But when he turned to wave, his friend had disappeared into the crowd.

It was true what John Pearce had said—that a young boy is always invisible to the adults around him. Nathan drifted in and out of places on the ship feeling awkward and wanting to speak to someone. But no one noticed him or asked what his business was. He overheard many conversations between sailors and soldiers about the forthcoming battle with the Turks. He was encouraged to hear that they felt the Turks were no match and it would all be over very quickly.

Suddenly he heard shouting and the men belowdecks began scrambling up the stairs. Nathan followed suit. Up on the main deck, he found a sea of men had packed onto the decks of the other ships and on the dockside. Some were scaling up rigging and hanging from masts in an attempt to see. Nathan shinned up the nearest mast to get a better look himself.

On the dockside, Othello was giving a speech in his great booming voice. He spoke about regaining Venice's past glories; then he said that the mighty Turkish fleet would go to the bottom of the sea faster than across it. The men cheered. Othello had clearly not lost the respect of his men, whatever the gossip about his marriage. Nathan was impressed by the mastery of Othello's showmanship. He whipped the men up into a frenzy of excitement about the impending battle and then he introduced his new wife. As he led out the beautiful Desdemona, more than ten thousand men murmured their appreciation. Othello took her aboard the ship that was to carry her to Crete, kissed her tenderly in full gaze of all, and parted from her. He then strode back to the platform and turned to the fleet of ships. "We sail," he shouted. "God go with you!" An almighty roar went up and the sea of ships became a swarming hive of activity.

Nathan slid down the mast and landed neatly at the feet of a grim-faced Iago, who inclined his head briefly in acknowledgment and then went below, without a word. Nathan wondered how Othello could be so blind to the fact that his ensign despised him. The general strode up the gangplank, followed by several aides, and began shouting orders and encouragement.

The flagship prepared to cast off as the great gates to the dockyard were open and the tide was high.

Ship after ship eased out of the dockyard and Nathan could see that six of the ships were towing the bulky galleasses, presumably because they could not maneuver well in open seas. Pearce's ship was towing a small pinnace, which would be used to flit between the ships and carry messages. By now, a crowd had gathered outside the arsenal, waving and shouting.

Belowdecks the men were stowing away their personal belongings and rigging their hammocks above the great guns. Nathan grabbed a canvas hammock and chose the only unclaimed corner of the deck in which to rig up. A burly German soldier, mistaking Nathan for a helpless city-bred servant boy, took his hammock from him and rigged it up, despite Nathan's protests that he could manage. The man spoke no Italian and just kept nodding amiably, while expertly tying the ropes.

"Thank you," Nathan said, offering his hand. The German looked pleased and shook his hand. Nathan looked around to see that Iago was making his presence felt among the men.

"We shall see some good action this time, men. What a shame our esteemed second in command will not be with us." He cast a sly eye in Nathan's direction. "Signor Cassio has a more important job to do—wet-nursing a bunch of women!" He laughed harshly and one or two of the men grinned. Nathan felt hot with anger but he pretended not to hear Iago's insult and feigned tying and retying his hammock ropes. Soon the whole deck was filled with swaying hammocks bulging with snoring men, but, too excited to sleep, Nathan decided to slip up to the deck.

As he emerged into the bracing air, he saw the solitary figure of the general, who was staring intently at the straggling vessels following in the flagship's wake.

Othello turned and noticed Nathan. His face broke into a smile.

"Marco! So you are to be a soldier sooner than you thought, eh?"

Nathan bowed slightly and nodded. "Thank you, sir, for giving me this opportunity to sail with you."

Othello put his arm around Nathan's shoulder. He was a powerful man, although not particularly tall, and Nathan felt the whole of his left shoulder being encompassed in his hand. As the general spoke, the movement of every muscle in his face showed and the tight curls of his hair glistened with salt spray. Nathan realized that he was captivated by Othello, not only because he was the first black man that he had ever known, but because he was filled with a great vitality that set him apart from others.

"Are you content to sleep on the gun deck?" Othello asked.

"Oh yes, sir," Nathan replied. "I like being with the soldiers."

Othello laughed. "Good, good. But you must come with me now. I would have you by my side when I meet with my officers. You will learn much of military strategy that way." Nathan felt honored to be so favored by the general.

The general's cabin was filled with maps and charts that were being pored over by the captain. Iago appeared, scowling, lamp in hand.

"Ah, Iago, well done. You have brought us some light just at the right time. Set the lamp here by the charts. Marco, sit down by me."

Nathan did as he was told and, ignoring Iago's stony look, sat down.

"Our last intelligence is that the Turks were massing a fleet at Cyprus but were still awaiting six vessels from the Gulf of Persia. When they arrive, our spies tell us that they will have a fleet of forty ships but"—Othello smiled triumphantly—"no galleasses. If we make fair passage, I intend to mass our fleet in the Ionian Sea and we will drill for a day with the galleasses in battle formation. Has the pinnace arrived yet?" Othello asked, referring to the light, fast ship tied up behind John Pearce's ship.

"The watch have reported sighting of it. It should be here shortly," the captain answered.

"Good," said Othello. "Then leave me to write my orders. We shall meet again tomorrow."

Iago and the captain bowed and withdrew. Nathan rose and made to leave too, but then he paused and turned back to the general. It was no good. His desire to know something was like a strong itch that he had to scratch. If the general thought him ignorant, then so be it. "May I ask a question of you, sir?"

Othello raised his head from the maps and nodded.

"Why is the fact that the Turks have no galleasses so important?"

Othello nodded his head again, pleased at such an intelligent question.

"In the Battle of Lepanto, which was our last great battle against the Turks," he began, "we brought six galleasses to the fight. You have seen them. They are broad and deep and very stable in the water. When all the guns are fired at once, the ship barely moves. And they have swivel guns on the prow, which can rotate to fire at the enemy from any angle. The long point on the bow is used for ramming vessels and such is the galleasses' power, that it can reduce a big ship, like the one you are standing on now, to firewood in a matter of minutes."

Nathan was impressed.

Othello continued, "You would think that the Turks, who lost at least twenty-five thousand men in that battle, would have constructed some galleasses of their own by now. But, it seems, that fortune smiles on us. Now be off with you, lad. I have missives to write and no doubt you could do with filling that belly of yours."

The next few days were interesting to Nathan, but the men seemed bored. They began to grumble at the inactivity and at the incessant weapons inspections. Even Nathan's mind began to idle and he found himself wondering how Pearce and the ladies were faring—their ship having left the fleet now, to make its way to Crete. On the flagship, there was a tension beneath the boredom. Every man knew that the battle would be soon and there was a strong desire to get it over with. But Nathan decided to busy himself and set about asking for work. He was given the job of soaking rags in oil and pitch and wrapping them around arrowheads. These would be set alight and fired at the enemies' ships when battle commenced.

After a week, their ship passed the coast of Greece and the gray sea of the Adriatic turned into the blue of the Ionian. The winds were still strong but the sun shone and innumerable small islands seemed to glint, like green and yellow crystals in the water. The remainder of that week was spent in battle drill, where, although no shots of precious gunpowder were used, the ships went through a silent dance of towing the galleasses in front of the fleet, which struggled in the increasing wind to maintain formation.

As the ships left the coast of Greece and hove out into the open sea, conditions began to worsen. The sea heaved mightily and the sky darkened. Rain tipped down with great force and the deck of the ship became a perilous sheet of running water. Sailors lashed themselves to masts, so as not to be swept away, and all soldiers were ordered to stay belowdecks. Iago suddenly grabbed Nathan by the collar and rasped, "You, boy! General Othello commands you to his cabin." Nathan obeyed, glad to be out of the mayhem of the gun deck, which was heaving with men baling the excess water that had leaked in through the closed gun ports.

Othello was writing letters when Nathan entered. The lamp swayed madly from the cabin ceiling and there were ominous creakings and crackings of timber. When the ship pitched badly and Nathan was thrown against the door of the cabin, he cried out in distress.

Othello grinned and hauled Nathan upright. "Don't be afraid, Marco. I have lived through greater storms than this." The general then proceeded to tell Nathan about his years as a slave, when he rowed in a galley, chained to the oars. "There were times when I feared that the ship would go down and I would die, dragged by my chains to the bottom of the sea. But I survived." He laughed heartily and slapped Nathan on the back. Nathan marveled at the courage of this former slave who was now such a mighty general.

As the storm raged, Othello told Nathan of all his adventures in battle. *How Enrico will envy me!* thought Nathan. Before he had met John Pearce and gone to Robey's school, he had never met a man whom he truly admired. Now he knew several. And, much as he loved and respected Pearce, Othello was now his greatest hero. To have survived hardship was enough but to then rise to glory was magnificent.

Eventually the rolling of the ship and the noise of the storm subsided and Nathan ventured out of the cabin to see how the ship had fared.

The decks were all awash and Nathan picked his way through the sloshing water, hoping that his leather boots would not tighten too much. He must take out his ankle knives later to dry and oil them. Above deck, exhausted men were unfurling the sails that had been taken in so that they could ride out the storm. There appeared to be very little damage. Nathan grabbed a nearby bucket and began to help bale out the water on deck.

In the days that followed, the men were beginning to grate on one another as the battle drew closer and their nerves were stretched taut in anticipation. Several times, the officers had broken up fights that had started over foolish things, like a piece of bread or a casual remark.

Nathan's biggest shock came when he was summoned on deck to watch a man being flogged. It was the large German soldier who had rigged up his hammock on the first day. He had been fighting and the sheer size of him had been enough to break an archer's bow in two when he reeled backward and fell on it. Damaging a precious weapon was punishable with fifty lashes and the man was tied to the mainmast, in the heat of the day, to have his punishment meted out. But the god of clumsy soldiers must have been looking down upon him that day, for no sooner had he received the third lash than a cry arose from above.

"Turkish ships on the horizon!"

The prisoner was untied without further ado, to prepare for battle. Nathan's mouth went dry as he stared out at the small dots on the horizon. The men were shouting and running to and fro, and in the midst of the maelstrom, he said a quiet prayer, *Please, God, let me live to be a man. Give me courage in battle. Let me not be a coward.* He was not sure which was worse—the fear of dying or the fear that he would not acquit himself with honor.

CHAPTER 16

"IN THE TRADE OF WAR
I HAVE SLAIN MEN"

THE Turkish ships grew larger on the horizon and the frantic activity of men in the Venetian fleet had stilled to an eerie silence. All that could be heard were steady drumbeats from the oar decks and the great oars scooping into the ocean with almighty smacks of power. Nathan had barely moved from his position near the mainmast. His mind had closed down to a numbness that he could not shake off.

The galleasses were plowing through the sea now, like great engines, to take up their positions in front of the fleet. Silent mariners were taking in sails, leaving just enough to maneuver with, and no more. The oars would direct the ships during battle.

Suddenly Nathan jumped as a deep voice spoke in his ear, "Marco, I have work for you." Othello was standing behind him, his sword in his hand, breathing rapidly and shallowly.

"I am ready to do whatever you ask, sir." Nathan tried to sound confident.

Othello smiled. "Marco, because you are the only one on the

flagship who has never fought at sea, you shall have the honor of starting the battle." Nathan's mouth gaped open in astonishment. "You shall fire the flaming arrow that starts the guns. Your master said you are a good archer. Is this true?" Nathan nodded, his anxiety causing his breath to shudder in his throat.

Othello led him up to the castle deck where a group of archers were facing toward the enemy, bows in hand, with a brazier of hot coals behind them.

"Men," Othello barked, and the archers sprang to attention. "It is my pleasure that this boy shall fire the signal arrow. Then"—he turned to Nathan—"if it is *your* pleasure, you shall have the honor of loosing more arrows at the enemy ships, alongside these men here. How say you?" Nathan nodded eagerly, unable to pry his tongue from the roof of his mouth to make an audible reply.

"Then take up a bow."

Nathan looked at the wooden rack which contained ready-strung longbows and chose the smallest and lightest. He took an incendiary arrow from the wooden barrels and, with trembling fingers, placed the end into the glowing coals. Immediately the rag began to sputter into life, and in a moment, it was burning brightly.

"Remember to turn away from the wind, young sirrah." A voice chuckled and Nathan turned to see a bald-headed, toothless man grinning at him. "Else you'll singe off your eyebrows when you draw the bow."

"Are you ready, Marco?" Othello's voice was hoarse with excitement.

Nathan took the flaming arrow out of the coals, nocked it onto the string and, turning with his back to the wind, drew the string back to his face. Although the flames were licking out away from him, he could feel their heat.

"Follow my hand," said Othello as he raised his arm straight into the air and pointed out to sea. "Ready . . . and fire!"

The arrow left Nathan's bow with a peculiar guttering sound and soared skyward in a graceful arc. Nathan's heart fluttered in his throat, as he feared that the flames would go out or that the trajectory was wrong.

But there was no need to worry. As the arrow hit the topmost point of its arc it seemed to balance in the air for a moment, then began its long descent toward the open sea. At this signal, hell opened up its doors and the Venetian fleet began its concerto of cannon fire.

Nathan's eyes closed at the ear-splitting volume of the guns. The deck on which he was standing shuddered, as cannon after cannon was fired on the gun deck below.

The Turkish fleet had ranged up in a crescent formation, while the Venetian galleys were in a V shape—the flagship being farthest away, with the galleasses in a line in front of the formation. The guns on the general's ship had the greatest reach. One of the soldiers had told Nathan that they were muzzle loaders, with a range of about two thousand yards. They were loaded with heavy iron balls for smashing into the hulls of the enemy's ships. The other ships in the Venetian fleet carried lighter guns, most of which spat out spike shot made of iron dice, for bringing down rigging. There was also the lethal scattering shot, which had the sole purpose of maiming the enemy crew.

The Turkish ships were now firing their own cannon. The whole crescent formation was spitting fire. Soon the smoke from over two thousand cannon was so thick that the sea seemed to be covered in a dense fog. Nathan could only see the masts and topmost rigging of the Turkish ships and he could hardly breathe from the acrid smell of burnt gunpowder wafting up from the decks below.

"When do we shoot?" he screamed at an archer standing by his side, for it was impossible to make himself heard any other way.

"When the general's drummer gives the signal," his comrade shouted back. "Aim for the topgallant masts on any of the fore, main, or mizzenmasts." The archer pointed at the front three masts of the Turkish vessels and upward to the top third of the masts where their flags flew.

The toothless man was standing by the glowing coals, arrows in hand. It was his job to set fire to the arrowheads and pass them to the archers. All the men made the sign of the cross and then turned to touch the toothless one's head. One of them shouted out to Nathan, "You must touch Zeno's head, for he has survived six sea battles and has the grace of God in him. Touch him and he will save your hide." Nathan hastily crossed himself and touched Zeno's balding head. "God bless you, son," Zeno shouted irreverently, as though he were a priest.

For a second, the guns on the flagship fell silent and each of the ships in the Venetian fleet followed suit. Then a flourish of rhythmical drumming came from the main deck. *Ratt-tat-a-tatt-tatt, ratt-tat-a-tatt-tatt.* "Now!" shouted Zeno and he plunged the arrows into the flames. Each archer scrabbled to pick a sputtering missile out and nock it onto his bow. Within seconds, a volley of sixteen hundred flaming arrows arced through the air toward the enemy and the guns started up again beneath their feet.

"Down!" screamed the man next to Nathan, dragging him down to the floor and the protection of the wooden walls of the castle deck. The Turks had answered the volley of fire arrows with their own volley. Three arrows landed within inches of Nathan. He rolled backward to avoid being burned and was rewarded by being doused with water by Zeno, who had nimbly grabbed one of the many buckets of water littering the deck. Nathan gasped for breath and spat out a mouthful of water, while the others laughed. "Better to be wet than dead," shouted Zeno.

Nathan was hauled up, and once again, the archers grabbed a prepared arrow. The next half hour passed in this rhythm of firing and ducking and putting out fires. One archer received an arrow in the chest, but as it was nearing the end of its trajectory, it did no more than bounce off his leather jerkin, setting fire to his shirt in the process. Zeno threw a bucket of water over him and he resumed his tasks but Nathan saw that the man's throat had been burned by the flames.

The half an hour of concentrated arrow fire seemed to last an eternity. Finally the guns suddenly stopped and the drums sounded a cessation. The archers slumped to the ground, flexing their cramped and aching string-hands and breathing heavily. When the guns started up again, a gang of men appeared to replace the archers. They were arquebusiers—handgun men—and their arrival signaled that the archers had done their job. The two opposing fleets were now close enough for the small guns to take over.

Zeno unceremoniously dragged Nathan off the castle deck. "We're needed belowdecks now, lad," he yelled, and he stopped and pulled out two pieces of linen cloth, which he dunked in a nearby bucket of water. He handed one to Nathan and motioned for the boy to follow his example as he tied the wet cloth around his face, covering his nose and mouth. Nathan obeyed, and as they stepped into the hellhole that was the gun deck, he realized that it would have been impossible to breathe without this mask.

The gun deck was appalling. In the gloom and smoke, all the men were stripped to the waist, sweating and screaming orders and covered in black grime from the discharging cannon. The noise was deafening and when Nathan's feet slithered on the floor, he registered that it was blood, and not water, that made the boards so slimy. There were three dead men—two of whom were lying by a gaping hole in the hull where a Turkish cannonball had found its mark. Zeno pulled Nathan into the center of the deck, just in time to avoid the recoil of a cannon as it hurtled backward after discharge. Zeno indicated that it was their job to remove the corpses. Two other archers had joined them and helped drag the two dead bodies out.

Nathan had a terrible pain in his head from the deafening noise of the cannon, but he kept his head down, staring fixedly at the corpse he was dragging by the feet. The man had a bloody hole where his chest had been, and at one point, they had to stop dragging him as his body almost split in two. Zeno grabbed one of the hammocks, which had been ripped down and flung in a pile in the corner, and together they scooped what was left of the poor soul onto the canvas and made a parcel of him. Nathan found it difficult to hold the thick canvas, his hands were so bloody, but eventually they hoisted the body up onto the main deck. Above them they could hear the popping of musket fire. Their way was impassable, there were so many Turkish arrows stuck into the planking. Zeno motioned to drop the body and he began to pull the arrows out of the deck and toss them over the side. Having cleared a path to the rail, they placed the wrapped corpse next to a line of six others and returned to retrieve another.

By the time they had got back down into the bowels of the ship, there were two more dead, this time from Turkish crossbow bolts. One man had been pierced in the head and another in the chest. Once more, they did their grim work of removing the bodies.

Later Nathan would reflect with surprise that he had not been sick at the sight of such carnage—but then there had been no time. His overwhelming reflex had been to fight and stay alive.

The second time they came up on deck, Nathan felt the ship turning. He realized, with terror, that the flags of the Turkish ships were spitting distance away. The two fleets were almost upon each other and about to engage in hand-to-hand combat.

The general appeared as if from nowhere—a sword in either hand and two pistols tucked into his belt. "Marco," he shouted, a wide grin on his face. "We have decimated the enemy. Now we fight at close quarters. Go to my cabin and stay there."

"But I can fight, sir," Nathan protested, but Othello would have none of it. "To my cabin," he roared. "That is an order." With that, he sprang to the side of the ship and armed men began pouring out from belowdecks, among them a blackened and bloodied Iago, sword in hand, charging forward to be at the general's side. Sailors were throwing grappling hooks across to the decks of the Turkish ship and hauling it toward them. There was a sickening crunch as the two vessels thudded into each other. All the men staggered with the jolt and then, with terrifying screams of bloodlust and fear, the Venetian soldiers leapt from their ship to the enemy's and the fighting began.

Nathan could not bring himself to hide away down in Othello's cabin like a coward but he knew that if he disobeyed the order and attempted to fight, he risked being flogged. He decided to hide himself somewhere so that he could at least watch the fighting.

He looked upward and saw that the crow's nest on the main mast was still in one piece. Swiftly he climbed up the rigging—a difficult job, as most of it was in tatters—until he reached the top. It was occupied by a dead sailor, a crossbow bolt in his stomach and protruding from his back. Nathan muttered a brief prayer and heaved the man over the side. He tried not to think about the thwack as the body hit the deck. Now he had a perfect view of the melee taking place on board the Turkish ship.

The enemy vessel was in a bad way. Two masts were sheared through and had fallen in a tangle of smoldering rigging onto the deck. The ship was listing, as it was taking in water from a hole in the bow. Othello and his men were fighting hand-to-hand among the debris on the main deck. The Turks wielded their strange crescent-shaped swords and a lone Turkish crossbowman was wreaking havoc among the fighting mass on the main deck by loosing off the occasional bolt, which, usually, found its mark in a Venetian.

Nathan knew the crossbowman had to be stopped. He reached down to the knives in his boot. His hands were bloody but the blood was beginning to dry. He wiped them hard on his thighs and took up the knives again. Every time the crossbowman made a shot he had to raise himself up to clear the wooden rail on the castle deck. Gauging the distance, Nathan lifted his right hand, and as the crossbowman straightened up, he threw his dagger with as much force as he could muster. The first knife whistled past the crossbowman's ear and the man, startled, loosed his bolt, sending it harmlessly into the sea. He looked up in Nathan's direction and saw the boy, second knife in hand. He began to load his bolt again—this time facing Nathan with murderous intent. For a moment, Nathan's courage failed him. But as the crossbow was hauled upward and the man took aim, Nathan let his reflexes take over. Leaping up to his full height, the knife left his hand with every ounce of strength he could muster and it struck the man's throat. The Turk crumpled, crossbow undischarged, onto the deck.

Nathan felt the gorge rise in his throat but he refused to vomit. Instead he stood there, and there he would have stayed, had he not caught the eye of Othello, who had witnessed everything. Nathan quickly dropped down out of sight but not before he had registered Othello's look of amazement.

He crouched in the crow's nest listening to the sounds of steel clashing upon steel and the oaths of men bent upon killing one another. They were the only sounds he could hear. The cannon had stopped firing—from both sides. Then, he heard a cheer go up. It started from a ship out on the edge of the fleet and spread like a ripple, until everyone in the world seemed to be cheering at once. Standing up once more, he saw that the remains of the Turkish fleet was turning into the wind, sails unfurling and heading for home. The battle had been won!

It had taken three hours for the Venetian fleet to claim victory, Nathan later learned. They had captured five Turkish ships, sunk eleven, and the rest had slunk away. Othello took great personal pride in boarding every Turkish ship they had captured and freeing the slaves, who were manning the oars. There were those who said that when the first slave hatch had been opened, the familiar stench had made the great general sick.

Nathan, meanwhile, climbed aboard the Turkish ship tied to the flagship and retrieved his knives. The dead crossbowman, eyes wide open, stared at him accusingly, so he took the grime-encrusted rag from around his neck and laid it over the man's face, closing the corpse's eyes as he did so. He would not easily forget the squelching sound the knife made as he pulled it from the man's throat. He picked up the crossbow and carefully removed the bolt. He would give it to Enrico as a souvenir.

After the blood had been washed away from the flagship's decks and the bodies of the men lost in the battle were wrapped in winding sheets and tipped over the side with a prayer, the general made all the survivors say a blessing for the lost Christian souls who had gone to the bottom of the sea in the sunken Turkish ships.

The Venetian loss was not great. Not by a general's standards.

Two hundred and three men had been killed; one hundred and sixty-two had been wounded. Two ships had to be scuttled, their damage was so bad: one galleass and one galley. Othello counted himself the victor at a small price.

No Turkish prisoners were taken. The doge had made it quite clear that he did not want the expense of keeping them. So those few who were still alive on the captured ships were gathered together, placed on the most disabled vessel, and set adrift. It would take them weeks to row themselves slowly back home—if they survived at all.

Those galley slaves who survived were accommodated on all of the Venetian ships, to be reunited with their families when the fleet returned to Venice.

Nathan was summoned by Othello and trembled all the way to the general's cabin. He wondered if he would be sentenced to a public flogging. That would require a different kind of bravery, one that he was not sure he could muster. But after Othello had finished shouting his displeasure at having his order ignored, he embraced Nathan and praised him for saving many men's lives by killing the crossbowman.

That night, Nathan slept in a bloody hammock in the battered gun deck and finally found time to think about the day's momentous events.

Today I have killed a man—maybe more than one—who knows what damage my fire arrows did? I have dragged dead bodies out of the gun deck and I may have saved the general. Does that make me a man?

He knew that killing someone in the heat of battle was different from killing someone in cold blood. Suddenly he longed for the comfort of home. His body smelled of the acrid sweat of fear and his bones ached from the relief of survival. Perhaps being a man meant knowing when the gods had smiled upon you and given you another chance at life.

CHAPTER 17

"THAT CASSIO LOVES HER, I DO WELL BELIEVE'T"

T took several days for the fleet to limp back to the island of Crete. Many masts and sails had been destroyed in the battle so, although the mariners were doing their best to effect repairs as quickly as possible, most of the journey had to be accomplished by oars.

The hammocks were taken down, laid flat on the deck, and scrubbed, the bloody water staining the deck red. The soldiers inspected and cleaned the cannon, archers repaired bows or threw the useless ones overboard, arquebusiers cleaned and oiled their muskets. Nathan borrowed some oil and some sharp sand, secreted himself away in a dark corner of the ship, and removed his boot knives. First he washed them, then he sharpened and smoothed them in the sand, and finally he lightly oiled them, before replacing them in his boots. Iago had once challenged him about the fact that he never took his boots off, even when asleep. Nathan had mumbled something about once having had some boots stolen—but he was sure that Iago had eyed him with suspicion.

There was a daily report about how many men had died of their wounds during the night. With only two surgeons in the whole fleet, they were stretched to the limit, ferrying between the ships, tending to wounds, performing amputations, and dealing with sickness. Some of the galley slaves had been sick with the fever and all were malnourished. Even basic ship's fare was too much for some of their stomachs and they died, worn out from years at the oars. Nathan reflected that liberation had come too late.

The landing at Crete was emotional. The ships docked, and soon the quayside was heaving with comrades reuniting on dry land. Men were shouting and embracing, shedding tears for the dead.

As soon as the flagship had settled into its berth, Nathan did not wait for the plank to be lowered but vaulted onto the rail and swung down one of the ropes, so eager was he to find John and Marie. Pushing through the frenzied crowd, he finally spotted Pearce and the ladies, standing talking to a gentleman of quality.

He wanted to fling himself at his friend and tell him how he had distinguished himself in battle, but remembering that he was supposed to be a servant, he contented himself with a low bow instead.

"Thank God, you are safe," Pearce said softly.

"Amen to that," whispered Marie, and Nathan gave her a comforting smile and nod.

"This boy is your servant?" the nobleman inquired.

"Yes indeed, Duke Montano. General Othello requested that he accompany him into battle as the boy has dreams of being a soldier one day."

Montano looked kindly at Nathan. "You must tell us all about your adventures, young man. Later, when you are rested." Montano turned to Desdemona and kissed her hand. "Lady, you must be glad now that your husband is safely returned."

It was then that Nathan noticed poor Emilia, standing on the quayside, impassively. *I wonder if she cares whether her husband lives or dies?* he thought.

Iago had now appeared, having vaulted off the docking ship, just as Nathan had done. He was on the quayside talking to his men and made no attempt to approach his wife. Nathan noticed that Emilia dropped her eyes and stared at her feet and that her cheeks looked a little flushed. *Ah, so she does care,* he thought. *But not about her husband, only about the shame he heaps upon her.*

Nathan was then aware that Iago was staring at him—or rather near him—and he turned his own gaze to see that Pearce had taken Desdemona's hand and was holding it reassuringly, while speaking quietly to her. Nathan saw Iago's eyes lingering on the clasped hands and he felt a lurch of anxiety. Had the ensign smirked before he turned away?

When the flagship had fully docked, Othello finally disembarked and rushed to Desdemona, clasping her in such a tight embrace that Nathan wondered if she could breathe. They stood, entwined, for some time, until Othello broke away and resumed his authority as commander in chief.

"Montano! Good to see you once more, my friend." He shook the duke's hand heartily. "Cassio, well done. You arrived safely. And you have taken good care of Desdemona, she speaks well of you." Othello was now happy and playful. "We have routed the

211

Turks and they have limped away to lick their wounds. And it was in no small measure due to your young servant here." He bowed ceremoniously to Nathan, who felt a flush of embarrassed pride. "I'm sure he will tell you of his adventures in due course."

Pearce smiled at Nathan but then quickly returned to business. "Shall we now attack Cyprus, General, as was your plan?"

Othello hesitated. "I think not.... The men have fought well and deserve a rest. Besides, I have not celebrated my marriage properly. I intend to let the men feast and make merry tonight, in honor of my union with the lady Desdemona."

Pearce was astounded. "But sir, will that not give the Turks time to regroup and fortify Cyprus?"

"We shall hit them doubly hard before the end of the week, have no fear. But I must spend some time with my lady." *He will not be swayed from his path,* thought Nathan.

Pearce forced an uncomfortable smile but it was obvious that he was not happy.

"And Michael," Othello added, "I have taken great pleasure in the company of young Marco. I would like to have him as my personal servant while we are here on Crete. Duke Montano shall provide a servant for your needs. Marco, find yourself a ride to the palace and seek me out in my rooms."

Before Pearce or Nathan could respond to the command, Othello and his new wife were away to Duke Montano's waiting coach.

Pearce looked grim and shook his head. "We shall lose every military advantage we have while this lovesick fool moons over his wife." He took Nathan to one side. "It seems that you are to be parted from me again, but perhaps it is to our advantage. You can keep me well informed of the general's plans if you are attending upon him. You have your code sheet?"

Nathan nodded and patted his chest, where the linen Vigenère Square was concealed.

"Good. Send me messages if you have anything to report. I think it is best that we communicate in that way, rather than in person."

Nathan agreed. "Iago is watchful of me. He has asked some awkward questions."

"Then it is good then that you have the protection of Othello. Remember I shall always be at hand if you need me." Pearce then said good-bye and returned to Emilia and Marie.

As Nathan watched the frenzied activity around him, he saw Iago reunited with his friend, Roderigo. *Whenever they are together, they are plotting something*, he thought anxiously, resolving to spy on them. Men were pouring off the ships now and it was easy enough for Nathan to disappear into the throng, so that he could edge closer to the conspirators.

Iago and Roderigo were sitting on some barrels by a warehouse. Nathan dropped to his knees close by, behind a pile of sacks. It was difficult to hear all of their conversation.

"...there is no doubt that Desdemona is directly in love with him...."

Iago was insistent. Nathan strained to hear more.

"It's not possible. Not with him," said Roderigo, clearly agitated.

Who are they talking about? wondered Nathan. It was so frustrating.

Roderigo seemed close to tears. "I cannot believe it of her. She is such a blessed lady."

Iago spat on the floor. "Blessed? If she is so blessed, what is she doing with the Moor? Open your eyes, man, she's the same as any other woman. I've seen her holding his hand. . . ."

Nathan knew then, with a deadly certainty, the man Iago had singled out as Desdemona's "lover."

"That Cassio loves her, I do well believe it . . . and she loves him, I am convinced," said Iago slyly. "But listen, Roderigo, I have a plan. Cassio barely knows you. What you must do, tonight, is find him and insult him—call him out—I shall be close at hand. When he loses his temper and fights you, you will best him and I shall ruin his reputation with the general. Meet me tonight . . ."

Just then, a cart rattled past and Iago's voice was drowned out by the horse's hooves on the cobbles. Nathan cursed that he had not been able to hear the full plan. Iago and Roderigo were now walking away down the dock, still deep in conversation.

He had to find Pearce, and find him quickly, before Iago's plan could be put into action. Nathan desperately scanned the dock but his partner had gone.

Suddenly a baggage cart laden with the trunks and bags from the ships trundled past slowly. Nathan sped over to the cart and vaulted up its side. To his great surprise Nathan realized that the driver was none other than Zeno, the sailor who had hauled bodies out of the gun deck with Nathan at the height of the battle.

214

Zeno winked, displaying his toothless grin. "Stroke of luck, eh? You can sit next to me if you like, young master. I'm delivering all this baggage to the duke's palace."

Nathan grinned and scrambled up to the front seat.

"Been to Crete afore?" Zeno asked.

"Never," said Nathan.

"Ah, it's a fearsome place."

Nathan looked up at the forbidding mountain ranges, which were twisted and tortured by ravines and black gullies. He could see what Zeno meant. This was nothing like the golden islands they had passed on their journey at sea.

"I never did learn your name, young master," Zeno said amiably.

"Marco," Nathan replied. He could see that the pair of work-worn horses pulling the cart were going as fast as they could. To distract him from his worries about Iago's plotting, he decided to let Zeno talk as much as possible.

"Tell me more about Crete," Nathan said, to encourage his companion.

Zeno smiled and gave Nathan the benefit of his great wisdom. "The whole strength of the Venetian Empire lays in the possession of Crete. It's like a crossroads, see. Placed smack in the middle of everything. But these Cretans, they don't like us, they don't like our religion, and they do all they can to cause trouble."

"What religion do they practice then?"

"Ach. Supposed to be Christians, same as us. But they like their Greek church. Make the sign of the cross different—don't believe in the Creed and such like. Heathens." Zeno spat again, this time in disgust. Nathan reflected that it did not seem like much of a difference but then he was not a very religious person.

A town was in sight. It looked, from a distance, like a small version of Venice. Nathan could see a bell tower, like the one in Saint Mark's Square, rising above the heavily fortified walls of the town.

"What is this town?" he asked.

"Iraklion," replied Zeno. "A home from home. See, there's the duke's palace and the Basilica of Saint Mark—that's the duke's private chapel. Over there is the armory and the loggia. Then there's the Cathedral of Saint Titus, with its bell tower; and the barracks of Saint George—where I'll be billeted, no doubt. We're going in through the Gate of Jesus now. Cross yourself, lad, and you'll be safe all the time you're here."

Nathan duly made the sign of the cross as they passed through the grand gate and into the main street of Iraklion. As the cart trundled along, he noticed some gates leading into what looked like a smaller version of the Jewish quarter in Venice. Zeno caught his gaze and nodded. "Aye, lad. That's the ghetto. Just like home."

Zeno reined in the horses and brought the cart to a standstill. "Announcement," he said by way of explanation. He pointed to a balcony above them where a herald had taken up position. People had stopped and began to form a crowd.

The herald raised his voice. "It is the pleasure of Duke Montano and of the great general, Othello, that all the citizens of Iraklion shall feast in honor of the defeat of the Turkish fleet and to celebrate the general's marriage. From five until eleven, bonfires shall be lit and there will be dancing and merriment."

There was some cheering from the Venetians in the crowd but the Cretans simply murmured.

"No one seems very enthusiastic about tonight," Nathan observed.

Zeno spat over the side of the cart. "Ach, it's like I said before, lad, the Cretans hate us. Mind you, they hate everyone. They've always been under the thumb of some empire or another, you see. Rome, Byzantium, Greece..."

Nathan could see how being under constant occupation might make a people resentful.

"There is one thing that is good about this damned place." Zeno chuckled, moving the horses along. "The wine! And it shall flow freely tonight. The general will see to that. Well, boy, here we are. The duke's palace."

Servants appeared and started to unload the bags into the courtyard. Nathan jumped down from the cart and saluted Zeno, who gave him a wink before he rode off in the direction of the barracks.

Nathan sped up the marble steps, asking directions as he went. He must waste no time in warning Pearce of Iago's plot. But he was only halfway up the stairs when he met an anxious-looking Emilia.

"Oh, Marco, thank goodness I've found you! The general is most insistent that you attend him at the marriage ceremony. He'd like you to be a page. Quickly now! You must wash and change, there is no time to lose!"

"But I must—" Nathan started to protest but Emilia grabbed his arm.

"Shh! Come, there's no time!"

She hurried him up the stairs, along a corridor, and into the general's room. Othello was dressed in a strange robe. Long and flowing, it was deep red and edged with gold patterns. Nathan had never seen anything like it before, but he thought that he looked very grand—like some exotic Eastern king. Othello grinned and paraded before him, arms outstretched. "You see me in my finery, Marco. Ready to kneel before the bishop and say my vows—and you shall be my page." Othello was excited, almost like a child. "Have you suitable clothes?"

"I have a best set, sir," Nathan replied. His mind was racing, wondering how he could get away and speak to John Pearce.

"Then that shall suffice. Emilia," Othello instructed, "show Marco to his room, where he may wash away the dirt of the voyage and dress. But hurry now! The bishop and my lady await us."

Emilia guided Nathan to a small closetlike room opposite Othello's. There was a bed and a table with a pitcher of water and a bowl upon it. Also on the table were candles, a candleholder, flint, paper, pens, and an inkwell. His bag, Nathan noted, was already on the bed.

"You are to be near the general so that you may serve him when he needs you," she said. "There is water. Do as your master bids now, and be quick."

"Emilia," asked Nathan as Emilia turned to leave, "are Signor Cassio and the lady Bianca to attend the wedding?"

"Indeed."

"And you and your husband?"

Emilia pursed her lips and shook her head, then closed the door behind her. *That will be another grievance Iago will bear against Cassio,* he thought. Nathan stripped hurriedly and poured water into the bowl.

He must warn Pearce of Iago's plot. He felt inside his jerkin and pulled out the Vigenère Square. He would write John a coded message that he could discreetly press into his hand at the service. Pearce would realize that it was important and then slip away to decode it. Nathan sat down at the table, took pen and paper, and concentrated. Using his code word NATHAN, he began to construct the message.

VAZV AAQ RHKEEVGH PAGRNW AO SVGAA YBH IG

AHR FTKLEG QO GVT PRAOL TUR PTSAPR THUITUT

(Iago and Roderigo intend to fight you in the street Do not leave the palace tonight)

He slipped the Vigenère Square back into his secret pocket and left the message to dry, while he dressed in his best clothes. Then he carefully folded the paper and placed it inside his boot. Now he was ready for his duties as a page at the marriage blessing of Othello and Desdemona. Although Nathan knew that if Iago had his way, the marriage would not be blessed—but cursed.

CHAPTER 18

"MENS' NATURES WRANGLE WITH INFERIOR THINGS"

THERE were two carriages in the courtyard of the palace. One held the bridal couple and the other Duke Montano, Pearce, and Marie. Nathan hovered for a moment, uncertain as to which carriage he should climb into.

Marie looked at him hopefully but Othello called out jovially, "Desdemona, here comes our page. He shall ride with us. Come, Marco."

Nathan did as he was told and took his place opposite the happy couple, frustrated at the lost opportunity to pass his note to Pearce.

The carriages set off smoothly, the horses' hooves clattering on the cobbles of the courtyard. Smiling, Othello took a chain from around his neck. Hanging from it were two gold rings, one large and one small. He handed it to Nathan.

"Guard these with your life, boy."

"I shall, sir," said Nathan firmly, and placed the chain around his own neck.

"When we reach the cathedral, take up your position behind us and proffer the rings when the bishop says the exchange of vows."

"I understand, sir," Nathan replied.

The carriages drew up at the cathedral and there, by the door, was the bishop and two clerics, who bowed deeply as the wedding party arrived. Everyone walked into the cool gloom of the cathedral and Nathan realized that they were the only people there. All the pews were empty. Nathan looked behind him at Duke Montano, who looked extremely embarrassed. He must have been expecting some of the important Venetians of the town to turn out for this occasion but the empty church spoke on behalf of the people of Iraklion.

The wedding party reached the altar and there was an awkward silence.

The bishop cleared his throat. "General, shall we begin?"

Othello looked uncertain for a moment, conflicting emotions flitting across his face. He spoke to the duke with contempt.

"I had expected some attendance at this wedding by the people whose lives have been spared from a Turkish invasion." Then he turned to the bishop and spoke disdainfully, "Excellency, this marriage shall be blessed whether any man like it or not. Begin!" Nathan hung his head in embarrassment. *Did Othello really expect the Venetians who live here to feel any differently from those back in Venice?*

The bishop bowed and the service began. Nathan found it long 221 and tedious. The bishop droned his prayers and evocations and the two clerics swung incense burners. Nathan found himself struggling to concentrate. A packed church would have given some spark to the proceedings, but as it was, the responses given by the bridal pair echoed in the emptiness and the proceedings were dulled by disappointment.

Once the general and Desdemona were pronounced man and wife, the tiny wedding party filtered out into the strong sunlight. The carriages made their lonely journey back to the palace, driving deeper and deeper into the depression that had settled over Othello. Nathan thought the general must be in shock. In one day he had gone from being the feted commander of the victorious Venetian troops to being the subject of narrow-minded disapproval.

Iago was waiting inside the hall and his expression of discontent changed to one of grim satisfaction when he saw the mood of the wedding party.

With a jolt, Nathan remembered the message that he had not yet given to Pearce. He turned to see if he could deliver it unobtrusively now. But Pearce and Marie had slipped silently up the stairs and Nathan had missed his opportunity.

Duke Montano was blustering to Othello, trying to make excuses for his subjects. Othello silenced him with a dismissive wave of his hand and told him to turn his attention to making sure that tonight's wedding banquet ran smoothly. "As the guests are to be my officers, we need have no fear that they will not attend," was the general's sarcastic parting comment.

Clicking his fingers in Iago's direction, Othello then summoned his ensign to follow him, and Nathan tagged along behind.

Desdemona was passed into the care of Emilia, with a kiss from Othello and instructions to rest. It was a grim general who strode into his room.

Silently Nathan helped Othello undress, while he listened carefully to the man's anger spilling forth to Iago.

"These people have treated my wife and me with utter contempt. I shall not forgive them for this," he raged.

Iago murmured sympathetic and understanding comments while Nathan reflected the difference between the general and Sir Francis Drake. *Drake would have had his men drag the Cretans out of their houses and into the cathedral,* he thought. He would never have endured such humiliation as Othello did today. Nathan felt pity for the general but he recognized that the man he admired so much was too soft. His lack of education, perhaps, his years of slavery, and the color of his skin made him need acceptance too much. Othello could do with some of Drake's high-handedness.

Iago was busy flattering the general.

"Venetians who live in the colonies feel themselves to be more important than they are," he ventured. "If they were in Venice they would see the high esteem in which you are held by the council."

Nathan saw that Iago's flattery had renewed Othello's confidence a little. As a general he had respect, even if as a bridegroom he had none.

"Dismiss these people from your mind, sir," Iago continued smoothly. "In a short while you will be amongst your men and then you shall bask in their approval and know yourself as the admired general that you are."

"Honest Iago." Othello laid a grateful hand on his ensign's shoulder. "I know that you speak plainly the truth as always. You may leave me now and tend to your own affairs." Nathan wondered how the general could be so blind as to invest so much trust in Iago. He remembered the hate that the ensign had shown toward Othello in that upstairs room back in Venice.

Iago saluted and withdrew. Nathan also made for the door but was stopped by Othello.

"Marco, can you read?"

Nathan turned. "Yes, sir."

"Then stay with me and read to me from the Bible. I have a pain in my head. Read to distract me."

Othello was holding out a large Bible and Nathan took it with a heavy heart. He had hoped to slip away and push his message under John's door, but what could he do?

The general lay upon the bed and Nathan sat in a chair.

"What shall I read, sir?"

"I would have you read to me from Numbers, chapter twelve," Othello answered, "when the Lord punished those who spoke out against Moses's marriage to an Ethiopian woman. Read it to me. It will give me satisfaction."

Nathan's hand trembled as he turned the pages, anxious to get the task over with. He felt a sense of mounting panic that he still had not been able to deliver the message to Pearce.

Nathan felt a cold chill as the general closed his eyes and smiled grimly while Nathan read the terrible story in which Moses's sister was turned into a leper because she disagreed with his marriage. *Surely such a deep sense of grievance is unhinging his mind,* Nathan thought. He was grateful when his task was over and he could escape from the room.

That evening, in the palace's great hall, Duke Montano tried to lighten the mood. Extravagant food was being served, musicians were playing sweetly, and the officers of Othello's army milled about, drinking freely before taking their seats. Desdemona, Marie, and Emilia were the only women. It should have been a cheerful gathering but the soldiers had heard about the humiliation of the wedding so the atmosphere was tense and all eyes were on the grim face of the general.

"This island is cursed," he declared to anyone who would listen. "Did you know that Crete is the place where the fabled beast, the Minotaur, killed and ate hundreds of young men? And that the whole of the ancient civilization that lived on this barren rock was destroyed by a great disaster?"

"What disaster was it, then, that could wipe out a whole people?" Pearce asked, attempting to make conversation.

Othello shrugged and helped himself to some wine. "Who knows? It was probably the justice of the gods being visited on this dreadful place. This island has no interest for me." He turned to Desdemona. "Now Cyprus—there is a beautiful island, with soft warm breezes. When we capture Cyprus and I am made governor, we shall live in splendor, my love, far away from Venetian prejudices."

Desdemona smiled but Nathan saw that Pearce looked a little uncomfortable. Nathan remembered that the doge had other plans for Cyprus; if it was to be retaken, an English governor would rule, not Othello. *Where will they find a home, if not on Cyprus?* he wondered, feeling a stab of pity for Desdemona.

Othello's mood lifted when he began to talk of the sea battle with the Turks. The duke looked relieved and threw himself into the discussion. Everyone was engrossed and Nathan saw his opportunity to press the coded message into Pearce's hands. *Finally!* he thought, with great relief. Pearce opened the message under the table and frowned. He caught Nathan's eye but there was no opportunity for him to leave the room and decipher it.

"Of course," Othello said loudly, "the true hero of the final hours was young Marco, over there." Everyone turned to look with interest at Nathan and he felt himself blushing.

"There we were," Othello continued, "fighting at close quarters with the Turks on board this captured ship and we were being decimated by a lone crossbowman on their castle deck. Suddenly a knife flashed through the air, from the direction of the crow's nest on our own flagship, and the Turkish crossbowman fell dead, a bolt still in his bow. I looked up and saw that the knife had been thrown by young Marco. Mind you, he disobeyed my orders by being above deck!"

There was general laughter and men volunteered to drink the health of the young lad who had been so brave. Marie had her hand over her mouth in shock but Pearce stood and raised his goblet in salute to his young friend. Nathan felt very proud, but aware that he was in the company of battle-hardened soldiers, he also felt a little awkward. He mumbled his thanks.

As the dinner progressed, Nathan kept watching Pearce, in the hope that he would excuse himself for a moment to read the message, but still he did not.

"It is now time for us to retire to our bed," Othello announced with a grin, as he raised Desdemona to her feet. "Cassio!" He turned to Pearce. "You are in charge of the guard tonight. Make sure that the festivities do not get out of hand."

"You may rely on me, sir," Pearce replied.

"Good, good."

Everyone applauded the couple as they left the room, and Nathan edged closer to Pearce. He had to speak to him. But Iago got there first.

"Lieutenant Cassio, will you come and drink to the health of the general with us, before we take the watch?" Nathan's heart almost stopped beating in his chest. All because he had not delivered the message earlier, Pearce was about to be put in danger.

Pearce shook his head. "No, Iago. I thank you but we have work to do tonight."

Iago persisted. "But it is early, sir, and some of your officers would like to get to know you better." With a wave of his arm he indicated a band of men who were standing nearby. "I have promised them that you would come."

Duke Montano joined in the urging. "You must come and toast to the health of the general, Cassio."

Much to Nathan's frustration, Pearce reluctantly agreed to go with the men but excused himself momentarily to talk to Marie. Nathan hovered, wondering whether Pearce would also speak to him but his friend then returned to the men and they left.

Marie came over and whispered to Nathan. "Pearce said to follow him, but keep out of sight. He may need you." Nathan gave her a grateful bow and sped off after his partner. Hopefully he would now be able to make amends for not delivering the message by thwarting Iago's plans in whatever way he could. If the ensign succeeded, then the whole mission would be in danger. Nathan cursed himself under his breath.

It was not difficult to follow the group of men. Nathan could hear Iago, laughing and joking continuously. The streets of Iraklion were busy—filled with soldiers and sailors who were taking the general's decree to enjoy themselves very seriously indeed. Drunks were reeling out from small tavernas, having been evicted by surly Cretans who had had enough.

As Nathan flattened himself against a wall to avoid yet another soldier who had been hurled into the street, he spied a man wearing one of the sinister Venetian half-masks. He knew, by the way the man walked and held himself, that it was Roderigo. He saw him touch his sword and stride off purposefully after Iago's group of revelers. Nathan knew that this was the appointed hour when Roderigo was going to challenge John Pearce to a duel.

Nathan quickened his pace. There was no point in trying to hide. Roderigo was too intent on his deed to notice if he was being followed.

As he turned onto a small square, Nathan noticed that Iago's group of men had seated themselves around a table in a large, open-fronted taverna. For a moment he lost sight of Roderigo and he anxiously scanned the milling crowds. Several of the Venetians were wearing masks. Nathan's eyes moved frantically from figure to figure—then he found him again, seated alone in a taverna on the opposite side of the square, downing a cup of wine. His eyes were fixed on Pearce.

Nathan took up position in a doorway, so that he had a good view of both sides of the square. He waited, breathing deeply to help himself remain calm. Then a great slap on his back sent him reeling forward.

"How are you, my lad? Having a good time?" A loud drunken voice shouted in his ear. It was Zeno.

"Ah... Zeno... I'm well... but a little busy right now...," Nathan stuttered, taken aback by the force of the friendly attack.

The jovial drunk clasped the boy to his chest. "Busy! Mustn't be busy. Not tonight. Come and have a drink with your old mate, Zeno. Come and have a drink."

Nathan struggled to free himself from the man's embrace. "Not now, my friend. I am on urgent business for my master." He pushed Zeno away with as much strength as he could muster. The man slammed into the wall with a surprised look on his face and slumped to the ground in a daze.

Suddenly someone shouted and Nathan's blood ran cold. Roderigo was standing in the middle of the square, calling out to John Pearce. His sword was drawn and he was asking for a fight.

"Michael Cassio, you pus-filled Florentine! Come out here, you scum! Desdemona will never look at your pretty face again, when I have carved my initials on it. Come out and fight like a man."

The square had fallen silent, except for a few shouts, encouraging the fight to progress, and a few laughs at Roderigo's choice of insults. Pearce's face was set in cold anger and Iago's mouth was frozen in an expectant half-smile. Nathan crouched and flipped both knives out of his boots, turning them upward in his palms, so that they were concealed in his sleeves. *My first dagger will be for Roderigo and my second for Iago,* Nathan vowed.

Pearce stood up and drew his sword. It gleamed in the torch-light and there were a few murmurs of appreciation from those who knew a good sword when they saw one. Then he slowly walked out to face his challenger.

"Who is it that speaks so fouly of the general's wife? Give me a name, so that I may know who has insulted such a noble lady!"

Roderigo said nothing. Nathan could see that he was drunk and John would probably best him—but he was alert, waiting for the slightest sign of intervention. It would give him great pleasure if Iago just moved one finger. Nathan smiled, picturing his dagger making swift passage to Iago's chest. All that training at the hands of the knife master, Bardolph, would not go to waste.

Pearce and Roderigo circled each other. Sweat trickled from under Roderigo's mask. Suddenly he lunged and Pearce, without moving from the spot, parried the thrust dismissively.

Roderigo made another pass and again Pearce flicked the sword aside. There were a couple more halfhearted clashes of steel and then Roderigo produced a concealed dagger. Instinctively Nathan flipped one knife out of his sleeve, holding it by the tip, ready to throw. Pearce, with a swift movement of his left hand, released his cloak from his shoulder and grasped it by the collar, ready to use as a foil for the dagger. Roderigo lunged again but his sword was skillfully parried. He waved the dagger wildly, trying to cut his opponent's side, but Pearce threw his cloak over Roderigo's head and, with a hard and well-aimed kick, sent the dagger flying from his hand. Then, almost as though he were dancing, Pearce brought one foot down and raised the other up, booting Roderigo in the chest and sending him reeling backward.

At that moment, Duke Montano foolishly decided to intervene and rushed across to the duel, just as Pearce was bringing his sword arm back. There was a collective gasp from the onlookers as the razor-sharp weapon cut deep into Montano's outstretched arm. Roderigo took advantage of the confusion and ran away while Pearce dropped his sword and used his cloak to stem the flow of the duke's blood.

Shocked, Nathan slipped into the doorway and put his daggers back into his boots. Then he ran over to Pearce who was standing, white faced, as a group of men attempted to lift the wounded duke off the ground.

"It was an accident. A foolish accident." Pearce was visibly shaken. "What possessed him to run up behind me like that?" He gathered his wits and looked at Nathan. "Run ahead and wake your sister," he whispered. "She must tend to the duke's wounds." Nathan was reluctant to leave his friend's side but he knew that Pearce was right—Marie had the skills to save the duke. He nodded and ran as fast as his legs would carry him.

When he reached the palace, Nathan ran up the steps, three at a time, and hurtled along the corridor to Marie's room. He burst in, without knocking, to find Marie playing a quiet game of cards with Emilia. They both looked up at him, startled.

"There's been an accident. The duke has been wounded. The master says you are to help him, my lady."

Marie sprang to her feet. "Bring a bowl of water down to the hall, Emilia. Marco, go to the kitchens and fetch clean cloths and honey."

"Honey?" Nathan was puzzled.

"Just do it, please. I must find my needle and thread. Go! Go!"

By the time the men arrived back at the palace, carrying the injured duke, Emilia, Marie, and Nathan were ready and waiting. Marie pushed her way through the men to the duke's side but Iago blocked her way.

"This is not your business, lady," he said curtly.

Marie flashed him a contemptuous look. "I know what I am doing, sir. Kindly leave the duke to my care." It was obvious that she would have no argument on the matter and the men laid Duke Montano on the table and backed away. With a knife, Marie cut away his sleeve and revealed the gaping wound, which had opened up the arm to the bone.

Montano was moaning. "I am done for, I am bleeding to death..."

"Nay, sir," Marie said firmly. "You shall not die. But we must stem the flow of blood. Be brave now. It will hurt."

Everyone stood in respectful silence as Marie poured brandy on the wound. The duke's moans grew louder as the stinging alcohol did its work. Then, her fingers bloody and wet, Marie deftly threaded a large needle with gut, and proceeded to sew up the layers of sinew and flesh. The duke was thrashing about with the pain and two men had to hold him down. Marie battled on, slowly, until the wound knitted together. Then she liberally smeared honey all over her handiwork, before bandaging the arm.

"What does the honey do, Bianca?" whispered Emilia, who had been her assistant throughout the gruesome task.

"The ancient Greeks used it on wounds. It stops pus forming." Marie spoke firmly to the semiconscious Duke, "This arm will heal, sir, but it will take many months. You have lost much blood and you must rest now."

"What in God's name has taken place here tonight?" a familiar voice thundered.

The men surrounding the table parted, making way for the formidable figure of Othello. He was not pleased at being disturbed and Nathan, seeing Iago close behind, suspected that the ensign had taken great pleasure in knocking on his bedroom door.

Pearce stepped forward. "It was an accident, sir. The duke tried to intervene in a duel and he got caught by my sword."

Othello's eyes blazed. "*You* were fighting a duel?!"

Pearce nodded and mumbled, "Yes, sir."

"My second in command—fighting a duel? Is this how you set an example to the men?" Othello's rage was volcanic. He raised his voice so loudly that it seemed to shake the rafters.

"If I might explain . . . ," Pearce began.

"YOU MAY NOT EXPLAIN!" Othello's face was a few inches away from Pearce's. "Michael Cassio, you are relieved of your command. I will not have any lieutenant serving with me who brawls in the street. You will take yourself back to Venice on the next available ship."

NO! No, that's not fair. Nathan was outraged and wanted to shout at the general and tell him how foolish this whole thing was. But he knew that if he spoke out forcefully, he would be abandoning his role as a servant and putting the mission in even greater jeopardy.

Othello turned to his ensign. "Iago, you must go and put an end to the festivities in the town. Take your men and round up all the drunks and troublemakers. Send the people to their beds. We have had enough folly tonight."

233

Iago bowed and Othello, with a final glare in Pearce's direction, accompanied the servants who were carrying the duke up to his bedchamber.

Pearce slumped into a chair, his head in his hands. "Well, that is my reputation destroyed," he muttered quietly to Nathan. "If I cannot be Othello's second in command, the doge will not honor his promise of an alliance." He was tired and shaken.

Iago came across the room, his face a picture of insincere concern. "Lieutenant Cassio, you must pay no mind to the general. He has his moods and he blows hot and cold. He is ill tempered because this day has not gone well for him. But, mark my words, he is ruled by the lady Desdemona now. If she were to speak well of you, he would listen. You should go and see her and ask her if she would plead your case."

"I will think on it, thank you, ensign." Nathan could tell that Pearce was wary of the scheming soldier.

Iago left the room and Nathan wandered casually over to the window. As he looked out into the street below, he saw a figure come out of the shadows. It was Roderigo, now unmasked. He was agitated and Iago seemed to be trying to reassure his friend.

Nathan felt deeply frustrated that he had not been able to get his coded message of warning to Pearce in time to prevent tonight's disaster.

Iago may have won a victory tonight, he thought, *but he will not stop plotting. Pearce is in mortal danger now.*

CHAPTER 19

"BEWARE, MY LORD, OF JEALOUSY. IT IS THE GREEN-EYED MONSTER"

THE events of the night hung heavily in the air like a putrid smell. Nathan had slipped, unobserved, into Pearce's room and found him decoding the message. The fact that the duel might have been avoided only added to Pearce's frustration.

Nathan watched his friend pace the floor and listened patiently as he fumed.

"If I do not participate in the retaking of Cyprus, then the doge may not honor the agreement. Perhaps if Othello were to know about the mission and why I am here ... I could show him Shakespeare's verses and I could give him the cloth so that he could read the code...."

Marie was sewing in one corner of the room. "You can't do that," she said nervously.

Pearce turned an inquiring gaze upon her and she flushed. "I ... I gave the handkerchief—the one with the strawberries—to Desdemona as a present."

235

"What?" Pearce and Nathan spoke as one.

"Well, I thought you had finished with it and . . . I had showed it to her . . . and she admired it. You said to be kind to her!"

"Of all the stupid . . . !" Pearce was almost lost for words.

Nathan tried to reassure his friend. "I'm not sure that the loss of the handkerchief is that important, John. Othello is becoming increasingly insecure. He felt deeply insulted that no one attended the wedding ceremony and it has played on his mind. Iago speaks malicious words in his ear, which make matters worse. If you tell Othello that a conspiracy between England and Venice took place behind his back, it will just make him angrier."

Pearce looked at Nathan with admiration.

"You're right, Nathan. To tell him of this now, when his mind is so unsettled, would be a mistake."

"Perhaps there is some merit in asking Desdemona to speak to her husband on your behalf?" asked Marie. "He will do anything for her."

"Maybe," Pearce said grudgingly. "Nathan, in the morning you must come and tell me when the general has left the palace. Then I will go and speak to Desdemona."

Pearce then lay down on the bed, to try and sleep as best he could. Marie withdrew to her own room and Nathan checked that no one was about before slipping out quietly and making for his own bed. If Nathan was to keep the confidence of Othello, he

must not be seen too often in Pearce's company.

In the morning, breakfast was a somber affair.

"I shall inspect the fortifications today," Othello announced curtly. Then he strode out of the hall to his waiting men.

Nathan hid in the corridor where he could still hear and see the general. He watched as Iago detached himself from the group and walked over to his wife. He grabbed Emilia by the arm and took her to one side. She looked very frightened. Iago's face was close to her ear and he was speaking very fast. Emilia nodded and her husband let go of her. Nathan wondered if Iago was drawing his wife into his plotting and vowed to watch her carefully from now on.

Horses were ready in the courtyard and Nathan stood at the window to watch the general and his men mount up and ride away. He then sped off to Pearce's room with the news that the general had left.

Pearce at once dispatched Nathan to request an audience with Desdemona. It was Marie who answered the door.

She smiled at Nathan. "Desdemona is anxious to help. She says to tell your master that he may come and see her after noon."

Nathan went back to tell Pearce the good news. His partner was now in a restless mood. "I am sick of being cooped up in this room," he said.

"Why don't we find some horses and go for a ride?" Nathan suggested. To spend the morning on horseback would lift both their spirits.

Pearce and Nathan rode out into the barren countryside and at the first opportunity, they urged the horses into a full gallop. It became a race between the two of them and laughter bubbled from their mouths as the wind coursed past their faces. Finally they slowed to a canter and smiled at each other—the demons of the night before exorcised and exercised away.

But one thought nagged at Nathan. Othello had told his

disgraced second in command to take the next ship back to Venice. "John, you would not leave Crete without us, would you?" he asked anxiously.

Pearce laughed. "Good God, no! There is madness brewing here, I fear. No, Nathan, from now on where I go, you and Marie go."

Nathan was relieved. They turned the horses toward the line of ships' masts that were visible on the horizon and cantered amiably toward the sea.

The dockyard was in a fever of excitement. Men were laughing and shouting. They both dismounted and Nathan held the horses while Pearce pushed his way through the throng to find out what was happening.

As Nathan waited, he was jolted by a nudge in the ribs. It was the toothless Zeno again.

"My old friend, Marco!" he exclaimed with glee. "Such news, eh? Such news."

"What is it? What has happened?" Nathan laughed to see the old man's face so gleeful.

"The Spanish have been humiliated. That's what's happened." Zeno did a little dance of mischief. "That English pirate, Drake, has burned all their ships in Cadiz harbor. The whole fleet—the whole blessed Spanish fleet—gone up in flames. Can you believe it! I bet old King Philip is spitting blood right now. Serve him right. T'ain't right that one country should have such a big empire. T'ain't right at all."

Zeno danced off to join the merriment. Nathan wondered how the news of Drake's piece of daring had been celebrated in the streets of London. He thought, with a pang, of all the revelry he would be missing; of how the theater in Shoreditch would be hurriedly putting on a play about Drake and his glorious deeds. He smiled at the thought that he would probably have been playing the part of some Spanish damsel in distress and decided that he was rather glad to have missed out on the experience after all.

Pearce pushed his way back through the crowd, a broad smile on his face. "Drake has sacked Cadiz," he said in disbelief.

"I know. One of the soldiers just told me. How has the news traveled this far?"

"A merchant ship, en route to Venice, was passing Cadiz when it happened. They watched it all, then they carried the news to the doge's palace as soon as they docked. The doge sent *that* ship from Venice with the news." He pointed at a small pinnace farther down the quay.

As they watched, a man of some importance, followed by two servants, disembarked and mounted their waiting horses.

"Doubtless, this messenger from Venice is off to find the general and give him the news. I need to speak to the lady Desdemona as quickly as possible, in case Othello returns early."

When they got back to the palace, Desdemona was ready to receive Pearce. Nathan waited outside the room. Surely Desdemona would try to get her husband to see reason?

There was a commotion outside in the courtyard and Nathan ran to the nearest window. Othello was bounding up the stairs, closely followed by Iago. The general did not look pleased. Nathan ran the length of the corridor and knocked urgently.

"Master, Master, the general has returned already!"

The door opened and Pearce came out. Desdemona stood behind him.

"Stay and hear me speak to my husband," she urged but Pearce declined, preferring to be summoned when the general had agreed to see him.

Nathan ducked into the doorway of his own room, a little farther along the corridor, and Pearce hurried away. But Othello had rounded the corner a second earlier, just in time to see Pearce leaving Desdemona's room.

Nathan heard the shock in his voice.

"Iago, I have just seen Michael Cassio come out of my wife's room. He hurried away, as if he knew I was coming."

There was an awkward silence and Nathan waited to hear how the devious Iago would exploit this situation.

"Cassio, my lord? Surely not? I cannot believe that he would steal away, so guiltylike...."

Then Nathan heard Desdemona speak.

"My lord! You have just missed Michael Cassio. He came here to ask for your forgiveness and to ask if I could talk to you on his behalf. He has just left. I beg you, call him back."

"Not now, Desdemona, some other time," Othello replied curtly.

Desdemona persisted, "But will it be soon?"

"Perhaps."

"Maybe tonight at supper?"

"No, not tonight." Nathan could hear that Othello's replies were becoming colder but Desdemona still carried on her pleading.

"Please, no more." Othello's voice sounded harsh. "I will see him when it suits me. Now go inside."

The door closed and Othello's voice said, "Come, Iago, I wish to speak to you." And their footsteps began to echo back down the corridor.

Nathan peered around the doorway and saw the two men turn onto one of the balconies overlooking the courtyard. He then ran, as fast as he could, up the stairs to the next floor, and out onto a balcony that lay directly above.

He could now overhear Iago and Othello's conversation.

"...I want you to be honest with me...," Othello hissed at Iago. "You suspect Cassio and my wife, don't you? You suspect that they are attracted to each other?"

Nathan felt his stomach twist into a knot. *Of course! Pearce is the obvious target for Iago's plot to ruin the general's marriage. This way he kills two birds with one stone.*

Iago's reply was smooth and calculated. "I have not said so, sir. Beware, my lord, of jealousy. It is the green-eyed monster that can make you suspect the ones that you love, for no good reason."

"I am so miserable." Othello sounded defeated, broken. Nathan was exasperated by the man's inability to see sense. "My wife is beautiful, loves company, has many talents, is of noble birth.... I must have proof that she is faithful to me."

"Yes, sir. You must." It seemed to Nathan that Iago spoke in a soothing manner, as though he were speaking to a distressed child. "You must watch your wife and Cassio. See how they behave together."

"Yes, you are right." Othello sounded grateful. "And if you see or hear any more of this matter, you must report back to me." His voice became harsh. "Leave me now."

Nathan heard the click of Iago's heels as he left Othello, and as he remained crouched on the balcony above the general's head, he was shocked to hear the sound of muffled sobbing. Nathan felt hot with embarrassment to hear such a great man cry. This was followed by pity for Othello's unraveling wits and then, finally, Nathan felt a great revulsion for Iago, who seemed to able to manipulate everyone around him.

Nathan knew what had to be done. He raced back to his room and began to prepare a message, warning Pearce not to attempt to speak or approach Desdemona again. He tried to hurry, fearful that Othello might summon him at any moment, but he made several mistakes. Eventually he had finished it to his satisfaction.

QO GVT FCETR TB QELKEZBNT HGNVN BA WVYL HULL ZADL OGUEESO SHRBVUF

(Do not speak to Desdemona again it will only make Othello furious)

Nathan silently sped along the corridor and pushed the note under John's door—just in time—for he then heard the general's door open.

"Marco," called Othello and the door slammed shut again.

Nathan hurtled along the corridor and knocked.

"Enter," came the command from inside.

Nathan entered and immediately noted that Othello's face looked strange. His eyes were glazed and he seemed distracted.

"I have had news," he said hoarsely. "You must take a message to your former master, Cassio, for me. A ship has arrived from Venice with a message from the doge. This ... messenger ... requests the presence of Lieutenant Cassio tonight at dinner. You must tell Cassio I wish him to attend, do you understand?"

Nathan nodded, fearful of the way Othello looked. *Is this madness?* he wondered. He had never seen a mad person before. But the general seemed deeply changed.

"There is one more thing." Othello's voice sounded cold. "Tell Michael Cassio that I do not wish his lady, Bianca, to attend upon my wife anymore. It is not fitting."

Nathan felt his face flush with shock. *This man has lost all sense of reason. What purpose does it serve to remove Marie? Desdemona will have no one for companionship except Emilia now.* With that thought, Nathan felt a pang of fear for Desdemona's safety at the hands of Iago and his wife.

"I understand, sir. Do you also wish me to return to my old master and cease being your servant?" Despite being convinced that Othello was on the verge of unpredictable madness, Nathan felt boldness was the best option.

"No," said Othello, sounding genuinely hurt. "You are my comrade, Marco. You are to be my protégé. You can stay with me as long as you wish."

Nathan was relieved that Othello did not consider him to be "the enemy" like his sister and Pearce. "Thank you, sir. I shall stay as long as you have need of me." With this lie on his lips, he bowed and left to deliver the general's message to Pearce. Walking down the corridor, he felt both fear and misery. Everything seemed to be unraveling. Pearce was in disgrace; the mission looked as though it was finished; and he himself seemed trapped in the service of a man descending further into insanity by the minute.

CHAPTER 20

"I AM BLACK AND HAVE NOT THOSE SOFT PARTS OF CONVERSATION"

ATHAN knocked on the door of Pearce's room.

"I have come with a message from the general, sir," he said loudly, so that any passerby would know why he was there.

"Come in." Pearce opened the door and Nathan saw that Marie was also in the room.

"I got your message telling me not to speak to Desdemona again," Pearce said quietly, after he had closed the door. "What has happened?"

"I believe that Othello has gone mad. He saw you leave Desdemona's room earlier and Iago has convinced him that you are her lover."

"What!" Marie and John exclaimed in unison.

Marie watched Pearce with a strange look on her face, then she spoke falteringly. "Is it true, John? Do you have feelings for Desdemona?"

John looked exasperated and Nathan snorted scornfully.

"Sweet Jesus, Marie, have you been infected by the plague of jealousy that rages through this palace?" His tone was sarcastic and Marie flushed a deep red.

"I am not jealous," she protested. But Nathan knew that she was.

"John, we must stop Desdemona from speaking to Othello on your behalf," he urged. "The more that she mentions your name, the worse the general will become."

Pearce agreed. "Marie, you are the only one who can warn Desdemona of the situation. You must speak to her at once. Tell her to be careful."

"No," Nathan interrupted, "that is not possible. Part of the general's message for you is that Mistress Bianca must not attend upon the lady Desdemona anymore. He feels that it is not fitting in the present situation."

Marie made a small involuntary noise of shock.

"I see." Pearce's voice was full of resignation.

"The rest of the message is that Othello commands that you attend the dinner tonight. The emissary from Venice has an important message, which he will not reveal to Othello until then, when you are also present."

Pearce raised an eyebrow. "This message from Venice could make the situation worse. We must prepare ourselves." He spoke with urgency. "Marie, pack all our belongings. We may have to run for our lives after this dinner. I shall go down to the stables and secure three horses, to be ready if we need them. Then I shall go down to the docks and see if I can procure a passage on a ship leaving tonight. You are both armed, I trust?"

Marie patted her bodice and Nathan his boot. Marie looked a little pale.

"Do not worry," said Pearce reassuringly. "Perhaps I am seeing danger where there is none. But we must be prepared for any eventuality. There has already been one attempt to kill me—I would not be surprised if there were another."

Buckling his sword, Pearce left the room and Marie set about her task of packing their few belongings. Nathan returned to his room to pack his own small bag. He felt desolate with a mixture of fear and relief. Fear that they were all in mortal danger and relief that Pearce had decided to abandon the mission and get them away from Crete. The palace was quiet and the heat hung heavily in the air. If there were more plots being hatched, then they were being hatched in the deep dreams of a sultry afternoon's sleep.

As darkness fell, the dinner guests began to arrive. Pearce returned, looking satisfied, and he nodded briefly to Nathan as he passed. "All is arranged," he muttered before bounding up the stairs to change his dusty clothes.

Duke Montano was still recovering from his wound and would not be attending but he had sent his servants around to the notable Venetian families of Iraklion, urging them to come. Whether they did so out of loyalty to the duke or their desire to hear the gossip of Venice from the doge's messenger, it was hard to tell, but Nathan overheard more than enough disparaging whispers about Othello and Desdemona to know that these people were not attending the dinner in a spirit of friendship.

Stewards were showing the guests to their seats and it became apparent that Michael Cassio and the lady Bianca were to be seated as far away as possible from the general and his wife. The honor of being on the top table went to Iago and Emilia.

When Othello and Desdemona entered, the assembled guests stood and broke into a halfhearted applause. Nathan watched the smile on the general's face falter a little and a cold glitter appear in his eyes. It was as if Othello was storing up grievances like a magpie hoarding pieces of tin. Close behind the couple was the messenger from Venice. He was introduced to the assembly as Signor Lodovico.

The talk of the guests, unfortunately, was of the news from Cadiz. All three tables were buzzing with the exploits of Sir Francis Drake and no one made any comment about Othello's victorious sea battle. The general became loud and boastful, and Nathan squirmed with embarrassment.

"This Drake is a pirate. No more," Othello said loudly. "He has no skill or strategy, he is merely an opportunist. When he sees a chance he takes it. Too many civilians pay for his boldness."

Lodovico, the Venetian emissary, responded quickly. "Surely seizing an opportunity is good. For example, General, if Drake had been in your shoes when you routed the Turkish fleet a few days ago, do you think that he would have regrouped in Crete or would he have struck at Cyprus while the enemy was in disarray?"

The whole room fell silent. Othello's face was immobile, not a muscle or sinew flexed under his skin. It was as though he had been struck in the face by a gauntlet.

Othello struggled to regain his composure. "The Spanish are not the Turks!" he exclaimed in a too-loud voice. "Have no fear, I will retake Cyprus very soon. I must. I plan to make it my home.

My wife and I shall live there, amongst friends, for the rest of our days."

The dinner faltered to its end. An air of defeat hung about the evening. All was not well between Othello and Desdemona. Several times she tried to cover her husband's hand with her own and every time, Othello's hand moved away as if he could not bear to be touched by her.

As the guests petered out, Lodovico strode over to Pearce, offering his hand. Nathan hovered nearby, pretending to clear the table. He was anxious to hear what the emissary had to say.

"You are Michael Cassio?" Lodovico inquired.

"I am, sir." Pearce bowed in acknowledgment.

"The message I bear must be heard by you. I request that you stay in this room while I deliver it."

"Of course."

Othello sat at the top table and watched this exchange between the two men. He was now breathing heavily and Nathan noticed that beads of sweat were appearing on his brow.

"Husband, are you not well?" Desdemona asked anxiously.

"I have a pain in my forehead," was the curt reply.

"Here, let me soothe it." She produced the strawberry-embroidered handkerchief, which was doused in cologne, and tried to press it to her husband's head but he roughly pushed her away.

"Let me alone," he growled. Nathan's eyes shot to Desdemona's face and registered her shock and confusion.

Lodovico now produced a parchment, bearing the doge's seal. Nathan moved farther along the table, still silently piling up dishes, safe in the knowledge that all servants are invisible.

"This is my message," Lodovico stated in a flat voice.

Othello broke the seal and Nathan observed the tremor in his hands as he did so. The general scanned the page and then he broke into laughter—the kind of laughter that strikes a chill in the hearts of sane men.

"My lord, what is it?" Desdemona whispered in fear.

Othello looked directly at her, a look of contempt on his face.

"Why, my dear. It is nothing. It appears I am recalled to Venice and Michael Cassio is to be commander in my place."

Nathan almost dropped the plates he was piling up. There was a shocked silence then Othello began to chuckle maniacally again.

"You see, my dear," he continued venomously. "The Council of Venice, in my absence, has decided I am not fit to command. Perhaps it is because I am black and have not those soft parts of conversation that courtiers have—or it could be that I am not as young as I was—or it could be the curse of marriage!" He spat the words at Desdemona and tears appeared in her eyes.

"I am glad," Desdemona said brokenly. "This place is cursed. Now we can go back to Venice and be happy."

With a violent burst of rage, Othello reared out of his chair and struck Desdemona a stinging blow across her face. She reeled backward into Iago. Marie screamed and Nathan dropped his plates. Pearce shouted a protest as he advanced toward Othello, but Desdemona held up one hand to stop him.

She steadied herself on her feet. "I did not deserve that, my lord," she said quietly and with great dignity, then she turned and left, refusing Emilia's offered arm.

Lodovico stared at Othello with cold disdain.

"My lord, this would not be believed in Venice. Is this the noble Moor who has the respect of the council? Are you mad to strike your wife in such a manner?"

Othello seemed disorientated and spoke as if from a faraway place.

"Sir, I am commanded home. I obey the mandate and will return to Venice." He looked past Lodovico to Pearce. "Cassio, you are welcome to Cyprus and its goats and monkeys. . . ."

Suddenly his voice seemed to strangle in his throat and he lunged backward, his body in a great arch, and fell to the floor, sending chairs flying. There he lay, uttering strange noises and twitching. Nathan ran toward him, convinced that the general's mounting insanity had caused him to try to take his own life with poison, but Iago barred his way and took command.

"Stand back, please! It is the epilepsy. I have seen it before. This is the second fit he has had in as many days." With that, he produced a leather strap from his belt and forced it between Othello's teeth.

"Is this a recent illness?" Lodovico asked with concern.

"No, my lord." Iago was struggling to hold Othello down. "The general has suffered from fits for many years. But only he and I know of his ailment."

Suddenly Nathan understood why Othello kept Iago by him and refused to see the flaws in the man. Iago must have nursed the general through many such fits and he had kept his secret well.

Servants were summoned, and once the general had stopped shaking and seemed to be quiet, he was carried up to his room.

Pearce and Marie left with Lodovico, and still shaken, Nathan began to clear up the broken plates.

He noticed that Desdemona's handkerchief was lying on the floor under the table, but Emilia immediately retrieved it. Nathan watched as she ran after her husband and furtively pressed it into his hand. Iago's half-smile of satisfaction caused Nathan a pang of concern. *What purpose could Iago have for Desdemona's handkerchief?* Nathan wondered.

After he had disposed of the broken crockery, he raced upstairs to the general's room. As he entered, Othello was vomiting into a bowl held by Iago.

"May I help the general, sir?" Nathan inquired, full of concern.

"No!" Iago spoke roughly to him. "This fit must have its quiet course or he will break out into savage madness."

The general vomited again and Iago relented a little. "Fetch me a wet cloth, boy. I need to wipe the general's face."

Nathan hurtled into the anteroom and grabbed a small towel, dunking it in the bowl of water on the stand. He gave it to Iago, who leaned the general back and began to wipe his face. "Dispose of the contents of the bowl, boy!" Nathan took up the bowl and held his breath all the way to the nearest privy. The deed done, he returned to Othello's room, but having caught the sound of voices from within, he paused and listened.

Othello was gabbling in a strange guttural voice. "Have you heard anything? Tell me, honest Iago!"

"Nay, nothing yet." Iago's reply was quiet and calming. "But you shall see some proof soon."

Nathan had no doubt that Iago had devised some further evil against John Pearce so he beat a hasty retreat to his partner's room to warn him.

Pearce was pacing the floor once more and Marie looked distressed. Nathan told them of the conversation he had just overheard.

"What happens now?" he asked.

"I don't know," Pearce responded honestly. "Lodovico told me some sad news that contributed to the doge's decision to recall Othello. Apparently Desdemona's father has died—they say of a broken heart."

Nathan bowed his head, remembering the last time they had both seen Brabantio, outside his house. He had been devastated by his daughter's marriage.

"But . . . ," Pearce continued, "it must be kept a secret. Lodovico does not wish to upset Desdemona further."

"Now you have been appointed in Othello's place, do you have to take Cyprus?" Marie asked anxiously.

Pearce smiled ruefully. "Apparently not. I am just to stay here and await orders. It seems that the furor caused by Drake's action in Cadiz has caused the doge to think again about the retaking of Cyprus. He feels the time is not right yet. I suspect he knows that the full fury of Spain will now be turned against England and we will not have the manpower to spare to guard Cyprus for the Venetians. Nathan, tomorrow I must visit the barracks and speak to the men. If the general is well enough, ask him if you may accompany me."

"I shall offer myself as a spy," Nathan said eagerly, "to report back on your actions. That should please Othello."

Pearce smiled appreciatively. "You truly are beginning to think like one of Sir Francis Walsingham's agents."

CHAPTER 21

"YOU TO DO YOURS AND I TO DO MINE"

THE next morning, Nathan knocked quietly on Othello's door and a somber voice told him to enter. Othello was sitting, staring out of his window. He smelled of sweat and vomit and had not been shaved that morning. His eyes were bloodshot and watery, and they turned upon Nathan with a look of sadness.

"Sir, I come to offer you a service."

"What is it, Marco? What service can you offer one who has fallen so low as I?"

All the fighting spirit seemed to have left the once-magnificent general, and Nathan felt a wave of pity, mixed with loathing. *How could he dishonor himself so? He was once so great a man—one I admired so much.* He pushed all sentiment out of his mind and steeled himself for his task of deception.

"Let me accompany Signor Cassio on his inspection of the barracks today and I shall be your faithful eyes and ears in all matters." Nathan tried to sound conspiratorial.

Othello's eyes flashed some spark of interest. "You would do me this service?" he croaked. "You would spy on your former master—for me?"

Nathan nodded. "It grieves me, sir, to see you thus and I would do what I can to help you."

Othello walked unsteadily toward him and put his hand on Nathan's shoulder. "I shall not forget this."

Nathan bowed and raced down to the courtyard.

As he mounted a horse, alongside Pearce, he reflected that he was heartily sick of crying women and mad generals, and in the soft haze of the morning, he breathed deeply, as if to rid himself of the suffocating atmosphere of the palace.

Pearce had assembled a party of officers to accompany them on their trip to the barracks. The events of last night had reached the men's ears and they were confused. It was only a couple of days since the general had dismissed Lieutenant Cassio and now they had been told that this man was replacing Othello.

Pearce had anticipated that the soldiers would be in this frame of mind and he addressed them firmly.

"Men, the general is ill, and orders have come from the doge stating that he must return to Venice. I am to command in his place. The general is not in disgrace—he must rest and the council needs his services in Venice." Nathan found himself in awe of Pearce's ability to turn around any situation with a few well-chosen words.

Several of the men nodded and the riders clattered out of the courtyard. Nathan looked up toward the balconies and caught a glimpse of Iago—a look of pure evil on his face. *What plot does he hatch now?* thought Nathan, as they rode out into the streets of the town.

It was no more than ten minutes' ride to the barracks, and when they arrived, the sentries were barely visible. One man was almost dozing in the growing warmth of the morning, another was chatting to a passing girl. Inside the gates, Nathan could see that many of the men were just lounging around aimlessly.

Pearce's face darkened.

" 'Hoy! You there," he shouted. "Make yourselves ready for a command inspection. Move yourself, man."

The sentries looked shocked. They blinked at Pearce—they barely knew him.

"I said, MOVE!" Pearce roared. "Go tell your company to assemble in the square, at double-quick time." A soldier hastened off to spread the news.

Pearce strode up to the top of the steps leading to the chapel and stood, waiting.

The men began to pour out of the buildings, some half dressed and pulling on boots and jerkins as they went. Tide after tide of soldiers gathered in front of the steps, until the whole square was a sea of heads. There was a silence as the confused army waited for Pearce to speak.

Nathan marveled at the way in which Pearce took command as though he had done so all his life. First he praised the men for their action against the Turks, then he rebuked them for their decline into slovenly ways. His delivery was so powerful—so persuasive—that by the end of his speech, the packed square was filled with men hanging their heads in shame. *I should like to have seen John when he was acting on the stage.* Nathan felt a surge of pride at the performance.

The speech finished with a command from Pearce that all men should wash, shave, and clean their quarters. He would inspect the barracks in one hour. There was an almighty stamp of boots in unison as they came to attention, then stampeded in all directions in an effort to meet the demands of their new commander.

Once the men had dispersed, Pearce allowed himself a sigh of relief and a shaky grin.

"That was a difficult job, Nathan," he whispered. "I would not care to do it again. Perhaps you could go and find us some ale? I have a great thirst now."

Nathan gladly obeyed and went to find the stores. He poked his head around a doorway, and his face broke into a wide grin as he recognized his old friend Zeno.

"Marco, me old mate!" Zeno was his usual jovial self. "What can I do for you?"

"I've come to get Lieutenant Cassio a drink of ale."

"Ah!" Zeno winked. "I should think so, after all that speechifying. Thirsty work, shouting at a square full of men." He bustled about, drawing some ale from a barrel into a pewter jug. "So what's this new commander like then?" he inquired over his shoulder.

"He's a good man. A great fighter. Very fair," Nathan spoke enthusiastically. Zeno cackled.

"We all hear'd that he was a bit of a ladies' man. In fact . . . ," his voice dropped to a conspiratorial whisper. "We all hear'd that he was involved with the general's new wife. I heard that Captain

Roderigo telling some of the other officers that he knew that the general's wife and your master were cheatin' on her husband. He seemed awful het up about it."

"It's rubbish, Zeno!" Nathan flared up in Pearce's defense. "Lieutenant Cassio is not involved with the general's wife."

"Ah..." Zeno seemed disappointed so he changed the direction of the conversation. "What's all this about the general bein' ill, eh? What's all that about?"

"He's sick in the head, Zeno," Nathan whispered.

"Ah." The old soldier didn't seem too surprised and handed over the jug of ale and two pewter cups. "Well, this is a pretty state of affairs, anyhow. Your lieutenant better watch his back." The old man spat on the first two fingers of his right hand, to ward off the evil eye. "I'll say a Mass for him—if'n I ever gets to church in the near future," and he cackled again.

When the barracks inspection was completed, the officers were gathered and Pearce efficiently set about drawing up a roster of duties and apportioning jobs. Nathan sat quietly in the corner of the room, listening and learning, once again amazed by Pearce's ability to assume command.

He told John of his admiration as they rode back to the palace alone. Pearce laughed.

"Playacting, Nathan. Just good playacting. But you knew that."

Back at the palace, Marie was waiting anxiously for their return.

"What is the problem?" Pearce asked, as he dismounted.

Marie shot him a warning glance. "Upstairs, my lord. I would talk with you privately."

Once inside John's room, Marie pointed at the bed. There, for all to see, was the embroidered handkerchief that Marie had given to Desdemona.

"I found it this morning." Marie looked at Pearce accusingly.

"I don't understand," said Pearce, bewildered.

"It was tucked under your pillow. Has she been visiting you?" Marie blurted out.

Nathan gasped at his sister's ridiculous question, but the look on her face made him realize that she really was jealous—to the point that tears were forming in her eyes.

"What is this folly?" Pearce said, laughing.

But Marie refused to be dismissed. "Have you been comforting Desdemona?"

"Well, have you?" said a deep, menacing voice from behind them.

They all turned to see Othello standing unsteadily in the doorway. It was not possible to read the expression on his face. His eyes were blank and staring.

"Has my wife been in your room?" He whispered the words with a kind of horror and Nathan felt himself trembling.

Pearce stood firm. "No, my lord. Never. I have no knowledge of how this handkerchief came to be here."

"My lord . . ." Nathan wanted to tell Othello that he saw Emilia give the handkerchief to her husband and he was sure that Iago was involved, but the general would have none of it.

"BE SILENT!" he roared.

"But, sir—" Nathan tried to protest but Othello grabbed him by his arm and threw him out of the door.

"THIS IS NONE OF YOUR BUSINESS, MARCO. BE-GONE."

Nathan found himself sprawled at the feet of the vile Iago, who was standing outside the door, smirking.

"You," said Nathan accusingly. "You put the handkerchief there. I saw you with it." Nathan lunged at Iago but the man was too strong. Iago clamped a rough hand over Nathan's mouth and pinned his arms to his side.

"Have a care, you little rat," he hissed in Nathan's ear. "You may think you have fooled the general—worming your way into his affections—but my friendship with Othello has lasted many years. You may not speak slander about me, the general will not have it. Keep your mouth shut, or it will be the worse for you."

Nathan struggled but Iago only held him tighter. Suddenly Othello came out of Pearce's room and looked his ensign. His face made Nathan's blood run cold. There were flecks of spit at the corners of his mouth and his eyes were glazed.

"Let both deeds be done," he said to Iago hoarsely. "You to do yours and I to do mine." Then he turned and wandered down the corridor, as if in a trance.

Iago flung Nathan back through the open door into Pearce's room.

"You may have your sewer spawn back, Lieutenant Cassio. I care not for his stench and the general has no further need of him." He laughed and followed his general, leaving Pearce, Nathan, and Marie in a state of shock.

"This is truly madness. We are no longer safe," Pearce

announced. "Tonight we shall leave as planned. The ship I selected is still at berth in the dock. The horses are in the stables. Our bags are packed. I shall leave written instructions for Lodovico and Duke Montano, to be delivered after we have left. Nathan, take Marie to her room and stay with her. Lock yourselves in. We must be ready to leave at sunset."

Bit by bit, during that afternoon, Nathan ferried bits and pieces of their baggage down to the stables. He did not want to be carrying things when they came to escape. He needed his hands free to defend himself.

He thought constantly about Iago's threats. He had no doubt that Iago would consider a servant boy's life very cheap and that both he and Pearce were in great danger now. As for Othello, there was no knowing what a man in his state might do.

The palace buildings were as silent as the grave. Nathan found the Mediterranean siesta irritating. Afternoons back in England had always been the liveliest part of the day, especially in the playhouse.

His task of loading the horses completed, Nathan sat in a small piece of shade and contemplated his future. The mission had been such a failure and he had lost all taste for adventuring. As a bee buzzed idly by his head and the searing afternoon heat made his senses dull, he thought with longing of his old life in the theater at Shoreditch. *Perhaps I will return there*—the thought gave him comfort—*I have had enough fear and death in this one mission to last me a lifetime.* He pushed the thoughts out of his head, realizing that he was feeling sorry for himself. For now, he had to concentrate on the matter at hand: getting out of Crete alive.

Once it began to get dark, Nathan went up to Pearce's room. He found his partner sharpening his sword and Nathan went to fetch Marie.

Without a word, the three of them crept down to the courtyard. The palace servants were beginning to stir and there were stewards coming up the stairs with lighted candles to rouse their masters. There was no time to lose.

In the stables, all was pitch black, save for some faint light coming in from the open door. It was enough for them to feel their way to the stalls where their horses were waiting. Nathan pulled out all the baggage from the hiding place and they began to strap them to the saddles.

"Stand away from the horses." The malevolent, whispered command came from a man silhouetted in the doorway. Pearce slowly drew his sword and pushed Marie behind one of the stalls. Nathan crouched down, ready to draw his knives.

"Do as he says," whispered another figure, who appeared beside the first man. Nathan saw a gleam of steel in their hands.

"They are double-armed," he warned Pearce, and there was a low laugh from one of the figures ahead.

Suddenly the first man lunged at Pearce, who parried successfully. There was plenty of space in the stables but it was dark and at the first clash of steel the horses reared back in their stalls.

Nathan now had both of his knives ready but in the blackness he could make out only flashes of light and form. He could not risk throwing his weapons in case he injured Pearce.

John was fighting a desperate battle with both hands against four weapons. He had drawn his dagger and was fending off the second assailant, while all the time trying to force both men backward, out into the better light of the courtyard. He had some advantage as the light was behind both of the attackers so every time they swung their weapons, he could just about make out their movements and retaliate. Inch by inch he pushed them back until they were outside. Nathan could now see that both men were wearing the sinister Venetian half-masks. He was sure that one of them was Roderigo. Nathan raised the knife in his right hand, aimed, and let fly. Just as the knife found its mark with a satisfying thud in the chest of the first man, the other man sliced his sword straight through Pearce's left thigh.

Marie screamed and Nathan yelled as Pearce fell back into the stables, cursing in pain. The man Nathan had wounded was writhing in agony out in the courtyard, but the second man turned and ran.

"Get him out into the light, get him out," Marie was urging through her tears, desperate to tend to Pearce's wound. Nathan dragged his friend out of the stables. Every move made Pearce yell with pain. When they got him outside, they could see that his thigh was split open and his blood was flowing fast. Marie pulled off her cloak and began to bind the leg tightly but suddenly she was roughly pulled aside. Iago had appeared from nowhere.

"Leave him be, Mistress Bianca," he said harshly. "This is work for a proper surgeon."

"No!" Marie was distraught. "I will not let anyone else touch

him. Let me go."

"What villains have done this?" Iago shook her angrily.

"There, over there!" Marie pointed to the body slumped on the ground, Nathan's knife sticking out of his chest.

Iago strode over to the man and removed his mask. "Roderigo," he hissed, and before anyone could stop him, he pulled out the knife and savagely stabbed the man again. Nathan recoiled as Roderigo gasped, "Damn you, Iago," before the death rattle came to his throat. Nathan felt acid bile rise in his own throat and he ran into the stables to vomit into a dark corner.

"Let us have some light. Send for the surgeon," Iago roared. Servants came scurrying from the palace with flaming torches.

"What's happening?" a voice called from the balcony above. It was Lodovico, the Venetian emissary.

"Cassio is hurt by villains," Iago called back. Nathan emerged from the stables, pale and shaken but he noted that Iago's sleeve and jerkin were stained with blood. But it was not new and wet blood from the stabbing of Roderigo. This blood had dried and it looked to be a spray of blood from a sword wound. Where did he suddenly come from? Nathan looked at Iago suspiciously. He was too quick on the scene. He must have been the other attacker. Here was a man who had tried to murder John Pearce and had then stabbed his own accomplice. *Probably to stop him from talking,* Nathan reasoned.

"Let me tend to him." Marie was frantic.

"No, madam. For all we know, you were a party to this injury. You may have wounded him in a fit of jealousy, or bribed Roderigo to perform the deed for you." Iago was shouting loudly so that all might hear these suspicions.

"No." Nathan was equally loud. "It was two men who attacked my master. Two men."

Iago did not comment, but fixed Nathan with a murderous

look. *He is a cold-blooded killer*—Nathan felt both fear and loathing—*and he would kill me and my sister with no more thought than swatting a fly.* He tried to think ahead, as John Pearce would, but he was too shocked by his seemingly invincible partner's injury at the hands of their enemy. All his fuddled mind could register was that he would probably be Iago's next victim unless he could find some kind of protection. *Othello is useless—perhaps Lodovico?*

The servants had arrived with a chair and Pearce was lifted carefully into it, to be carried upstairs to his room where the army surgeon would do his work. Indeed, before they had ascended the first flight of stairs, a cart came clattering into the courtyard, bearing the surgeon and the tools of his trade.

John was laid upon the bed. The cloak binding his leg was now so stained with blood that it was a dripping rag. Pearce was unconscious and Nathan feared for his life. The surgeon pushed through the throng and dismissed everyone at once.

"Too many people. Leave, leave." The two men who had accompanied the surgeon were now tying John Pearce's arms to the bed with strong ropes.

"You will not take off the leg?" Marie almost screamed in fear.

The surgeon unwrapped the bloody cloak and surveyed the wound. Then he shook his head.

"No. We can save the leg, for the moment. Provided it does not fester afterward, he will have two legs to walk on."

Marie smiled through the tears coursing down her face. Nathan knew that she would bring all her skills to bear in nursing John back to health.

Both Marie and Nathan were allowed to stay while the operation took place. Nathan held the torch while the surgeon swiftly sewed up the leg. He knew, having seen his sister work on the injured Duke Montano, that she was more skillful than this surgeon. But he was powerless to intervene.

When the work was finished, the surgeon left. The room looked like a slaughterhouse, blood was everywhere. Marie sprang into action.

"Help me now, Nathan," she whispered. "We must act quickly."

Under her direction, Nathan ran to fetch brandy, honey, and as many beef bones as he could beg from the cook. The kitchen staff looked bemused but Nathan was so insistent that they complied with his request.

When he returned to the room he found, to his horror, that Marie had opened up the wound again.

"Are you mad?" he cried.

"Do you want me to save him?" Marie hissed as she poured brandy into the wound and mopped it out again. She then began to sew—with neater, closer stitches than the surgeon's—so that the skin puckered around the leather thread. Then she liberally smeared the honey over her work, before binding it tightly with a clean cloth.

"Now give me one of your knives."

Nathan obeyed. Marie took the knife and began to scrape out the marrow from the beef bones.

"What are you doing?" Nathan was puzzled.

267

"He has lost a great deal of blood. I shall feed him this bone marrow when he wakes. It will help him to get his strength back."

Nathan marveled at his sister's knowledge of healing. He took his other knife and began to help. Soon they had a bowl full of the brown marrow.

Nathan wiped his hands and both his knives before putting them back in his boots.

"Will he wake soon?" Nathan scanned Marie's face anxiously.

"No. But sleep is good. His body will repair itself. When he is awake, he is in pain and not healing so well. I shall give him some herbs later to make him sleep as long as possible."

"Then we are trapped here in this place. We cannot leave now."

Marie nodded, and brother and sister looked at each other fearfully. They were inexperienced agents—how would they cope without the guidance of their friend? An attempt had been made to murder him, and for all they knew, another attempt could be made on *their* lives. They could not leave without Pearce and they were surrounded by enemies. There was no way of escape.

CHAPTER 22

"HAVE YOU PRAY'D TONIGHT, DESDEMONA?"

ATHAN and Marie sat in silent vigil over the unconscious body of their friend. Nathan had locked the door and was desperately trying to focus on a way out of their plight. Suddenly there was an urgent pounding on the door. "Help me, Marco," cried Emilia, "you must help me."

"What is it? What has happened?" Nathan opened the door a crack and could see that Emilia was in extreme distress.

"Desdemona ... I fear for her safety. She was getting ready for bed when Othello appeared. He looked so strange ... so frightening. He spoke harshly to me, telling me to leave and then he asked her if she had said her prayers. Before he closed the door on me and locked it, I saw her sweet face. It was a picture of terror. I am so afraid! I have knocked and knocked but he will not open the door...."

"Let both deeds be done. You to do yours and I to do mine." Othello had spoken those words to Iago. A cold fear crept into

Nathan's stomach. Was it that Iago should kill Cassio, and Othello would kill his wife?

"He means to murder her," Nathan cried in panic and Emilia's hand flew to her mouth.

"What are we to do? I cannot find my husband or Lodovico. I can rouse the servants but ..." Emilia was becoming frantic.

"Do that," Nathan said, thinking fast. "Get the servants, and try and break the door down. I will find another way into the room."

Emilia rushed off and Nathan grabbed the ropes that had been used to tie John Pearce to the bed. He told Marie to lock herself in when he had left, then he sped away to the nearest staircase.

Up and up he bounded, the ropes across his shoulder. Once he reached the battlements of the palace he ran along the roof, looking down at the windows below, trying to gauge which was Desdemona's room. Having decided, he tied the rope around one of the crenellations and pulled it with all his might. He planned to climb down to the window, and to do that, he knew he would have to remove his boot knives in order to make his ankles more flexible. He would hold his weapons between his teeth.

Nathan dropped the rope over the side of the battlements and, vaulting up onto the edge, turned around and picked up the rope with both hands. He cursed that he was not gloved as he began to walk backward down the wall. The rope burned his palms. He decided to descend another way, to save taking the full weight of his body on his hands, so he bent his knees, kicked away from the wall and clamped the rope between his boots. As he thudded sideways into the wall he hung there for a moment to get his wind back, then he began to inch downward. He looked down, to judge how much farther he had to go. He felt his stomach lurch at the sight of the great drop below the palace walls. He had forgotten that this side of the palace was built on a sheer rock face. The ravine was pitilessly deep.

Slowly Nathan descended, his breath coming in short gasps between his teeth, making the knives shudder against his lips. Although he had wiped the knives, they tasted of beef fat and the greasiness made them slip in his mouth.

Finally he came level with the windows, although he was midway between two and unsure which was the window he wanted. He listened carefully and he thought that the sound of a door being rammed was coming from the right-hand window. He needed to get farther over by at least four feet.

Slowly he began to sway his body so that the rope swung from side to side. But it was obvious that he was not going to be able to get across to the window. Then he remembered his escape from the oubliette at Robey's school. He gripped the rope between his feet and held on with one hand. With the other hand, he carefully removed one knife from his mouth, and reaching as far as he could to his right, he jabbed the mortar between the bricks with the point of his knife. Finding a crack, he pushed the knife in, up to its hilt. He leaned slightly toward it and hung on it a little, to be sure that it would take his weight, then he let go of the rope with his feet and hung, in a crucifix position, against the wall of the great palace—his left hand gripping the rope and his right hand gripping the knife in the wall. Then, gambling his life on the strength of the knife in the wall, Nathan let go of the rope completely, flipped himself around so that his back was against the wall and, in a split second, reached out his left hand and grabbed the iron bars of the window. As he did so, the hilt broke away from the knife and went plummeting down to the unknown depths of the ravine below. He struggled, momentarily, hanging by one hand from the window bars, before flipping himself around again and grabbing another iron bar with his right hand. His breath was now coming in painful gasps.

His strength was failing fast and he was on the point of tears when he heard a muffled scream coming from inside the room. This sound of distress gave him the added impetus to haul his body up onto the window ledge.

The glass window beyond the bars was fastened from the inside. Nathan could see that Othello was holding Desdemona's face roughly in one hand. He was shouting at her. Nathan steadied himself on the ledge and removed the knife from his teeth. He pushed it through the middle of the two windows and began to lever the catch upward. Twice he almost had the catch flipped over and twice it fell back down again. All the time he kept one eye fixed on the demented Othello as he raged at his terrified wife. On the third attempt the catch fell backward and Nathan pushed the windows wide open through the bars.

Desdemona was now screaming.

"Kill me tomorrow; let me live tonight. Let me say one prayer!"

"It is too late," came the unnatural reply from her husband and he closed both hands around her throat and began to squeeze.

"No!" Nathan shouted out in horror. He aimed his knife. Othello heard nothing—not the clamor outside the door, nor Nathan at the window shouting for him to stop, nor the whipping sound of the knife as it spun through the air to pierce—not his flesh—but the bed hangings beside him.

Nathan screamed in anger and frustration. The knife, wet from his spittle and slimy with beef marrow, had slipped from his fingers a second too quickly and missed its target. Desdemona's body hung lifeless in Othello's hands and her throat made a rattling sound, just as the door cracked in two, spilling armed men into the room.

Nathan sat on the window ledge, his aching shoulders shaking with sobs. His fumbled knife throw had not saved Desdemona. Everyone had arrived too late.

Emilia screamed and threw herself over Desdemona's body, "Oh, lady, speak! Sweet Desdemona, sweet mistress, speak!"

The men stood in silence. Then Emilia turned on Othello and spat in his face.

"You black devil! How could you have done such a thing?"

Othello looked broken, defeated, and suddenly quite old.

"She broke our marriage vows. She was in love with Cassio. She slept with him."

Emilia was incredulous. "Never! This is a damned odious lie. You have killed the sweetest innocent that ever lived."

Othello flew into a rage. "It is true!" he ranted. "Ask your husband. It was he who told me of the affair between Cassio and my wife."

Nathan saw Emilia's face turn from the redness of rage to the whitest white of shock. She swayed a little on her feet with the horror of it all.

"My husband?" Her voice was barely audible but there was a

flinch of disgust in her face. "My husband lied from the depths of his rotten soul." Nathan felt a wave of relief, almost like nausea, that at last Iago would be exposed for the terrible man that he was. But he also felt a deep, deep sorrow that it had not been before such tragedy had occurred. Emilia's face and voice turned to cold fury. "Your wife, sweet Desdemona, loved you dearly—even though you were not worthy of her and brought her nothing but misery. You ignorant, stupid man!"

Angrily Othello grabbed Emilia by the throat and the armed men were aroused from their frozen state of shock. There was a clank of metal weapons being directed toward the madman but he had not tightened his grasp on her throat. Emilia's look of utter contempt had stopped him, more surely than any sword could.

"Kill me too, if you want," she spoke in a voice that bordered on pity. "Add my murder to the terrible murder of your wife. I care not." Her voice suddenly rose to an unearthly scream, which made the blood drain from Nathan's face.

"YOU MURDERER! YOU FOUL MURDERER!"

Othello let her go and put his hands over his ears to try and block out the terrible words. The noise had summoned more people. Nathan saw Duke Montano, Lodovico, and Iago pushing their way through the men at arms.

"What has happened? Oh no...no," cried Montano as he pushed through and saw Desdemona's corpse.

Emilia saw Iago and her body trembled with anger and hatred toward her husband. She flew at him, her hands clawing the skin on his face, ripping thin slivers away with her nails. His blood welled into livid stripes of shame on his cheeks.

"You villain! You evil man!" Her mouth was surrounded by the white spittle of fury.

Iago threw her away with great force, so that she thudded into the bedpost, winded.

"Are you mad? Get yourself home," Iago said viciously through gritted teeth. But Emilia was no longer afraid of him.

"You told a lie, an odious damned lie." Emilia's voice was guttural—strange—possessed. Nathan shivered. "You said Desdemona was false with Cassio and your damnable lies have caused this murder."

"I did not lie. All I said was true." Despite his arrogance, Nathan could sense that Iago was rattled.

Othello began to tremble, the full enormity of the murder beginning to sink in. He flung himself down on his wife's pale body and wept.

"No, no. It cannot be. She was unfaithful. She was."

Emilia looked down at his face, wet with tears.

"Where is your proof, man? Where is the proof that she was unfaithful to you?"

Othello spoke like a little boy pleading to be believed.

"Iago knows that she was a thousand times unfaithful. I myself saw her handkerchief . . . I saw it on Cassio's bed. . . ."

"Oh God . . . oh heavenly God . . ." Emilia was shaking once more.

Iago now drew his sword, hissing at his wife, "Keep your filthy mouth shut."

"I will not." There was no stopping her now. The men at arms moved slightly, ready to defend her. Emilia crouched down on the opposite side of the bed so that her face was level with Othello's. She wanted him to hear and understand every syllable. "That handkerchief that you speak of—I found it on the floor—Desdemona dropped it when you struck her last night." Othello's face flinched at the memory. "I gave it to Iago because he wanted me to steal it for him. He threatened to beat me if I did not."

"You lying whore!" cried Iago in a fury, and he lunged with his sword. Men sprang forward to disarm him, including the general, who had leapt to his feet. Nathan grabbed the bars of the window. "No! Save her," he shouted as loud as he could but the shouts of the men drowned him out. Iago was so enraged that it took three of them to overpower him, but as they fiercely pulled him back, Emilia silently slid to the floor. Nathan saw the blood and hid his face, as he realized that the brave Emilia had been mortally wounded.

Iago gave a low laugh, which snapped the assembled men back to reality, and Othello answered with a cry of pure rage.

"Devil incarnate!" he screamed and hit Iago across the face, his rings splitting Iago's cheek open to the bone.

"ENOUGH," Lodovico roared as he stepped forward. "NO MORE BLOODSHED. We have seen evil enough today."

He held up a piece of paper.

"This letter to Iago was found in the pocket of the slain Roderigo. It speaks of Roderigo's great dissatisfaction with his friend. How Iago had promised him Desdemona but never delivered her and how Iago expected Roderigo to help him murder Michael Cassio. It is all here. Proof that Iago has, for a long time, planned this villainy." He looked at Iago, who was sullen in defeat, and at Othello, sick with despair. "You are both under arrest."

Iago raised his head. "I shall tell you nothing," he said with a wicked smile.

Lodovico set his mouth grimly. "Believe me, you will speak under torture. Take him away." Iago was led off, leaving a fine trail of blood spots behind him. Lodovico now turned to Othello. "You, sir, shall be returned to Venice under close arrest. The council shall decide what becomes of you."

Othello turned away and everyone saw Nathan crouched on the windowsill.

"By all that is holy!" Lodovico exclaimed. "How long have you been there, boy?"

"Long enough, sir," Nathan replied through chattering teeth. Shock and his feat of great strength had made him cold through to the bone.

"Men, go up to the battlements and rescue this boy."

There was a flurry of activity as the men left on their mission. Only Lodovico and Othello remained in the room with the bodies of the two dead women. Othello stared at Nathan.

"Marco ... were you here when ... when my wife was still alive?" Othello could barely frame the question, yet he needed to know.

Nathan looked away, unable to look at the once-great general— unable to speak to the man who had sunk so low from such heights. Othello put his hand gently through the bars and turned Nathan's face, but when he saw the pity and confusion in the boy's eyes, Othello closed his own in shame.

There was a shout from above and a large basket was lowered down next to Nathan's left shoulder.

Othello grasped the iron bars.

"A word or two before you go . . . ," he implored. "I have done the Venetian state some service. I hope they will remember it. But you . . . once my comrade." He looked deep into Nathan's eyes. "When you relate these terrible deeds, speak of me as I am, do not make excuses for me or paint me as a monster. Speak of a man who did not love a woman wisely, but loved her too well. Speak of a man who was not normally jealous but circumstances and the interference of others whipped him up into an insanity. Speak of a man who, like an ignorant savage, threw a pearl away that was richer than all his tribe, and now sheds bitter tears for it. . . . Will you?"

Nathan fought back the tears, feeling both revulsion and pity for the man he had once so admired. He managed to nod and Othello, satisfied, turned away to the bed and the corpse of his beloved wife. He bent over her and kissed her cold lips, then as he straightened, he caught sight of Nathan's knife hanging in the bed curtains. Their eyes met and each knew what he meant to do. In the moment that Nathan's arms stretched through the iron bars and his mouth framed the word *no,* the general had seized the knife and plunged into his own chest. Lodovico shouted and Nathan could hear the men calling from the roof.

"The general has killed himself!" Nathan bawled up to the men above, before burying his face in his hands in despair.

Lodovico stood, surrounded by three bodies and a great pool

of blood, and looked hopelessly at Nathan. "I did not think he had a weapon."

Nathan looked hopeless too, numb with the horror of it all. "My knife," he said bleakly. "It was my knife." He would utter these words over and over again in the nightmares that would haunt his sleep in the days and weeks to come.

EPILOGUE

"THIS HEAVY ACT WITH HEAVY HEART RELATE"

H E voyage home from Crete was a quiet and somber journey. Many on board spent the days lost in thought. Nathan could not banish from his mind the images of that cursed room in the duke's palace. But by far the most heartrending experience had been standing with the small knot of people who had laid the bodies of Desdemona and Emilia to rest in the cathedral crypt. Something cold and dark had settled down in the pit of Nathan's stomach and would not allow him to cry anymore.

Even fewer people had assembled outside the city walls to bury Othello. Denied a church burial because he had taken his own life, his body was unceremoniously dumped in a deep hole on the side of a hill. As the dusty Cretan earth thudded down onto the tarpaulin in which Othello was wrapped, Nathan vengefully hoped that Iago was somewhere inside the prison, screaming in pain and praying for death.

The sea, as if sensing the lack of spirit in the ships of the Venetian fleet, was calm and untroubled for the whole voyage. This meant that Pearce was able to sleep up on deck for most of the time while Marie watched over him like a hawk. By the time the great arsenal of Venice hove into sight, Pearce was sitting up, the waxen pallor of his skin changed to a pale gold. He was even complaining that the stitches in his leg itched.

Nathan looked over the side of the ship. The wonders of Venice were no longer so magnificent to him. He could not see things through the same eyes as before.

Lodovico went to report to the doge and the council, while Pearce, Marie, and Nathan took a gondola to Graziella's house. Their conversation fell silent as the boat passed by the house where Desdemona had once lived with her father. The shutters were closed and the house looked as dead as the family that once occupied it. Nathan turned his head away.

Later that night, Nathan was beginning to relax and feel that, even though their mission had failed spectacularly and there would be no alliance between England and Venice, he would be wiser and stronger to face his next adventure. Two weeks ago in Crete he had resolved to go back to the theater as soon as he arrived in England. Now he was having a change of heart. Venice, while shocked by the deaths in Crete, was buzzing with the news of Drake's attack on the Spanish Armada and it reminded Nathan that England was facing war. His services would be needed now more than ever.

On the long voyage back to England, his nightmares had stopped and it was an older and wiser Nathan Fox who gratefully set his feet upon English soil again when the ship docked at Dover.

Stefan and his gypsy troupe were waiting in the port when they disembarked. They had been there several days, Walsingham having alerted Stefan to the impending return of his family. Nathan warmly embraced his father. He thought of the desolate Brabantio and he realized that all fathers must give over a large part of their heart to their children. This time it was harder for Nathan to say good-bye.

"Shall I see you again?" he asked, sticking his head out of the carriage window.

Stefan nodded. "Soon. I shall send word." Then he melted into the crowd.

When they reached London, John Pearce escorted Nathan and Marie home before making for Westminster Palace to meet with Sir Francis.

As they parted, he gripped Nathan's hand firmly. "You have proved the best partner a man could have. I am only sorry that our first mission was so hard on you. I would not judge you badly if you wished to end your spy work here."

Nathan smiled and shook his head. "I am resolved to continue, John. Besides," he added, "you cannot do without me now."

John laughed and limped over to Marie. He bowed. "My lady, I thank you for saving my life."

Marie blushed and murmured some unintelligible comment. John kissed her hand and in confusion she fled into the house.

WALKING around Shoreditch and into the silent theater, Nathan felt detached from everything around him. He had tasted the high drama of life. The low drama of the theater would never hold the same appeal.

He had been hardened by what he had seen and done, of that there was no doubt. But as he sat by a dying fire and told Will Shakespeare the full tragedy of General Othello—the man who was once a slave and by his own genius had raised himself up to be commander of the armed forces of Venice; the man he had fought beside in battle and who had been his friend; who out of weakness had ended his life and that of his beautiful Desdemona—the tears fell silently down his cheeks.

Shakespeare scribbled down the story at a furious rate, too absorbed to notice a silent figure slip in through the door behind Nathan.

"Master Fox," growled a deep voice that made them both jump. "I hope you did not think that because John Pearce is resting at his mother's in the country, that you will be doing the same?"

Robey stepped into the glow of the fire, his eyes shining with amusement. Nathan sprang to his feet.

"Master Robey! I . . . I had not expected . . ."

Robey raised an eyebrow in mock disapproval.

"Tut, tut. Now is not the time to rest on your laurels. You have more training to complete. Sir Francis gave me very little time before your Venice assignment. Now Bardolph, Pistol, and Nym would like to tutor you with . . . more leisure. I have a horse waiting outside. You must say your good-byes and meet me downstairs." Robey bowed courteously then turned on his heels—leaving only a bemused Will Shakespeare behind, and Nathan Fox standing by the fire with a broad smile of anticipation on his face.

Thank you for reading this FEIWEL AND FRIENDS book.

The Friends who made

possible are:

Jean Feiwel, publisher

Liz Szabla, editor-in-chief

Rich Deas, creative director

Elizabeth Fithian, marketing director

Barbara Grzeslo, associate art director

Holly West, assistant to the publisher

Dave Barrett, managing editor

Nicole Liebowitz Moulaison, production manager

Jessica Tedder, associate editor

Liz Noland, publicist

Allison Remcheck, editorial assistant

Ksenia Winnicki, marketing assistant

Find out more about our authors and artists and our future publishing a
www.feiwelandfriends.com.

Our books are friends for life